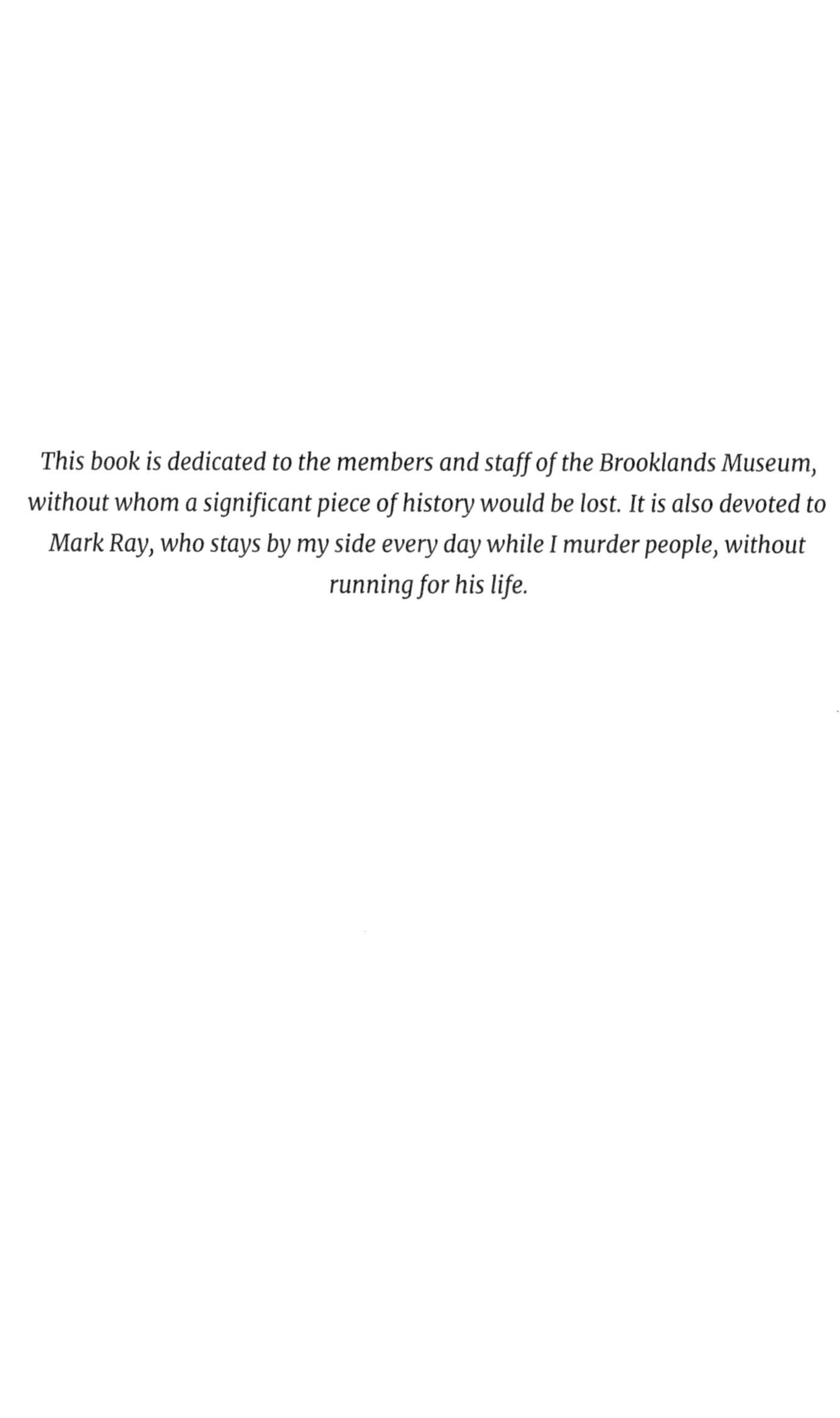

This book is dedicated to the members and staff of the Brooklands Museum, without whom a significant piece of history would be lost. It is also devoted to Mark Ray, who stays by my side every day while I murder people, without running for his life.

1

Chapter 1

Be patient? Don't you realize I've been working here... well, two whole hours now?

-How to Succeed in Business Without Really Trying, 1967

"Oh, good day to 'ya, sir! Your Mum is in her sanctuary and is expectin' ya 'pon your arrival. So good to see ya. And the Miss, too," gushed the housekeeper. She pulled the pair across the threshold into the Elliott ancestral home in West Sussex. "Miss Regina, you will need to follow, but not till Mr. Elliott has had his, um, audience with the Missus."

Tucker and Reggie followed the faithful Myra through the foyer and into the study, where refreshments were waiting. It had been quite some time since Reggie had been to the family estate. That was when she first met Alene Farthing Elliott, Tucker's stern but loving mother and head of Farthing's Fine Teas, the biggest of the family businesses.

"Thank you, Myra. I'm sure she's expecting an update on our... well, these!" Reggie said as she modeled her footwear for the woman.

"Oh, they're lovely, Miss. I'm sure she's waitin' for some good news on that front. This one don't keep her up to date on anythin'," she said behind her hand as she jerked her head at Tucker. "All she gets is the headlines and not the good 'uns."

"Alright, I'm off," said Tucker, downing the last of his scotch and giving Reggie a peck on the cheek.

"Don't I know it," said Reggie.

Myra smiled happily at Tucker and quietly closed the doors to leave Reggie to her thoughts. She groped through her briefcase, pulling out sheets of facts and figures showing that they hadn't spent their entire time chasing murderers in Florida, whether at the Sea Gables Tea Room or while on Useppa Island, while seeking an escape from the tea room murders. Even though Alene knew the circumstances, she still expected progress on the company task with which she had entrusted them when sending them to the States.

"These reports look rather respectable," Reggie said. "At least the damn company's off life support."

She wondered how it was going in Alene's lair and was glad it was Tucker and not she who was literally on the carpet.

"Alright, time to freshen up and make my appearance. If I only knew where I was going in this museum. Myra!"

###

"Hello, old girl," said Tucker, enveloping his mother. "How's things with the empire?"

"I might ask you the same, darling. Anything other than headlines so far?"

"I suppose Regina will have all the intel on the flops, love. She's handling that section of business for us. She knows all, that one."

"And how goes the other front, son? She's a lovely girl, you know. How are you two getting on?"

"Wonderfully, but then you knew that, didn't you? Have you ever lost on a gamble, Mother?"

"Not to date, darling. I know my son well, and I know our Miss Regina. If anyone were to lasso you and make you behave, she would be the one. She's a highly perceptive young lady."

"That she is. I never stood a chance, did I, but then again..."

"Yes, I knew that, as well. Sit, please, darling. Onto more important matters."

Tucker patted the "hot seat" in front of the power desk and glared sternly at his mother.

"Still not electrified, I hope?"

"Not since the last time you were summoned in front of me. Oh, sit, dear. And try not to fuss. I'm just going over the responses for the Tea Ball."

Tucker could never resist snickering at this double meaning: a fancy-dress ball or a tea infuser? He'd been going to these company galas since he could walk. Each year brought a new experience, a new friend, and a new challenge as he grew older and became the heir apparent to the throne of Farthing's Industries.

"So, who's gracing us with their presence this year, Mum? Any royalty, rock stars, competitors?"

"All of the above, darling. As I sift through these, I am beginning to be more concerned about security. I know Brooklands has top-notch people, but I do believe we need to hire more. This is quite a group, Tucker," she said, handing him the list of attendees.

"Bloody hell, Mother, look at these people."

"Language, Tucker. Please just tell me your thoughts. Do I need to call in Stricklands?"

"May not be a bad idea, Mum. These are some high-level guests. Oh, how fun. I haven't seen him in a while. So glad he's coming. Bringing any family? I didn't know he was in the UK. Actually, I thought he was on tour in the States."

"No, this leg has brought him a bit closer to home. He may be bringing a couple of children with him. Remind me to find that out."

"Bollocks, Mother! You can't mean this?" burst Tucker, looking further down the list.

"Tucker, mouth, please. And yes, I do. I'll leave you to call Stricklands. This group will be coming with their own security, but we just can't leave it at that. Please see to it."

"Yes, ma'am."

"And answer the door, darling. That will be Reggie."

"I didn't realize her attendance was mandatory here."

"She's your hired nanny and running this show for now, darling. Please let her in."

She did not look up from her mounds of paper.

Tucker advanced on the door as if expecting an enemy coalition. He jerked it open to find the lovely and talented Miss Regina Winter, all gorgeous five feet eleven inches of her, and tastefully, yet promotionally dressed.

"Oh, Reggie, dear. Please come in. You do look lovely. What's that I see on your feet?" Alene asked, with a glint in her eye.

"Why, Mrs. Elliott, it would be the newest in the footwear line for Flipping for Flops! Aren't they beautiful?"

"Yes, they most certainly are, which leads me to believe they're not from the line with which the previous management was using to sink the ship."

"Oh, no, ma'am. It's the insolvent little company I found and asked you about before we went on vacation to Useppa Island. You know, the one that was having difficulty with their designers and their payroll? I took the liberty of stepping in and rescuing the best of the lines. So, they are all now 'Flipping' for us, so to speak."

"Oh, yes, right," said Alene. "I remember now. Well done, dear."

"I'm sorry, when did you do this?" asked Tucker.

Reggie had the decency to look contrite and reprimanded. Tucker shook his head and rubbed his temples in a fruitless attempt to fend off a fresh headache.

"I instructed her to go ahead," said Alene, barely looking up from her notes.

"You were busy with our friend Laird catching a murderer. Again. By the way, they are coming, yes?"

"Oh yes, Mother. Dahlia should be getting in any time now, and then Dulcy and Laird will follow tomorrow. They wouldn't miss it. Looking quite forward to it."

Tucker's childhood friend, Dahlia Porter, was fresh off a grand opening of her tea room, a faked death, and the involvement of her manager with the "copper" who solved the case. John Laird also turned out to be FBI, as luck would have it.

"That's wonderful, dear. So, how do you like them?" she asked.

"How do I like what?"

"The new strappy, gorgeous flops. Please do keep up, dear."

"They're... spectacular," said Tucker, ignoring the shoes and running an eye over the rest of the stylish woman in front of him.

"I'm glad you approve. Maybe one day, you'll actually look at the shoes she's wearing and adding to the inventory. That should about do it for now. Please take care of what I've asked, yes?"

"Of course I will. Coming Reg?"

"She'll be along in a bit, dear. We have a few things to discuss," said Alene, peeking at him from the piles of acceptances and regrets.

"Yes, ma'am. I'll inform you of the plans moving forward. Thanks for seeing me, Mum."

"Thanks so much for coming, love. Now off you go."

Tucker smirked and blew a kiss to Reggie as he shuffled to the door and slid through it, wondering what had just happened.

"There. Now that he's buggered off, tell me everything!" said Alene. Reggie drew up a chair and leaned in with a deliciously mischievous grin.

2

Chapter 2

Jack Butler : Wanna beer?
Ron Richardson : It's 7 o'clock in the morning.
Jack Butler : Scotch?
-Mr. Mom, 1983

Dahlia marched up the steps as the door was thrown wide, and Jennings' smiling face greeted her as he grabbed her bag.

"So nice to see you again, Miss Dahlia. Your parents are waiting for you in the conservatory. I shall be bringing your 'tea' along shortly. Is there anything else I can get you at the moment?"

"No, Jennings, thanks awfully. Just make sure the 'tea' is neat, please."

"Yes, Miss. One scotch, neat. Ice on the side?"

"Oh, yes. Please do."

Dahlia wandered through the massive foyer to the sanctuary of the conservatory as the irrepressible butler scurried off to the pantry. The conservatory was her parents' favorite room, and truth be told, hers as well. Her mind floated back to the last time she had sat here, trying to sort out the strange events that had nearly shut down her tea room and bed and breakfast. She desperately hoped she wouldn't have to dive behind a potted plant this trip. She gave her backside a slight pat and opened the doors.

"Hullo, Mum, Dad. How's everything?"

"Hello, darling. Good trip?"

"Oh, yes, just a bit tiring is all. Everything ready for the Tea Ball?"

"As far as we know. Tucker and Reggie got in earlier and are handling last-minute details. From what we hear, it's quite a guest list," said her father.

"It usually is," she said.

She was feeling thirsty, and as if on cue, Jennings set a highball glass in front of her, along with a side of ice. Now, she was settled in. She'd enjoy her cocktail and then check on the Elliotts.

"Alright then, I'll chat with them in a bit. And then I'll have to go shopping before zero hour. I haven't a thing to wear!"

###

"Do you see the car, Dulce? I'm not sure what I'm looking for."

After a long overnight flight and country train ride, tea room manager Dulcy Dandeneau and Agent John Laird finally disembarked at the station, where they hoped Tucker would be patiently waiting. Laird's long legs had been cramped since they landed, so he stretched and meandered to sort them out.

"Oh, over there. I see him now. It's a bit brisk here, isn't it? Hope I brought enough clothes."

"I don't believe there was anything you didn't pack, darling. Small as you are, it's still a lot of clothing."

"John Laird, you try packing for fall in England, casual outings, and a dress ball. It was everything I could do to stuff that gown into this teeny case."

Her blue eyes were flashing, and her curly reddish hair bounced with her indignation.

"Hullo, you two. Good trip?"

"Yes! How go the preparations, Tucker?" asked Dulcy, beaming her freckled face at him.

"Oh, the usual. Food, security, tea, and seating arrangements to keep everyone happy. I think we've managed brilliantly. No one feeling murderous because they have to sit next to a dodgy relative."

Dulcy winced and shot him a look that should have made him fear for his life.

"Sorry, love. I can't seem to stop putting my foot into it. This shall be a lovely, high-end event. No murderers allowed," he said.

John laughed to himself. Dulcy wasn't even grinning, so he threw the bags in the boot and opened her door. The ride was pleasant and scenic, and they were at the manor in no time.

CHAPTER 2

"Feel like a cocktail?" offered Tucker as they relaxed in the Elliott study and waited for Alene to appear.

"It's barely one o'clock," said Dulcy.

"Well, no time like the present to get on the UK schedule. Oh, hullo, Dad. You remember Dulcy and John Laird, my accomplices in crime fighting from Dahlia's tea room."

"I seem to remember a certain high-trafficked closet in her B&B, son."

"Oh, that has been retired and renovated," said Dulcy. "You should just see the hidden dining room now. It's beautiful and booked out months in advance."

"Glad to hear it, then. Brilliant idea, there. We'll come back to try it out as soon as we get through this Tea Ball business. Don't tell your Mum, son, but I'm ready for this to come off already. Been a beast of a planning nightmare. Ready to be well shot of it."

Again, as if on cue, Alene Farthing Elliott marched into the study, trailing Reggie behind her, wearing yet another pair of sexy, strappy flip-flops with just a smidge of a heel.

"Hello, you two," said Alene, giving Dulcy and John a dual hug while Reggie waited for her turn.

"How was your trip?"

"Oh, fine. Slept most of the way so we'd be bright and fresh for today," said Dulcy. "Have you seen Dahlia?"

"Not yet, but she should be stopping on in a bit. She suddenly had to go shopping. She neglected to bring the formal wear of all things."

"Oh, she didn't neglect to bring it; she just wanted to shop," said Dulcy.

"So, Regina, what are those trendy things on your feet?" asked Tucker.

"I'm just giving you all quick glimpses before we launch the new models in Cleveland."

Tucker spit his scotch across the rug as Alene handed him a napkin and gave him a short, sharp rap on the back.

"Again, darling, do keep up. The new styles will launch when you get back to the States. We're at a wonderful venue, The Music Box, in downtown in what they call The Flats. It's right on the river. Reggie will give you all the details. You must have missed the announcement. Sorry, love."

"No, you're not, Mother. Honestly, is there anything else I should know?"

"No, I think you're up to speed now. And Myra's busy in the kitchen, so Reggie, would you be a dear and please let Dahlia in before she breaks down the front entrance?"

Before Reggie could head for the foyer, the study door popped open, and Dahlia breezed through, juggling shopping bags and a magnificent bouquet.

"For you, Mother Elliott, and hullo, you two! So nice to see you here. Everyone ready for the big event?"

"As we'll ever be," said Tucker.

A light knock on the door revealed Myra with a tray of champagne glasses and a still bubbling bottle ready for a pre-ball toast.

"Here's to a successful tea gala with plenty of happy guests, new tea flavors flowing..."

"And no murders!" added Tucker.

A thump of glass was heard hitting the carpet as Dulcy's flute dribbled its champagne and rolled under the sofa.

3

Chapter 3

"Welcome to the party, pal!"
- Die Hard, 1988

"This is lovely," said Reggie, glancing around the spacious grounds of The Brooklands Museum's newly refurbished Edwardian Clubhouse. "What a great choice for a venue. Do you always have it here?"

"Oh, no," said Tucker. "We have it all over; usually places with guest cottages and the like, but always somewhere unique and interesting. Last year, it took place at Highgrove House, one of King Charles's houses with gardens. The house and grounds are part of The Prince's Foundation, his educational charity for design and architecture for people and their communities. It was a spectacular event. He even popped in for a minute to congratulate us on our new line. Wonderful, really."

"They've done a great job setting up everything. It's lavish and elegant, yet it's somehow homey, if that makes any sense."

"Perfectly. That's the tone we usually aim for. Glad to see it worked. Brilliant, really. You've no idea how difficult it can be to try for the same feeling but do it differently each year."

"I have a small idea about that difficulty," she said, scanning the room. "Look – there's Dahlia, Dulcy, and John. They look right at home."

"Dahlia should. She's been coming to these things as long as I have. Ah, and my favorite nanny before you came along, our Mr. Sidney Tolliver. You shall meet him directly."

"Is that the man your mother sent to Las Vegas to 'babysit' you?"

"Yes, and he's brilliant. Nice chap, and as I said, given name Sidney, but we call him Tolliver. Just doesn't seem like 'Sidney' fits him."

"Can't wait to meet my predecessor. Wait a minute - is that ... a Beatle?"

"Yes, it is. He comes to a lot of these. Brings the family much of the time as well. Would you like to meet him?"

"Oh, I'd love to, although I think I'd be too nervous. Okay, let's meet him. You can...

"Hello, Elliott. At it again, are we? Still trying to come up with new trends in tea? Good luck staying in the spotlight with my brands out there. As always, you'll be in my shadow this year, but good luck to you anyway," said the man, looking Reggie up and down with a lascivious leer, then waltzing off.

"Uh! Who was that odious little man?"

"Oh, just someone who thinks he's better than he really is. That's the head of our competition in the tea world, J. Winston Weatherford. He's brash, bombastic, and unforgettable."

"Unforgettable? I'm not sure I'd use that word."

"Unforgettable, but not in a good way. You only remember him because he's so rude and boorish. He's turned behaving badly into an art form. And odious is a brilliant word for him, Reg. Well done."

"Oh, no. Our Beatle is gone. I guess I'll just have to meet him later. Hopefully, he'll still be here."

"Should be; I'm sure he'll stay for a cuppa and a nibble of something. Sorry about him," Tucker said, sliding his eyes toward Weatherford. "Only thing is, the more you try to ignore him, the more he irritates you. Rather like a rash that gets worse with the heat."

Reggie had been sipping her wine and nearly spit it on Tucker as she stifled a laugh and tried not to stare in the man's direction. He was abusing a new target as she sneaked a peek his way.

"He's abusing a new victim judging her face," said Reggie. "Last time I saw a look like that, the woman had stepped in dog poo."

"Well said, Regina. Uh oh, I see our friends over there in harm's way. Poor Dahlia. He'll latch onto her like a disease. Maybe we should help."

"I would think 'poor Weatherford,'" said Reggie. "I can't imagine Dahlia letting some old fool push her around. Oooo! Did you see that?"

"I did. Never mind the rescue. Poor clueless bastard, Weatherford," said Tucker, echoing Reggie's thoughts. "I do believe she's left a print on the man's face. He should put some ice on that."

As they took a turn around the room, Reggie spotted more high-profile figures and watched as they mingled with other guests as though they were old friends. She was watching a vaguely familiar young woman when her husband joined her. Reggie nearly dropped her glass.

"Tucker! Is that..."

"Oh, yes. Must go say hello. We do get a bit of royalty at these things. They're quite lovely, so come along and we'll make introductions. Mum would fire me on the spot if I didn't punctually acknowledge them."

They were weaving through the pods of chatting guests when, just as they had almost reached their quarry, Winston Weatherford edged in front of them, blocking Tucker and Reggie's path.

"Odious little man," repeated Reggie. "How do you stay so calm? I'm so angry I could give him a swift kick."

"He'll cock it up, Reg. Just give him a minute. She's too gracious to say anything, but you watch; she'll sidestep him and be off."

Just as Tucker said, the nimble royal moved away with a curt nod and a full back turn to Weatherford. Reggie looked over to see Tucker sipping his drink with a satisfied smirk.

"How do you know this stuff?"

"Seen it before. He offends one and all, not just me and mine. Besides, the royals serve our tea, not his."

"And it is your gala, not his."

"Exactly. There he goes. Oh dear, he's going for Mother. This won't be good if he gets to her before I do, especially for me."

Reggie watched as Tucker shoved his drink at her and crossed the room to Alene's aid, guests delaying his mission any number of times. Pushing his way through various attendees, he could hear the brewing of something other than tea talk.

"I shall ensure everyone knows you stole my blends, Mrs. Elliott. It won't be hard to tell; mine are exclusive and have proprietary ingredients where yours..."

"Do not finish that sentence, Winston, unless you wish to be wiping more than that smirk off your face," said Alene with a cold, frightening stare that froze Tucker's heart.

"I wouldn't fight me, Alene. You won't win. You'll take my designs and my research over my dead body."

"That can be arranged," she said, pressing her face into his, as Tolliver hovered protectively in the background.

"Now, now," said Tucker. "Mother, we have a young guest who would like to meet you. She has expressed a keen interest in learning the business and would love to tour the facilities and pick your brain. Right over there, see? Yes, she's waving to you, Mum. Off you go. Tolliver, mate, introduce her to the young Miss, please," he said, pushing his mother out of the horrible man's face. Tucker turned full force on him.

"I think it's time you push off, Weatherford. I'm not even sure why she keeps sending you invitations. Always takes the high road. Unlike you, who always seem to be under the ass... excuse me, throat tickle, phalt. Goodbye, Weatherford. I think you know where the exit is."

"Oh, I'm not ready to leave just yet. I'll have to find my wife and tear her away from the old crones she insists on dragging with her everywhere. I'm sure Olivia will want to stay on for a while."

"Well, let's see if we can find her," said Tucker, grabbing Weatherford by the elbow and shoving him through the crowd.

"Ah. See there? She's right by the champagne fountain. Shall we?"

Tucker pinched the man's arm until he thought it would bruise before managing to steer him to the fountain. As they neared the ladies, a striking woman in a fabulous ball gown dripping in jewels stepped up and planted herself in front of her husband.

"What have you done now, Winston?" she asked, sneaking a slight glance at Tucker.

"Only told the truth, dear. Mr. Elliott seems to think maybe we should call it an evening."

The woman turned amethyst eyes on Tucker and summed up the situation.

"It was also a request from Alene," said Tucker softly. "You are welcome to stay, Olivia, but as for..."

"Yes, I know as for. You fool of a man. Must you do this everywhere we go? I'll find my own way back. Please leave, Winston. I've just about had it with you. I'll not take much more of this," she said, turning her back on them.

J. Winston Weatherford grinned from ear to ear and leered at the ladies before nodding to Tucker and making his way through the crowd.

"I'm sorry, ladies," said Tucker. "Please give my apologies to Mrs. Weatherford."

"Oh, sir, no need. He's a raving lunatic. Why she bothers with him, I cannot understand," said an elderly lady in a gown that threatened to swallow her whole.

"Honestly, Agatha," said Dame Flora Abbington. "Now he's gone and run her off again. And just as I had something I wished to ask her. Only a bit of gossip, mind you. It can wait, I suppose. Odious little man."

"Seems to be the consensus," thought Tucker as he nodded his exit to the ladies.

Being tall was a plus for Tucker as he scanned the crowd for Reggie. He spotted Winston Weatherford heading for the door, glaring back toward his wife as she glowered at him through narrow slits that would shoot bullets if they could. With one slap of the door, he wedged his mass through it and was gone. Tucker spotted Reggie watching the man leave and made a beeline for her.

"Uh! Such an odious little man."

"Odious little man, yes, that does seem to be the definitive word for him," replied Tucker.

"What does the 'J' stand for?"

Tucker kissed her forehead and smiled.

"Jackass," he said, leading her in the opposite direction.

4

Chapter 4

Larry Wilson: We could call the cops, Richard, but you know where we'd be spending our weekend. In some... goddamned hot police station answering questions we don't know the answers to.
-Weekend at Bernie's, 1989

Tucker spotted two women talking as they watched Weatherford exit the party. They were nodding together, and Tucker wondered what he had done to get under their skin.

"See those two there?" asked Tucker, pointing out the women to Reggie.

"Ye-ess."

"The one on the left is Candace Corbyn. She's the event coordinator for Brooklands, and the one on the right works for us. That's Audrey Ratliff, who Alene highly regards. She's incredibly organized, efficient, and doesn't miss a trick. Mum stole her from somewhere or somebody, but that happens a lot in this business. They were talking about Weatherford. Did you notice?"

"I wasn't sure, but if you say so. Wonder what he did to them?"

"Dunno, love, but we're going to find out. I don't need any surprises tonight."

They made their way to where the pair were engaged in quiet conversation while trying to appear inconspicuous.

"Candace, Audrey, how are you both this evening? Candace, everything is just lovely tonight. You have outdone yourself. Have you met my new assistant?"

"Thank you so much, Mr. Elliott, and no, I haven't," she said, turning light green eyes on Reggie.

"Miss Regina Winter, may I present Miss Candace Corbyn and Miss Audrey Ratliff?"

"So nice to meet you both," said Reggie. "You've done a beautiful job, Candace, and this is such a marvelous venue. I'm so glad you could host for us. And I've been looking forward to meeting you, Audrey. I haven't been to the UK recently, so I hope we can get better acquainted on this trip. I can catch you up on some of the things we're doing with the footwear line that was, well, losing traction, shall we say?"

"Oh, yes," said Audrey. "I did hear something about that. I'm hoping I can join you in Cleveland for the launch."

Reggie felt Tucker stiffen. She patted him on the shoulder and stepped aside.

"We're working hard on those plans and hope to be at full speed soon. We've had a few... distractions lately," said Tucker.

"Oh, yes. We heard," said Audrey. "That was so scary for Dahlia. And you all as well," she said, turning to Reggie. "So glad everything came out alright."

CHAPTER 4

Reggie had barely gotten over the tea room murders when they found themselves right back in it again on their lovely island escape. She had higher hopes for this quick getaway and annual event.

"And how is everything going here this evening?" asked Tucker. "Is there anything you need?"

The two women shot each other a glance as Audrey let out a huff and beckoned Candace to answer.

"We were just discussing it. You've already taken care of it. We were having a small challenge with one of the guests, but we see that he has taken his exit, so we don't anticipate any other... difficulties."

"Oh, damn," said Tucker, looking from one to the other. "What did he do to you?"

"It was more like what he was doing to you. And to Mrs. Elliott," said Audrey. "He was telling the guests that our new lines were actually his and that Alene had stolen them from him."

"And he was in the kitchen earlier," said Candace, growing an angry shade of red. "I thought Chef Dumont was going to walk out. Mr. Weatherford told him the menu looked like a backstreet public house and probably tasted like it. I moved the meat cleaver before Chef could think to use it."

The smile faded from Tucker's face as he sighed and shoved his hands in his pockets. The "odious little man" had struck again. Thank goodness his wife had competently dismissed him.

"I'm terribly sorry. I will go and apologize to Dumont. Is he sufficiently calm, or should I wait a tic?"

"Oh, I should think he's fine. He's quite busy with his preparations and overseeing the servers, so I'm hoping..."

"Thank you again," said Tucker, shaking his head at the man's audacity.

He was turning toward the kitchen when two others Reggie did not recognize joined the group.

"Ah, hello, Roswyn, Bella. How are you this evening? Reggie, meet two of our most esteemed team members: Mrs. Roswyn Walsh, our head of research and formulation, and her invaluable assistant, Bella Fielding. They are the lifeblood of our company."

"Why, thank you, Tucker, and it's nice to finally meet you, Reggie. We've heard so much about you. Welcome to the family," said Roswyn, extending her hand, Bella standing to her right.

"It's nice to meet you all," she said as Tucker looked impatiently toward the kitchen. "I'm looking forward to getting to know you better since we'll be in the UK for a bit."

"If you'll excuse us, please," said Tucker. "I better not wait to make my visit to Chef Dumont. Come with me, Reg."

Candace and Audrey watched as Tucker led Reggie by the hand toward the back of the venue. They gave each other a slight smirk and snickered.

"Wonder what she really assists him with?" whispered Candace.

"I know what I'd like to," said Audrey.

###

Alene Elliott was working the crowd when she saw Tucker drag Reggie into the kitchen at a speed that would make the racecourse drivers envious.

"Oh, what the devil now?" she muttered. "Excuse me, please, I must tend to something."

She instructed Audrey's assistant, April, to take over entertaining the valued guests milling about like geese in a gaggle. She squeezed through the crowd, bearing down on her son like a locomotive.

"Just what the devil do you think you're doing, Tucker? Regina? What is the meaning of this?"

"Come here, Mother," said Tucker, leading her away from Chef Dumont, who looked on with angry curiosity.

"Our 'friend' Weatherford told Chef Dumont that his food was backstreet pub fare, which made the man apoplectic and required Candace to remove the meat cleaver. Mother, the man is a menace. Why do you insist on sending him invitations every year?"

"Because if I don't, I will have stooped to his level, which will make things much worse in the end, dear. Let me handle Dumont. Please take Reggie out and mingle. The idiot man is no end of a pest. I wish he'd just go jump off the nearest bridge and be done with it."

"Be careful what you wish for, Mother."

Tucker ushered Reggie out and held the door as she hurried through it. The last thing he saw was his mother advancing on a haughty Chef Dumont with the most gracious of smiles and folded cash between her fingers. Mother knew how to solve matters most expeditiously. He glanced over to where Candace and Audrey had been and noticed they were gone. When he glanced at his watch, he saw why – it was almost time for the presentations, the introduction of the new flavors, and the awards for top performances for the company.

"Do you see Audrey anywhere, Reg? And do me a favor, please, and fetch Mum from the kitchens. She should be about finished with Dumont."

"Well, no, I don't, and do you think I should interrupt? I don't want to set off our temperamental chef again. Oh, wait – here she comes. Finished already?"

"How long does it take to hand a man a fistful of pound notes?" he mused.

"What?"

"Nothing. Round her up when you can, and I'll be at the podium with Audrey."

Reggie headed toward the kitchen while Tucker pushed through the crowd to the stage. On his way, he ran into Dahlia, Dulcy, and Laird, enjoying themselves with acquaintances passing from the buffet to the bar.

"Hey there! How's it going? We haven't seen you since we got here. Everything running smoothly?" asked Laird.

"Yes, like dropping rocks into a blender and watching them grind."

The three eyed each other and watched as Tucker blended with the crowd till he reached Audrey and April, clipboard at the ready. They could see him reviewing the program and watching intently as Reggie led Alene to the podium, Tolliver hovering like a watchful mother.

"What was that all about?" asked Dahlia. "Nothing going wrong, I hope. I don't like the look on his face. And I really don't want to see what happens if he spots 'her'."

"Who?" asked Dulcy.

"See the young lady over there? That is Lydia Kent-Williams, former Farthing's Fine Teas employee, and, wait for it, former Tucker Elliott love interest."

"Oooo! Juicy," said Dulcy. "What happened?"

"It ran its course, but not before he found her using the company lab for her personal projects. She's quite brilliant and has a couple of science degrees."

"What's she doing here?"

"Alene still invites her. She looks different. She's cleaned up a bit."

"Was she dirty?" laughed Dulcy.

"She was a bit unpolished, shall we say? Tucker may not even recognize her."

Dulcy watched as the young woman mingled with the other guests while maintaining an eye on Tucker. Was she keeping tabs or trying to stay out of his way? Tucker was all business and grim determination approaching the dais.

Alene took the stage while Tucker reviewed the program on April's clipboard. With a last glance at his watch, he signaled Alene to call the attendees to attention. A loud tapping noise caused a ripple in the crowd as she smiled and greeted the gathering guests. Movement slowly died out as all eyes were on Alene Farthing Elliott, the grand dame of the gala.

"Welcome, everyone! Honored guests, our loyal employees, and patrons. Thank you all so much for being with us tonight as we recognize those who make this event possible year after year. We're also excited to showcase our new flavors and invite you to sample every one of them. At this time, I'd like to present our son and ambassador, Tucker Farthing Elliott, to introduce this year's seasonal best. Tucker, please come forward."

Tucker kissed his mother's hand and took her place on stage to thundering applause. He had given his opening remarks and told a quick joke when he noticed a commotion in the back of the room. He watched as several people parted way to accommodate a frantic woman rushing through the back doors, screaming at the top of her voice.

"He's dead! He's dead! I tried to wake him. I thought he was drunk, but he was... dead!"

With a guttural groan, she turned a mottled gray, fluttered her eyes, and slid into the arms of the ever-present Tolliver.

5

Chapter 5

“Oh, as I hold this cold meat, I’m reminded of Winston. God rest his soul.”
-Mrs. Doubtfire, 1993

Tucker bolted from the stage, Reggie falling in behind, ball gown billowing through the guests.

“I’ve got this one, sir,” said Tolliver as Tucker passed him and the fallen woman.

He ran out the door, staring wildly into the night with Reggie in hot pursuit. He had no idea where to look or who he was supposed to see. And then he saw it – a form seemingly asleep on the “friendship bench” by the front entrance. How ironic, he thought. Reggie pulled up behind him, staring at the prone figure with a tide of revulsion welling in her stomach.

“Do you think the woman’s right?” she asked.

Tucker leaned over the man as the sound of sirens could be heard in the distance. Seeing nothing obvious, he waved Reggie closer. He scanned the area for security cameras but could detect nothing. Every venue had its own system.

"Go find Laird. This man is certainly dead. Where are the security teams, by the way? Maybe someone saw something useful."

"I think they're all inside now because of the special guests. Most everyone had already come in, plus there was security at the gate. I guess they didn't see a need to be out here, thinking the cameras would back them up."

"On second thought, I'm sure Laird will find us. Help keep this area blocked off. I don't want to touch the man, but I don't see anything to indicate what happened. I don't think there's anything we can do for him now."

True to form, Laird was soon looming over the scene, eyeing Tucker intently. Tucker shook his head and listened to the sirens coming closer. He looked at his watch. It had only been forty minutes since anyone had seen Weatherford, but that had been enough time for whatever had happened.

"Who is this man again?" asked Laird.

"J. Winston Weatherford, our main tea competition and all-around nasty bit of goods. He threatened Alene earlier this evening. Speaking of, where is Mum?"

"I think she's still near the stage trying to restore order."

"Reggie! Get Tolliver to fetch Alene. I'm sure the woman is fine now."

Tucker watched her hurry through the throng as Laird held back the growing, crowd. Tucker checked once more for a pulse, knowing it was too late. He gazed at the position of the body and searched for weapon evidence. He found no sign of trauma; no indication of a bullet, knife wound, or other obvious entry points. He was checking for signs of a fight when he caught a glimpse of something clutched in the man's fist.

"What is that? He's got something in his hand just there."

Tucker took out his handkerchief, grasped the object, and pulled. It was a sample gift packet of Amethyst Herbal, one of the new lines of Farthing's Fine Teas. As he was checking for other clues, he spied a spilled cup under the bench. Had he been drinking this, or was it a coincidence? Tucker was dying to grab the cup but didn't want to interfere with what would be an ensuing investigation.

The ambulance and police pulled in together, and Tucker gave one last glance at the scene before giving it up to them. He saw a stretcher and uniforms cutting through the crowd as his mother was exiting the entrance with Reggie and Tolliver. One look at her, and Tucker could see it would be a rough night ahead.

"Bloody ass. Leave it to him to pick my event for his final exit," she whispered to Tucker. "Has anyone found Olivia?"

Tucker and Laird shot each other a glance while Tolliver nodded and re-entered the building. He needed to find her quickly before she stumbled onto the scene herself.

"I found something," said Tucker to Laird.

"What? And where is it now?"

"I promise I am not interfering with an investigation, but take a look at this. It's one of our new blends debuting this evening. I found it wadded up in his fist. That's not all – look under the bench. It's a sample teacup spilled right underneath him."

"What are you saying, Tucker? What does this mean?" interrupted Alene.

"Excuse me, I'm Detective Chief Inspector Campbell, CID," said a man, flipping a badge. "Who's in charge here this evening?"

"Good evening, sir, Alene Elliott. This is my son and associate, Tucker. We were having our annual tea gala here when this unfortunate incident occurred. We have no idea what happened. I believe it's in everyone's best interests to end the event for the night, don't you?"

"Stevens, get these people back inside, cordon off the area, and you lot, come with me," he said, noticing Laird. "And you are?"

"Agent John Laird, FBI, U. S."

"You're a bit out of your jurisdiction, aren't you, Agent?" he said with a smirk.

"Strictly social, DCI Campbell. Until now."

A flurry inside the doorway ushered in Mrs. Winston Weatherford's arrival, steamrolling over everyone in her path.

"What is it now? Oh, Winston, not again. This drunken behavior has got to stop, or I'm leaving you."

"Uh, madam, I'm afraid he's already left *you*," said DCI Campbell. "This man is dead."

Olivia Weatherford's stately figure began to crumble, coiling into a human puddle and falling into, yet again, Sidney Tolliver's capable arms.

6

Chapter 6

"I'd agree with you but then we'd both be wrong."
- Russell Lynes, AZQuotes.com

The questioning continued through the evening until everyone was excused to return to their accommodations with a warning from DCI Campbell not to stray too far. The group was huddled in the Porter's study with Jennings attending to the ruffled feathers of the Elliotts.

"I'm so sorry, Alene. It was a beautiful evening. Mostly," offered Delia Porter.

"Until it wasn't. Blast that man for ruining my lovely gala. He'd go to any lengths to irritate me."

"Uh, Mother, I don't think he'll bother you anymore," said Tucker. "The man is dead, love."

"What did you say to me earlier?" asked Alene. "Be careful what you wish for? If it were that easy, I'd get rid of all my competition."

"Please drink this, Mrs. Elliott," said Jennings, slipping a considerable measure of brandy into her hands as the others watched in stunned silence.

"I do believe she's in shock," whispered Reggie to Tucker as Tolliver nodded in agreement.

"Is there anything I can get anyone?" asked Jennings.

"No, mate, I think you've done a brilliant job. We'll just relax for a minute and then pop off home and to bed. Tolliver, why don't you just bunk in at the Elliott house this evening? Much easier for you."

"Thank you, sir. I would appreciate that."

"So, what next?" asked Mr. Porter, as all eyes turned to Laird.

"All I can say is that they have their investigative methods here, and no one should interfere. Is that clear? Just answer their questions, don't volunteer anything, and don't nose around anywhere. I'm sorry, Mrs. Elliott. It was a beautiful setting and a nice gathering."

"Till it wasn't," she said again. "Tucker, you and Reggie will have to step in and help with damage control. We'll need to reroute the launch and go ahead with the new lines. And no, I didn't steal them from Weatherford. Pompous ass."

"We know you didn't, love. He has no credibility. It's not worth getting ruffled feathers, now is it? It's late and I have a guess that it's going to be a bugger of a day tomorrow. I'd be ready for early calls from our CID friends," said Tucker. "Dahlia, we shall see you tomorrow, yes?"

"Of course. Try to get some rest, Mother Elliott," she said, patting Alene's arm and blowing her a kiss before heading to bed.

"I shall sleep like a baby, dear. No worries. It's whoever rid the world of the not-so-dearly departed Winston Weatherford that should have a bit of trouble resting. Not in peace, as it were."

"Let's get her moving home, Reg," said Tucker. "I think she's had about enough. And it will be a huge day tomorrow."

The group disbanded in a barrage of hugs and kisses and made for their separate quarters to sleep the sleep of the innocent. Hopefully.

###

The morning revealed a brilliant blue sky as the households rallied and began their day, unsure of what was in store.

"Good morning, Tolliver. You're up bright and early. What's up?"

"Well, sir, I couldn't really sleep. Not that the accommodations weren't more than one could wish for, but I just don't understand a few things."

"Well, mate, when you say you don't understand something, I listen. You seem to have a second sight. How do you come by this, Tolliver?"

"What I mean, sir, is that there are a few things I don't quite follow."

"And those would be?"

"The cameras, sir. I don't understand the cameras. Why didn't anyone instantly ask about those? In my humble opinion, sir."

"Fair point, Tolliver. Something to ask Campbell, I imagine. Maybe we missed something there."

Tucker stared at the eggs piled on his plate, the bacon encroaching on them, and the toast and tomatoes hovering on the side like vultures. His appetite fell a bit. What Tolliver said filled his brain with more questions that he would now need the answers to. He had looked for them last night, but they had eluded him. He had put these things out of his mind until Tolliver brought them back in a rush.

"Hello all!" said Reggie, streaming into breakfast, looking like an ad from a fashion magazine.

She was again impeccably dressed and, of course, sporting yet another pair of flip-flops that would leave an impression on anyone, let alone the man responsible for the welfare of the entity itself.

"I'm sorry," said Tucker, "but do please back up a pace and let me admire those gorgeous things on your feet. They're sexy, enticing, and please tell me they're ours."

Reggie was sporting a pale-yellow flip-flop with a tiny heel. The colors splashed all over them like a Jackson Pollack painting, exactly matching the patterns in her tailored blouse and flared A-line skirt.

"Oh, I would, but then I'd be shooting a huge arrow through your wonderful heart-shaped bubble, wouldn't I?"

"They're not ours," he stated, disappointment enveloping the room like an English mist.

"Almost," she said," but there are a few details still to work out with the company we're laying to rest. And then there's the rest of the inventory as well."

"Gawd," said Tucker. "Just do it and don't tell me about it."

Reggie grabbed a plate and chose various items to graze upon. She also grabbed a glance at the two men at the table, picking at their food like children refusing to eat their vegetables.

"It looks like I interrupted," she said. "I may not be the first nanny, but I am the second, and I sense a... conundrum, shall we say? What's going on?"

"Oh, Miss Reggie, we were just discussing something I was trying to figure out last night. It's probably just me," said Tolliver.

"Oh, don't believe that, my girl. When this man thinks he sees or doesn't see something, best watch because what follows is usually a carefully deduced, systematic means of getting at the truth."

"You don't mind if I eat alone?" teased Reggie, stalling at the buffet.

Tucker and Tolliver watched her slather a plateful of breakfast grease to her heart-healthy choices. She graced them with a dazzling smile and moved to the other end of the football-field table to ignore them and eat in peace.

"We've mucked it up, haven't we?" asked Tucker.

"I'll just make some notes, sir, if that's alright with you."

"Mr. Elliott?" said the housekeeper, shyly poking her head into the room.

"Yes, Myra, what is it?"

"Sir, if you please, Detective Inspector Campbell would be wantin' to see ya, sir."

Tucker pushed his plate away, glanced at Tolliver, and stared down the table at Reggie, who continued to dig into her breakfast goodies as if no one else in the world existed.

"Well, Tolliver. Shall we?"

Tolliver gave his plate a wistful glance, rose, and trailed after Tucker like a puppy heeling to its master.

###

"Good morning, sir," said DCI Campbell, stepping through the door before being invited.

"Please, come in," said Tucker sarcastically. He grimaced and shot Tolliver a command to follow and be ready to defend the hallowed halls and all those within.

Reggie sighed and gave into the intrusion in the front hall. She could stand it no longer. The two men had been marched from their breakfast to face the bombastic and blunt detective inspector. She popped one last strawberry into her mouth and abandoned her dish on the sideboard. She headed to the foyer where she saw the three men dancing around each other like dogs sniffing butts.

"Anything I can help with?" she said, advancing on the trio watching her every move.

Tucker was eyeing her feet.

Tolliver was staring past her.

Campbell smiled and attempted to head off Tucker as he moved quickly to her side.

"It's Miss Winter, is that right?"

"Why, yes, Detective Inspector. Thank you for remembering. I want you to know that if there's anything you need, just let me know."

"Thank you, Miss Winter. And you are involved how again, please?"

Tucker snickered while Tolliver tried to hide in plain sight. Reggie lightly laughed.

"I am Mr. Elliott's assistant. I help with everything related to the business, mostly on the American side, but you can call on me for whatever you wish."

"Thank you so much, Miss Winter. I'll be getting back to you once I've had a chance to speak with these two. Mrs. Elliott has already given your credentials," he said, sporting a patronizing smile that Reggie wanted to smack off his face.

"Shall we go to the study, Campbell?" said Tucker. "I regret to say that my mother has yet to come downstairs this morning."

"Please don't trouble yourself," said DCI Campbell. "We'll have plenty of opportunity to speak with Mrs. Elliott. I know she's not going anywhere, and there are things to clear up."

"What things?" asked Tucker.

"Well, we do have some questions for her. There were accusations last night from the deceased, and we will need to sort those out."

"What kind of accusations?" asked Tucker. Tolliver took out a small pad and began jotting notes.

"I believe you know there is an alleged rumor that the deceased had accused Mrs. Elliott of stealing his formulas for the, uh, tea ... launch," he said, flipping hurriedly through his notes.

"You've got to be joking," snorted Tucker. "No one would ever take those accusations seriously. He was intoxicated and, once again, taking advantage of my mother's good intentions and good nature."

"How so?"

"I actually asked her," said Tucker, leaning into the man's face, "why she continued to extend invitations to this wretched piece of ... dryer lint. She said she refused to stoop to his level and that if she did, it would only be worse."

"Why would that be? Sir."

"It would only be worse for her because he would continue to twist her words and shovel his preposterous lies," finished Tucker.

"So, she had every reason to see him out of the picture or the teapot, if you catch my train of thought."

"What? No! I only mean..."

"What do you mean?" said a voice from the study doorway.

"Good morning, Mother. How nice to see you. How are you?"

"That depends. What is it you're trying to do? Defend me, or send me up for the rest of my life?"

"Oh, now, Alene, you know..."

"If I may," said Tolliver with a slight cough, "was there something that the officer needed to ask Mrs. Elliott? Since she is now here, I think maybe we can clear things up."

Tucker watched as Reggie walked up behind his mother and held onto her. Alene squeezed Reggie's hand and advanced into the room and the face of DCI Campbell before gracefully placing herself on the settee. Reggie eyed Tucker warily and leaned against the door, anticipating a scene.

"Mrs. Elliott, I will get to the point here," said the DCI. "You were accused of pirating Mr. Weatherford's formulas for your own launch."

Alene Farthing Elliott was not one to be trifled with. She rose to her full height and stared down Campbell like one of her errant children.

"If you think for one minute that I consider his accusations anything other than the ramblings of a has-been and desperate man, then you are sadly mistaken. I would think you would have better things to do than to take that direction. So, please tell us what you've found to help find this killer, who is obviously still among us."

"Nothing other than that everything seems to be pointing at you, Mrs. Elliott."

Alene stared down the inspector with a practiced eye.

"You can't be serious."

"I'm sorry, Campbell, I don't like where you're going with this," said Tucker. "You must have other people to question. Other avenues to consider."

"We can't ignore certain points, sir," said DCI Campbell, "and I think we've found our suspect in Mrs. Elliott here. We're just following the evidence.

She seems to be the one with the motive, the most to lose, and a damning confession."

"What?? What confession?" she said, leaning into the man's face.

"Do you deny that when Weatherford said he'd give you his new formulas over his dead body, you said that could be arranged?"

"Yes, but, well, I..."

"And weren't you overheard later in the kitchens saying that you wished he'd just be thrown off a bridge and be done with it?"

"How dare you! Those are retorts in the heat of the moment with no meaning whatsoever. I will not stand here and be accused in my own home of ridding the world of this old sod."

"That's fine with me, Mrs. Elliott, because as of right now, we are taking you to the station for questioning as the chief suspect in the murder of J. Winston Weatherford."

7

Chapter 7

It's true what they say: Cops and women don't mix. It's like eating a spoonful of Drano; sure, it'll clean you out, but it'll leave you hollow inside.
-Naked Gun: From the Files of Police Squad, 1988

"Tucker! Call Chalmers. He hasn't been of any use so far, but he needs to earn his retainer. Now!"

"Right on it, Mother. Tolliver, you heard the woman, call Chalmers. Reggie, a moment, please," he said, opening the study door and colliding with Myra, who was pretending to be cleaning something.

"Myra, do actually go clean something, love. Mother won't be happy when she comes back from the nick, and things aren't spic and span."

"Oh, sir, I can't abide it," she said, sniveling and blowing her nose.

"It will be fine. We'll sort all this out; just wait and see. Now, off with you."

They watched as Myra listlessly wiped her cloth over an already spotless antique buffet.

"Reggie, this is a bloody mess. Do me a favor, please, and help Tolliver while I follow Alene to the station. This Campbell bloke is a right sneaky bastard, and I'll need to be holding her hand. Call Dahlia, Laird, and Dulcy and get them moving as well. This ought to cock up the day worse than the buggered launch gala."

Reggie listened as Tucker reviewed the duties and delegated basic details to her. She worried about Alene making new "friends" in Stir. Her heart went out to him, and she gave his hand a squeeze.

"I'm sorry, I really am. You know you can count on me to help in any way I can. You go with Alene. Tolliver and I will hold the fort. He knows what to do in a situation such as this."

"Thank you, lovely assistant. What would I do without you?"

"Oh, let's not find out," she said with a firm pat of his hand. "Now go. I've got this."

"Yes. Yes, you really do. He drew her close, kissing her tenderly before grudgingly releasing her.

She watched the lanky man pivot to the door and then disappear. Peering into the study, she found Tolliver perched on the vacated settee, brooding over his notepad.

"Hello, Tolliver," she said, gently lowering into the wing-back chair opposite. "So, it looks like it's just you and me. If I may ask again, what is your given name?"

"It's Sidney, Miss. Sidney Tolliver."

"Alright, Tolliver, let's get moving."

"Moving, Miss?"

"Yes. Spring into action. Get to work. Dive right in. First, let me go over what Tucker needs done. What is it, Tolliver?"

"Well..."

"You're still buggered about the cameras, to use Tucker's terms, aren't you?"

"Yes, Miss. It just seems like something's wrong there."

"Are you sure? They're not exactly obligated to share their investigative findings with us, you see. How do you know they haven't already gone through the footage and found something of use?"

"Then they wouldn't have taken Mrs. Elliott. I'm sorry, Miss, I just can't get it out of my head."

"Noted, Tolliver. Did you manage to find Dahlia and the others?"

"I left a message with Jennings. Nice chap. Efficient. Have always liked him," he said, wandering from the subject.

"You've no idea. He's a wonder, really. He reminds me a bit of you, actually."

Tolliver reddened and buried his face in his notepad. And as usual in these instances, Reggie's busy mind was already off and running and formulating a plan.

"Tolliver."

"Yes, Miss?" he said, relieved to be rescued from the embarrassment of her compliment.

"You said you left a message with Jennings. So no one was up and about at the Porter residence?"

"If they were, he didn't know it, Miss."

"Doesn't sound a bit like Jennings. They must still be sleeping or at least relaxing before getting going. Jennings knows when the mice move in that house."

"The Porters have mice?"

"Just an expression, Tolliver."

Reggie's idea was growing larger by the minute, and the more she thought about it, the more she felt the pressure of time against them. They had to act before Laird could stop them.

"Tolliver, my dear," said Reggie, eyes glistening. "Have you any thoughts on where to start with damage control?"

"No, Miss. I was hoping Mr. Elliott would be more specific with you as to whom he would like me to call first, but I can forge ahead. It seems obvious; I need to speak to, let's see, Miss Corbyn and Miss Ratliff. We will have to reschedule the gala. That's going to be a sticky one, but Miss Corbyn will most likely take care of that."

"I'm sure it'll all work out, but that's not what I'm thinking about right now."

Tolliver watched Reggie quietly as her brain chugged along at a rapid pace.

He could almost see her thoughts gathering steam. It reminded him of Tucker, in Las Vegas, happily defying every order and command Detective Nick Stone had given him. A light was dawning, and he began to feel queasy. This scene was all too familiar.

"Oh, Miss, I'm getting a familiar feeling here. And not a particularly good familiar feeling."

"That's just the queasiness, Tolliver; it will soon pass. Take heart; all will be well. Now, here's what we're going to do..."

###

Dulcy rolled over and reached for John Laird but found only crumpled pillows and ruffled sheets. She lazily rolled back over, slowly recalling the events of the night before. They were not good events. She scanned the room but found no trace.

"Now, how did I lose a six-foot, three-inch, hunky, handsome cop who I swear was just in my clutches?"

"You didn't lose me. You can't get rid of me that easily," he said, crawling through the sheets and landing face-to-face with her.

"Oooo, you're wet."

"And you're not. I've showered, checked my messages, and rang for Jennings while you lounged in bed like a countess on vacation. Don't you want to know what's going on out in the world?"

"If it's anything like last night, no," she said defiantly, throwing the covers over both of their heads.

"Come on, my love, rally. We need to find out what's happening with the Elliotts. I'm going to wheedle my way in at the station and get information on the postmortem. I don't think Campbell will help much there, but I know my way around a morgue. I want you to find Reggie and Tucker and see what's happening with them."

"So, your idea for our lovely Christmas vacation is to rummage around the dead bodies in a morgue on another continent?"

"It's not rummaging around. They're very thorough here. I plan to get the preliminary findings as soon as possible. The faster we sift through this, the less damage the tea business will see."

Dulcy felt properly chastised. She groaned, stretched, and raised herself onto her elbow with a sigh of resignation. She had every intention of giving the FBI agent a piece of her mind when a knock at the door interrupted her before she could get in a word.

"Good morning, Miss, Sir. I took the liberty of bringing a full breakfast for you. Eat hearty, then. It's going to be a rather busy day," said Jennings. "And Miss Dahlia will be resting this morning. She finds that her headaches go away much more quickly if she can shut herself in a dark room till they subside. You'll just need to press on without her."

"I'm sorry to hear that, Jennings. So, it appears you know things that we don't, then?" said Laird.

"The Elliotts have already had their wake-up call today, so it's time to be on your way."

"What's happened, Jennings?" asked Dulcy, twisting in the sheets and sitting upright.

"I shall give you the quick version, Miss," he said. "As Mr. Elliott and Mr. Tolliver were scheduling today's duties for damage control, DCI Campbell arrived to continue his investigation. The ensuing actions were less than favorable for the Elliotts, I'm afraid, as Campbell collected Mrs. Elliott and removed her to the local station for interrogation on suspicion of murder. Mr. Elliott and senior have followed to lend aid and assistance."

"What?" squeaked Dulcy.

"Would you like me to repeat the message, Miss?"

"No, no, no, we got it the first time," said Laird, jumping from the bed and grabbing the tray from the man. "Thank you, Jennings. Anything else I should know?"

"No, sir, only that Mr. Elliott did request that you meet him at the police station. You will find the address on the sheet provided," he said, pointing to a piece of house stationery with the Porter crest at the top. "A car has been pulled from the garages and is at your disposal. Do you require a driver, or are you comfortable motoring here?"

"I've got it, Jennings. What are the rest of them doing, do you know?"

"Mr. Tolliver and Miss Reggie are working with the necessary staff to handle the press and keep the launch on schedule. As I understand it, they are at work as we speak. Will there be anything else, Sir, Miss?"

"No, Jennings, thank you."

Dulcy reclined on her pillow and sighed. She stared at the goodies, wondering if she now had any appetite to even enjoy them. Laird was dressing as he munched a butter-slathered scone.

"So, breakfast, but no dessert."

"Later, my love, later," he said as he kissed her and pulled off her sheets.

###

"I demand to know with what I am being charged," stated Alene Elliott, towering over Constable Downs, who was out of his element and visibly uncomfortable.

"You're not being charged, madam; you are just being questioned. May I get you a cup of tea?" he asked. He then reddened to the shade of a fine wine.

"I require nothing except my attorney. Tucker, have you found him yet?"

"He's on his way, Mother, not to worry."

"Dad, walk with me, please. Tell me what you can. You said when we first got here that you'd be glad when all this was over. I didn't think much of it at the time, but was there a specific reason why you said that? Were there problems with this launch?"

Douglass Elliott had stayed happily hidden in the background, avoiding questions and the limelight in his usual manner. But there was a gloom in his face that Tucker hadn't seen before. There were shadows, and those shadows were concealing something, and Tucker meant to find out what it was.

"What aren't you telling me, Dad, because I can see there is something," he said, guiding his father to a quiet corner of the station.

"I never could keep anything from you, son. You always seem to draw it out of me."

"Then there is something."

"Yes, but I don't think...

A sound like a tornado ricocheting through an empty building reached them as Attorney Chalmers's blustering and blathering form came into view. Constable Downs poked his head out of the interrogation room and flinched as the attorney came closer with each step. Alene held steady behind him, smiling sweetly as the man bore down on them.

"I won't forget about this, Dad. You've got to tell me what's happened. It could mean everything. It certainly might point us to who killed Weatherford. I'm fairly certain you don't want them hanging onto Mother."

"Gawd, son. I'm fairly certain they don't want to hang onto her either," said the senior Elliott, and the two chuckled for the first and last time of the day.

8

Chapter 8

I know my behavior can be erratic at times.
-American Psycho, 2000

Reggie was organizing while Tolliver was in the background, pacing and darting worried glances at her. His familiar feeling was making itself right at home. He was having flashbacks to Las Vegas when Alene had dispatched him to keep Tucker Elliott from creating his usual headlines - the unattractive ones. His efforts had not only failed but failed spectacularly. By no fault of their own, the company was maligned by alleged drug trafficking, two unfortunate murders, and an accidental death. The two got themselves in it up to their necks, landing Farthing's Teas in a publicity nightmare, much to the dismay of Alene and company. Tolliver couldn't shake his growing uneasiness and searched for a means of escape.

"Hang in there, Tolliver," said Reggie, watching him pace. "Don't go running on me just yet. I have a brilliant idea which will not only be simple but will cure all your ills."

"You have a gun on you then, Miss?"

"Oh, stop, Tolliver. This will be helpful. Let's go before we lose any more time."

"Or the others catch us in the act."

"And then there's that."

"Shall I drive, Miss?"

"Yes, please. You drive, and I'll direct. We'll get your questions answered, and you'll be feeling fine in no time."

"Yes, Miss," replied Tolliver, feeling the same angst as when babysitting Tucker.

"Do you mind my asking where we're going, Miss?"

"Not at all. We're going to Brooklands, of course."

Tolliver's angst turned to acid, and his stomach took a pitch as he pulled out of the Porter drive.

"But that is certainly not on the list for today, Miss. Are you sure this is where Mr. Elliott wants us to be going?"

"Of course he doesn't want us going to Brooklands, but I'll never get your full attention unless we settle the camera angle. Ha Ha. Camera angle."

Tolliver returned Reggie's laughter with a smile that looked as though he'd sipped rancid tea.

"What do we hope to accomplish there, Miss?"

"We'll hunt down Candace and get her to show us the security cameras. It'll be killing two birds with one stone – you get your camera question answered, and we can knock out our business with her while we're there. On the way home, we can drop by the offices and see Audrey. Lord only knows she's probably having a nightmare of a day."

Tolliver could only focus on the busy road and pray that Tucker Elliott had his hands full with DCI Campbell. If not, they would likely be around his neck. Traffic was moving at a brisk pace, and before Tolliver had time to think of something else to worry about, they were pulling into the entrance of The Brooklands Aviation and Motoring Museum.

"Such a lovely spot," said Reggie. "It's even prettier in the daytime with all the flowers and lovely antique cars. Oh my, is that the Concorde, Tolliver?"

"Yes, Miss, this is its permanent home now. The museum holds all kinds of motor racing cars, collections, exhibitions, history of the site during the wars, the motor course years. It's a wonderful tribute to racing and flight. This was actually the world's first motor racing course where both men and women made history and broke records."

"How amazing! I can't wait to find out more. I hope we can still have the launch here. It's fantastic," she said, secretly thrilled that Tolliver was distracted by the venue details.

They drove to the car park and were looking for a space when Reggie had a thought. Why park out here when they had business inside the gates with Candace?

"Tolliver, do me a favor, please, and just run the car up to the front of the museum. We'll find Candace, and she can point us to the cameras."

As Tolliver rounded the bend toward the front of the museum, the stark reality dawned on them. Bands of blue and white tape emblazoned with "POLICE" were strewn across the clubhouse entrance, including the now-infamous bench of J. Winston Weatherford's unexpected departure.

"Here then, what's your business, Miss?"

"I'm so sorry, Constable, but we have an appointment with Candace Corbyn. We were part of all this last night," she said, pointing to the crime tape swinging in the late morning breeze.

"I can't let you in there, Miss. If you'd like, you can wait here while I see if she's available. Who might I say is calling?"

"It's Regina Winter, Farthing's Fine Teas, representing Alene Elliott. This is Mr. Tolliver, one of our associates. Unfortunately, Mrs. Elliott has been detained and was unable to accompany us."

Tolliver coughed and wheezed as the constable peered around Reggie, eyeing him intently.

"Wait here, please."

"She's been detained, Miss? Couldn't you have said something else? Anything?"

"Oh, Tolliver, it doesn't have to mean she's been hauled off to jail. It can mean she's too busy to make the appointment. It's just syntax."

"It feels more like my head on a block, Miss, when Mrs. Elliott finds out."

"Really, it'll be fine. Besides, we've got bigger worries at the moment."

"And those would be?"

"Well, the big fat appointment lie we just told, if she's even on site, and most of all, how will we ever get to see the cameras if everything is blocked off?"

Tolliver was holding his head in his hands when the constable quickly returned to Reggie's door.

"If you please, park the motorcar in that area there and follow me."

Tolliver eased the car into a small space not far from the Concorde. The sight was majestic and awe-inspiring, and the two almost forgot they had a constable waiting for them.

"Well, we're in, Tolliver. Just follow my lead. It'll be fine."

All Tolliver thought was, "Where have I heard that before?" but he trotted off after her anyway.

###

"I can't think when I've had a more miserable morning," pronounced Alene Elliott as she blew into the family study.

Tucker and Douglass Elliott treaded carefully behind, signaling Myra for a stiff round for all. Dulcy and Laird had made their appearance at the station just as it had gotten interesting and were following once Laird had coaxed whatever he could out of DCI Campbell.

"I'm sorry, Mother, not a great way to start your day, I know. Things haven't been going so well so far, have they, Dad?" he said, leveling an intense gaze on his father. "Let's have it, then."

Douglass Elliott walked slowly to the settee and eased himself onto it for the duration. He gently picked up Alene's hand and held it in his own as Myra entered the room with the restoratives.

Thank you, Myra," said Tucker. "Have you seen Miss Reggie and Mr. Tolliver about?"

"No, sir, all's I know is that they went off in the motorcar. Mr. Tolliver was drivin'. They didn't say as to where they was goin', sir."

"Thank you, Myra," said Alene as she accepted her drink. "Say again, Tucker? Let's have what?"

"Thank you, Myra. Dad? I want to know all of it."

For the first time since he had arrived, Tucker saw a momentary flutter in Alene's face. She was a tough old bird, but even she couldn't hide what her husband was about to reveal. He could see it in her face, in the sudden sag of her shoulders and the cast of her eyes.

"I didn't want to bother you with it, Tucker, because it's nothing. Just a nuisance to deal with, is all. For some time now..."

"Miss Dulcy and Mr. Laird, ma'am, if you please," said Myra as she led the two into the tense situation.

Tucker could see John Laird stiffen as he assessed the scene. He politely ushered Dulcy before him and seated her while he stood nearby.

"Mr. and Mrs. Elliott," nodded Laird. "I feel like we've come at a bad time."

"No, no," said Alene. "You've come just at the right time. The time for all this to be discussed and finally gotten out in the open."

Tucker sat quietly, afraid to move for fear of breaking the trance that held the room. Dulcy reached for Laird's hand as Alene shifted, took her hand from her husband's, and folded it in her lap.

"As I was saying, for some time now, we've been at odds with the Weatherford Company, and it's only gotten worse as the gala came closer. What you heard last night was not the first of his accusations. As it happens, he's been sending us the most damning correspondence. I wasn't sure how he was getting his information, but with each letter, he seemed to know exactly what we were doing and when."

"And how," added the senior Elliott. "We've been gathering the evidence and comparing it."

"Comparing it to what?" asked Tucker.

"His formulas, ingredients, and processes," said Alene.

"And from everything we've seen, it appears there's only one conclusion," said Mr. Elliott.

"And that is?" asked Laird.

"That we did indeed steal his formulas," announced Alene.

9

Chapter 9

Hammond: You know, you're real stupid for a cop, man. You're following this guy too close.
Cates: Yeah, well, most cops are pretty stupid, but since you landed in jail what the hell does that make you?
-48 Hrs., 1982

"I'm sorry, Mother, I'm not following. How could you have possibly stolen his ideas and formulas? You have your own development people. He has his. What could possibly make you believe such an utterly ridiculous claim?"

"It's a scare tactic," interjected Laird. "He was trying to get you to lose faith in yourself and disrupt your new releases and, of course, your popular galas. If he's been sending you communications, he's harassing you. Did you keep these notes?"

"Not at first," said Mr. Elliott. "We burned the first few, and when they kept coming, we hid them away in a file."

"I hated keeping something so scurrilous," said Alene. "And what was so disturbing was that it was as if he knew everything we were testing and was claiming it as his own. It's been quite stressful."

"I hate to bring it up, but you know you'll need to turn those letters over to Campbell," said Laird.

"Well then, he really will think I killed him. I don't think that's a wise decision, do you?" she asked, staring down Tucker.

"I think you need to fetch the file and let us see these letters. You're not interfering with their investigation; you're just not giving them all the information you have. Let's look them over and then decide what to do," said Tucker, turning to Laird.

"I agree. Besides, if you're telling us everything and you haven't stolen his proprietary information, you've nothing to worry about, and he's the one who should be investigated. Sounds like just the opposite to me."

"What do you mean?" asked Alene.

"It's suspicious to me," he said. "How did he know everything you're doing? How could he be right on the money with every accusation?"

"I don't know," said the senior Elliott, "except the only thing I can think of is that someone has been feeding him our information."

"Exactly," said Laird. "You've got a leak, Mrs. Elliott!

###

"Good morning, Candace," said Reggie, extending her hand. The young woman entered the clubhouse foyer, looking calm and relaxed despite the disarray around her. "How is everything today?"

Tolliver glanced around at the red tape marking the indoor off-limits areas. He wondered what clues the police were looking for when the man was found outside, rather than inside, where he was no longer welcome. Discreetly scanning the taped area, his eyes fell on the Farthing's Fine Teas sample table, complete with a full product selection.

"Oh. Pity," he thought. "What a waste of all that."

Candace had been telling Reggie about her morning. It sounded like the opening chapter of a suspense novel where the innocent young woman finds herself in it up to her eye sockets with no clue as to how it happened.

"After we left last night, I thought they would finish and be done with it. Imagine my surprise when I arrived this morning, and a whole fresh hell greeted me as I walked into the clubhouse."

"How did you even get in?" asked Reggie. "We were stopped immediately by the young man who came to find you."

"I came in the back way. There was no one there, and I didn't think anything of it until I entered the kitchen to what looked like a showing of a CSI episode. I do love those shows you have in America. We get some of them here," she said, eyes shining brightly.

Reggie shot Tolliver a glance. This naïve young thing was in more trouble than she possibly knew. As Reggie thought it over, she had to admit that they were as well.

"I'm sorry you're having to deal with all this, Candace. Is there anything we can do to help?"

"Yes! You can reschedule the gala and help stifle the ugly rumors about our venue. We've had three cancellations this morning alone, and no matter what I say, I know they don't believe me. 'We've had a change of plans.' 'We're no longer going to have a big event.' 'We found a better price for our gathering.' One woman even said she couldn't possibly enjoy an event at a venue where a murder had been committed. Our donations are going to plummet if we don't solve this quickly."

"You know it has nothing to do with you, right? It was just a bad blood war between Farthing's Fine Teas and Weatherford's Brands. You can't possibly be blamed for all this."

"I know, but try telling our clientele that. I swear I could just kill that old goat myself if someone hadn't beaten me to it."

Tolliver flinched, and Reggie winced as Candace stomped her foot to punctuate her statement.

"Try not to worry. And for God's sake, be careful what you say. Alene wished the old man would jump off a bridge and be done with it, and look how that turned out. She was dragged to the station to be questioned for murder."

The two stared in silence, then burst out laughing, much to the dismay of Tolliver.

"Is there somewhere we can sit and talk?" she asked. "I'm sure we can find some way to help. We need to get our launch back on track, and there's no time like now to get that done."

"Of course," said Candace. "I should probably get Audrey involved, although I called and left a message and haven't heard back yet. I'm sure she's probably in her own little hell as we speak."

"Just one thing," said Reggie with a pleading look. "May I use the ladies' room? It has been quite a morning."

"Oh, of course. Just 'round the way there by the disgraced tea sampling table, and then on your left. We'll be over there in that office off the hall by the kitchen."

She led Tolliver around a short corner toward a narrow passage. As they passed the historical portraits, Tolliver saw DCI Campbell enter the kitchen. He began giving the crew new directives. Tolliver wondered what those could be when he heard the name Alene Elliott. His heart stopped for a beat, and he struggled to listen to the rise and fall of the conversation.

"Questioned her, evidence of poison, tea samples and the most damning of all – find the person or persons who prepared those tea samples" were all that Tolliver could glean from Campbell's barking. Whatever road they were taking, it looked as though it led straight to the Elliott's doorstep.

###

"So, what do you think?" asked Dulcy as they left the Elliotts. "Is Alene in big trouble, or is this just a little scrape?"

Laird sat silently thinking about the scene in the manor house, his mind on driving in the country in a tiny car on the wrong side of the road. He wasn't satisfied with what he saw in the small, local station full of "coppers." Things were spinning out of control at an alarming rate.

"I need to speak with Tucker alone," he said as they were driving back to the Porter residence. "He can help more than he knows. I'm American, not local, and I present a problem for them."

"Why? You're just a visiting copper. Did I say that right?"

"Yes, but because I'm involved by default, and I'm sure they don't want me to be. Others inviting themselves into your investigation isn't always welcome. Or never, mind you."

"What should we do next?"

"I don't even want to say."

"Oh, my gosh; you're going to pull a Reggie!"

"I'm not going to do any such thing. I don't even know what that is."

"You're going to go just a little outside the law, my dear. And I'll help. I wonder where that girl is? She wasn't at the house. She was supposedly with Tolliver doing damage control. Uh oh, what do you think?"

"I think she's probably doing more damage than she is control. We'll need to find her as soon as possible."

###

As Laird and Dulcy were heading back to the Porters, Reggie and Tolliver were wrapping up details for rescheduling the tea launch with Candace Corbyn. It would be as impressive an event as the original but without the murderous touch. It would also be a saving grace for both parties while giving Reggie more time to investigate the murder.

"This really is a fascinating place," she said, glancing again at the cordoned-off tea sample table. She had seen Tolliver looking that way and wondered what he was thinking.

"Would you like a tour?" asked Candace.

"Of course! Oh, and look at our lovely sample table," she said, wandering over to the cordoned-off area. "Such a shame. It's a nice presentation that shall have to be tossed, every last bit of it."

She was leaning in to view the dainty sample packets when Candace brought her attention to the other end of the display. The elegant tea urns were still in place, name placards solemnly gracing the plates in front of them.

"Oh, what a shame," repeated Reggie. "Such a waste, don't you think?"

"Oh, well, this is all evidence," said Candace. "They're being transported as soon as possible to the police lab for further testing. I would have thought they would already be gone, but here they sit. I can't possibly imagine why they're still here. I guess because they're not done with Chef Dumont's area yet. I've never seen such haphazard investigating."

"Have you seen a lot of investigations?" asked Reggie.

"No, of course not, but it would just seem that, well, you know... "

"Why don't we take that tour and let the constables get on with their duties?" Reggie said, taking Tolliver's arm.

Tolliver wondered what Miss Regina was up to now, given everything happening around them. Candace guided them to the rear, where just a short time ago, Chef Dumont had practiced his culinary artwork, been offended by Weatherford, and been bribed by Alene Elliott.

"This is our state-of-the-art kitchen," she said, leaning over the crime tape as she went to the back entrance. "We'll go out this door so we stay out of their way."

Reggie peeked at Tolliver and winked. She hoped to get information on the investigation inside before they were forced to leave, but she had prepared for any interference.

“What did you do?” whispered Tolliver.

Reggie just smiled as she followed Candace to the sleek, sexy Concorde sitting proudly off to the side. People were milling about in awe.

“We have daily tours of the ship with a special deluxe tour for the adults. Actual Concorde pilots teach you the history and take you on a virtual flight in a real seat, all while you sip champagne. It’s rather a big draw for us, you know. We’d love for you to experience it while you’re here. I’ll get you tickets before you go.”

“That would be wonderful! We’ll look forward to that, of course.”

“Follow this way, and you’ll see the areas where we keep our collections, our exhibitions, and the actual racecourse. This is the birthplace of motor sports, plus our aviation history. We’re very proud of that honor, you know.”

As they were wandering the grounds, a ruckus from behind drew their attention to the front of the clubhouse and the violated bench. DCI Campbell was waving his arms and barking orders to constables who were scattering in every direction.

“What is that about?” asked Reggie as the three turned to watch the scene.

“I don’t know, Miss Reggie, but it might be time to pay a visit to Audrey. I think these gentlemen may mistake our presence here,” said Tolliver.

“I did want to see the racing course, but maybe another time.”

“Of course,” said Candace. “When you come for the Concorde tour, we can also see the track. If that’s everything for now, then I’ll take you to your car.”

"Oh, dear. I've left my purse in your office, Candace. I'm sorry, but we'll need to get it," Reggie said, nudging Tolliver.

Tolliver winced, now knowing what Reggie had done back in the museum. He glanced at her and cringed as she winked at him again.

"Shall we go the back way, or do you think we should walk through the front door?" she asked.

And then Reggie was marching toward the front entrance before Candace could stop her. She was bearing down on DCI Campbell, who looked anything but cordial.

"Oh, Gawd," breathed Candace. "We'd better go get her."

Tolliver lagged behind, looking like a beaten puppy, as Reggie greeted the inspector with the full force of her charm.

"What are you doing here?" he demanded, refusing to take her hand.

"I would think that would be obvious."

"Back to the scene of the crime, then? Was it you?" he barked.

Reggie had the decency to look clueless and confused as the copper backed her away from "Weatherford's bench".

"I'm sorry? Was what me?"

"The missing evidence. There was a cup here last night. It was a crucial piece of evidence, and it's gone."

"What would I have done with it? I didn't even know it existed. I would think you would have confiscated that last night, along with everything else that still seems to be here."

The inspector was glaring at her as she was searching the upper perimeter for the original purpose of their trip – the security cameras. She scouted the museum eaves, eyeing a few telltale points that confirmed her suspicions. The cameras were present but decoratively concealed so as not to take away from the historic design of the building. Tolliver followed her gaze and let out the breath he hadn't realized he was holding.

"You know, I think we can answer the sample cup question by checking the security cameras," said Reggie, smiling attractively at Campbell.

"We've already checked them. Unfortunately, the bench is out of range of the equipment. We know the cup was there, but we don't have it, and neither does the museum staff, so they say. You have a vested interest in this investigation, Miss Winter, and I suggest you start talking, or I will have you as a guest at the station as well."

Tolliver coughed while Reggie stared down the inspector with a dangerous gaze. Candace backed away as the scene took on another level of intensity.

"I won't stoop to even acknowledging that remark," she said. "You know we had nothing to do with this... this odious little man. He was an equal opportunity offender of just about everyone here last night, including the Royals as well as his own wife! I suggest you start looking elsewhere for your suspect, Mr. Campbell."

"It's DCI Campbell, and me thinks the lady protests a bit much."

"It's 'the lady doth protest too much, me thinks, '" said Reggie, rolling her eyes at the man. "You could at least get the quote correct if you can't get anything else right."

That was it. The laser beam eyes shot straight through her as Campbell had finally had enough.

“Let’s take a drive, Miss Winter,” he said, guiding Reggie toward his official vehicle.

“Tolliver, be a dear and run in and get my purse from Candace’s office, please.”

She was squinting her eyes at him and angling her head in the direction of the sample table rather than Candace’s office.

Tolliver had it in one and was through the entrance before anyone could stop him. He pulled out his phone, hit the video button, and captured the entire area before changing direction to head to the office.

“Here then, sir, stop please,” said an official-looking gentleman as Tolliver crossed the foyer. “What is it we can do for you?”

“My associate. Her purse. It’s in Miss Corbyn’s office. She’s being...”

“Yes, I see. I’m sorry, I’m Alex Aldeworth, museum director. This has been quite an unfavorable circumstance for us, Mr...”

“Tolliver, Sydney Tolliver, assistant to Alene Elliott, and the Farthing’s businesses, sir. We only came to reschedule the event, but it seems to have gone wrong along the way. I came in to retrieve Miss Winter’s purse before she’s taken down to...”

“Yes, yes. Let me take you there,” he said, watching Reggie being shoveled into the inspector’s car.

They were hurrying to the exit when Tolliver took one last glance at the sample table. Something was amiss; something looked different. Or was it his imagination? Was it there when he came in? At the top of the sample cups sat one that was slightly askew. Tolliver was racking his brain. Was that there before, or was it indeed his imagination? He discreetly shot a picture out of the sight of Director Aldeworth and marched out the door.

10

Chapter 10

"You're tearing me apart! You say one thing, he says another, and everybody changes back again!"
-Rebel Without a Cause, 1955

"Paging Miss Ratliff! Miss Ratliff to the main center, please."

"Oh, what the bloody hell is this about? Can't a girl get a cuppa before the storm blows in?"

Audrey continued to her office and attempted to throw her purse on the chair reserved for guests. Glaring at the phone, she decided it could wait.

"I need..." she said.

"Miss Ratliff, would you like your tea now, then?" said the young girl in the doorway. Audrey straightened from pitching her purse like a shot put.

"Oh, yes, please, April. It's been a monstrous night and morning."

"It is an awful thing. Even though he was a pill of a man, does it mean he deserved to die?"

"What? Oh, yes, no. He was an awful little man, but he did not deserve to die, especially in the middle of our lovely tea launch. Odious little man," she added. "What did you see last night, April? You were buzzing about like a starving bee. You must have seen something useful."

"No, Miss, I was trailing after Mrs. Elliott, trying to keep track of the people we'd need to be contacting next week. I didn't even have time to use the loo," she said, eyes flashing. "Um, I think they want you in the lobby, Miss. I'll bring your tea to you there."

"Oh, right. They did page me, didn't they?"

"Yes, and Mr. Tolliver called to say that he and Miss Winter had met with Miss Corbyn and that the tea launch has been rescheduled. At least you don't have to worry about that."

"What? Who had them do that? Why wasn't I informed? Please get Mr. Elliott on the phone while I handle these... policemen."

"Mr. Elliott had only just returned from the station where they took Mrs. Elliott for questioning in Mr. Weatherford's murder, and as I understand from Mr. Tolliver, he is heading back there again as they have now taken in Miss Winter for questioning. It's been quite the morning."

"What the bloody hell happened between the time I went to bed and this absolute minute? I feel like Alice in Wonderland. Which rabbit hole is this?"

"Um, policemen, Miss."

"Oh, yes, right."

She glanced around her office as if looking for a good hiding place, gave it up as a bad job, and walked gracefully to the lobby like a good English girl.

"So, how may I help you, gentlemen?"

"We just have a few questions for you, Miss, if you'll follow us over here."

Audrey was not the least bit intimidated by the officers; on the contrary, she was not in the habit of being told what to do on her turf. This was not the way she wished to start her day.

"I beg your pardon, but is this where you wish to conduct an interview? Wouldn't you rather go to my office, where it's more private?"

"It's up to you, Miss; we'll question you anywhere you like as long as you answer. We don't wish to take you to the station."

"Sounds like it's a full house there anyway," she sighed.

"Sorry?"

"Nothing. What do you need to know?"

"Where were you at the time of the gentleman's death, please?"

Audrey narrowed her eyes at them. Who would know that? When did he meet his untimely demise? She was immediately on her guard and was thinking how to answer when April descended upon them with her tea.

"There you are, Miss. Nice and hot and as you like it. Sirs? Anything I can get you?"

The constables grimaced at her till April shrugged her shoulders and sauntered away.

"I'll be in my office if you need me," she said to the captive woman. She gave her a meaningful stare from behind the tea tray.

Audrey watched her slide away like a bat and wondered what was going on in that slick head of hers when the police brought her attention back to the scene at hand.

"I'm sorry, what was the question?"

"Where were you, Miss, at the time of the death?"

"That's what I mean," she said, regaining her thoughts. "When *was* the time of death? How am I supposed to know where I was when I don't know when he died?"

The two shot each other a glance and moved on.

"When do you first recall that there actually was a death?"

"When that blessed woman came in, pitched to the floor, and the whole place went up like a Guy Fawkes night. People running, yelling, calling for police. Highly irregular for a gala."

"Do you know what time that was, Miss?"

Audrey stood staring at the floor. There was something about the time. There was something she was trying to remember. It caught her attention at the moment, but she was scrambling to recall it.

"Oh, I know! It was as the program was starting—eight o'clock or so. Mrs. Elliott was getting ready to start the ceremony. Mr. Weatherford had been asked to leave. We had been discussing it with Mr. Elliott before that, and then she took the podium. But I could swear I saw Weatherford again even before that."

"What do you mean, Miss?" asked the constable.

"Well, he was annoying the other guests, and his wife had dismissed him. We watched that from where we were standing. He was also a bit of a rotter in the kitchen earlier. He almost cost us our chef!"

"And then what?"

"When Mr. Elliott went to the kitchens with Miss Winter, I saw him slip back in and pour something from the tea sample table into a cup, and then he was gone again."

The constables only slightly raised their eyes, compared notes, and hurriedly excused themselves.

###

"And here we are again," said DCI Campbell. "What is it with you lot? Shall we get you a courtesy room? You seem to be spending quite a bit of time here."

"DCI Campbell," began Reggie. "I know this is all just a big misunderstanding. You know I didn't have anything to do with this. I just got here. I'm an American. I know very few of these people. And the ones I wanted to meet got waylaid by that..."

"Before you dig yourself in any deeper, Miss Winter, please just answer the questions and refrain from trying to dictate any further proceedings."

Reggie had the smarts to smile graciously and sit upright in her chair, anticipating their questions. Her mother would be proud if only for her posture.

"What were you doing out at Brooklands today? Spare the tales you manufactured for me."

"I'm quite sorry if you think we...

"Short version. Now."

"We went to reschedule the gala. Simple."

"And there was no other reason you went out there other than to set a new date?"

Reggie read the situation. They were baiting her, and if she didn't tell the truth, they would find out.

"I wanted to see what the security cameras had to say as well."

"So did I," said a voice from the doorway.

Heads swiveled to see Tucker Elliott standing in the opening, arms crossed against his chest, Agent John Laird looming directly behind him.

11

Chapter 11

Oh, boy. Think, think, think. What to do with the body?
-The Emperor's New Groove, 2000

"Tucker! So glad you're here," said Reggie. "We were just discussing the fact that we have rescheduled the launch."

"I heard security cameras. What was found on them? And Miss Winter, I shall have to give you the definition of damage control. It's actually more of a public relations activity where you suss out the trouble and assure the parties involved that we are doing everything in our power to secure the situation. It is not inflicting more damage than control."

DCI Campbell was stifling a chuckle during this exchange, which made Reggie place sharp, dark eyes on him. She gave Tucker an engaging smile as he redirected her like a bad child.

"To answer your question, we reviewed the film only to discover that the bench is just out of camera range. So, there was nothing useful to be found. I hope that answers your question."

Tucker felt as though he was trying to land a large fish, fighting with all its might. The harder you tugged on the line, the more the fish pulled and ran.

"DCI Campbell, what about the other cameras? Was there anything useful on any of those?"

"Not that we've seen. Whomever the person is, they managed to stay out of range. They must know the venue well or have had help from someone who does. We have lots of footage of people chatting and wandering about. We were able to follow you quite well, Mr. Elliott. You had a busy evening. You also had several encounters with the deceased, which did not paint a pretty picture."

"Mr. Campbell, if I may..."

"It's DCI Campbell, and what is it, Miss Winter?"

"As I was about to say, the 'deceased' should be the one being investigated. In his short appearance, he not only offended royalty, but he also insulted Miss Porter to the point where she slapped him across ..."

"Stop there," he said, taking out his notepad. "That explains the mark on his face. It did look like a hand print. Go on."

"He taunted Mrs. Elliott and accused her of stealing his formulas, offended the chef, almost causing him to leave, and had an argument with his wife in front of other attendees who witnessed her dismissing him like a schoolteacher. That's when he left and expired on the 'Friendship Bench.'"

Laird shot Tucker a glance and raised his eyebrows. She summed it up as efficiently as a prosecuting attorney. There wasn't much more to add.

"Yes, well, except that he didn't expire on the bench. From what we've found in our investigation, the late Mr. J. Winston Weatherford met his death somewhere else. His body was moved to the bench, and once again, no camera views to tell us where the murder may have taken place."

###

"Tolliver, you've been rather quiet throughout this interview. Anything to add, mate?"

Tucker had caught the man by surprise and instantly regretted it. There was obviously something Tolliver had bouncing around his massive brain. But would he tell it here in front of the law? And did he want him to?

"I was bothered by the security cameras, sir. The lack of interest seemed odd to me, and I didn't understand why the investigating team wasn't concentrating on them."

"Shall I remind you that this isn't a 'team' building exercise and that we don't have to give you a minute-by-minute report of our findings?"

"Of course, Campbell," said Tucker. "I understand what Tolliver is saying. There was so much happening last night that it was hard for us to notice what was going on in the background. The last thing we want to do is interfere with your methods."

"That's a nice speech, Elliott. Is this your damage control at work?"

"I don't feel the overwhelming need to answer that, Campbell, so if it's all the same to you, we'll be off."

With the appearance of Chalmers, they rose, gathered their things, and headed for the door.

"I did not dismiss you," said Campbell.

"You have now," said Chalmers. "Good day, DCI. I expect not to see you again today."

The group was herded out the door and the building. Tucker slowed his pace, waiting for Reggie to catch up as they bid a fond farewell to Chalmers, who only shook his head and waddled off down the sidewalk. They followed Laird and Tolliver, their heads bent in quiet conversation. They reached the street, where they gathered in silence, staring at the sidewalk.

"So the body was moved," said Laird.

"That's what the bloke said. I can't believe it, though. He left the building. Maybe he went to the Sunbeam Café."

"Oh, the little restaurant in the back there," said Reggie. "We saw it this morning when we were taking our tour with Candace. Quaint little place, right Tolliver?"

"Yes, Miss. Sirs? Maybe Weatherford met someone there. The café was closed last night. Maybe that's where it happened."

"That's a possibility," said Laird. "I didn't know it was even back there. I wonder if there are cameras in that area."

"We need to find out," said Reggie. "We need to go back. To Brooklands."

"We need to do nothing of the sort," said Laird while Tolliver stared back at the station as if it were listening.

"Maybe Candace can help," Reggie said. "We have to find out what happened. They're still accusing Alene and, for some reason, even me, and it seems that you're not too far off that list either," she said, leaning toward Tucker.

"Shocking," he said. "But if the body was moved, it's a whole other situation now."

"Agreed, but we have to be careful," said Laird. "And I agree. You don't come off too well in their footage, Elliott."

"Then let's head that way after checking in on Mum. Tolliver, maybe we can find out more about your cameras," he said with a sly grin.

Tolliver helped Reggie into the back seat while Tucker headed for the driver's side door. As he passed Laird, he grabbed Tucker's sleeve, stopping him.

"I meant to ask you earlier, Elliott. What does the 'J' stand for in Weatherford's name?"

Tucker stopped, grinned, and laughed.

"Jackass!"

* * *

"I need to tell you about the call I had earlier," said Alene.

"What??"

"Oh, Douglass, nothing earth-shattering, but it was from Olivia Weatherford."

"As in Mrs. the late J. Winston Weatherford?" he asked.

"The same."

"What did she want, dear?"

"She wanted to make sure we came to the funeral. It takes place on Wednesday at eleven o'clock at St. Mary's in Steyning."

Dulcy stared in silence while the senior Elliott turned to look at his wife.

"Are...are we going?"

"Yes, Douglass, we're going. But there's more, dear."

"And that would be?"

"I've arranged a visit to Olivia. I'll pay my respects and see what I can find out while I'm there."

"I'm not sure, Alene. I'm not sure if this is a good idea. What about the DCI? The Campbell bloke? How will he look at this?"

"I don't know, and I don't care, Douglass. It's the right thing to do. Not to worry; I'll be taking Dame Abbington with me."

"Flora? Upon my word, Alene, why ever would you do such a thing? She's the biggest gossip there is."

"She was at the gala. She must have seen things."

"And heard things," said Dulcy. "You sneaky woman, you. I like it."

"Now I just have to tell Tucker."

"Tell me what?" said a voice from the study entrance.

Tucker Elliott seemed to be popping into all kinds of doorways today.

###

"I have some correspondence to attend to," said Alene after filling them in on her social call schedule. "Douglass, are you coming?"

"Uh, no, dear. I think I'll stay and chat with Tucker. I'll see you for cocktails in a while."

Tucker watched as his mother leisurely left the room to do her "correspondence." He was curious; he knew she was up to something, but he would find out what soon enough. His father would tell him, of that he could be sure.

"Uh, sir? There's something I need to bring to your attention. It's something I found at the Clubhouse."

Reggie and Dulcy straightened and stared at Tolliver.

"What did you find? Was it when you went to get my purse?"

"Yes, Miss. It goes back to that tea sampling table. When I went inside, it just seemed like there was something wrong. Something was off about the scene. I couldn't figure out what it was, but as I was leaving, I took another picture. Here..."

The four gathered around Tolliver's phone and strained to see the miniature image. It was clear, but the gist of what he was saying wasn't.

"I'm not seeing it, Tolliver. What am I looking for?"

"Look at the video first, I think, sir."

Tolliver took the camera and opened the video. They reviewed the footage and then reviewed it again. Tucker stared into the screen, its message unclear.

"I don't see it, mate," he said tiredly.

Tolliver took a screenshot of the video showing one section in particular – the sampling cups. He then scrolled to the next photo, which showed the same section. It was ever so slight, but there was a difference in the pictures.

"That wasn't there in the video shot," said Laird. "This cup is sitting crooked on top of the stack. Look at the first picture and then look at the second."

Their heads were bent as they examined the second photo, which revealed a small sample cup, slightly askew atop the stack of straight, snug shot cups.

"That wasn't there earlier," said Tolliver. "That means that in between the time we left the Barbara Cartland room with Candace, someone dropped that cup on top of that stack. That means it's someone at the museum. Someone at the venue is involved. Who in the world could that be?"

###

DCI Campbell was relaxing at his desk as the constables walked into the station, notes in hand from Audrey Ratliff. He was picking through the others' information when the two bounced through the door, looking like they'd solved the case.

"What? What's going on?"

"Nothing that's a problem, sir. We just found some interesting information."

"Go on then."

"It was something we discovered when we interviewed their associate, a Miss Audrey Ratliff. She tells us that after the deceased was asked to leave, she saw him come back in and pour something into a cup and then leave again."

"Well, that changes things a bit, then, doesn't it? So, he was still alive at what time?"

"It was before the presentations began, so maybe seven-thirty."

"That makes a difference. And he was found shortly after eight. What did he do between the time he came back in and the time he was found on the bench?"

The constables looked at each other, shrugged, and gazed back at Campbell.

"We have to find out who he was with during that time. Let's get on it, boys!"

12

Chapter 12

I was at lunch with an old friend who pointed to two elderly ladies across the room, and she said "That will be us in ten years." I said, "That's a mirror."
-someecards.com

"C'mon," said Tucker.

"Are we going where I think we're going?" asked Laird.

"We need to get back out to Brooklands and find out what's going on in that clubhouse," said Reggie.

"We'll stop and check on Audrey at the office," said Tucker. "Tolliver, you told her about the rescheduling, yes?"

"Yes, sir, well, no; actually, I left a message with Miss April because Miss Audrey was unavailable at the time."

"Right. We'll have a chat with her before we go to Brooklands," said Tucker.

"You're doing exactly what I told you not to do," said Laird. "You start interfering with Campbell's men, and you'll be back at the station in no time."

"But we're not going there to nose around," said Reggie. "We're going for lunch at that cute little place in the back. The Sunbeam Café."

Tucker grinned, and Laird leveled a classic "cop" stare at Reggie.

"Oh, yea!" said Dulcy. "I'm hungry. Besides, he can't deny us lunch any more than he can tell us where we can have it."

"You will all need to behave," stated Laird. "Or the station you end up in will be the one with the choo-choo trains that take you out of here rather than the High Street police station."

"Please don't get your knickers in a twist, mate. Oh, and Christmas is coming up, Dulcy," said Tucker.

"That's nice, Tucker, but what does that have to do with this mess?"

"Try to find a nice sense of humor for Agent Laird here. His seems to have gone missing."

###

"Why, hullo, Mr. Elliott. We weren't expecting to see you today," said a young girl at the lobby desk.

"Good surprise, I hope, Gillian," he said, glancing around the area.

"Oh, of course. Is there anything I can help you with? Are you going to your office or do you need to see someone?" she said, reaching for the phone.

"I think I'll head on along to my office. If you would, please call Audrey and have her meet me there. Thank you, Gillian."

Tucker led them to an elevator and picked the top floor as the girl watched them with interest. His office was down the hall in a well-lit and spacious corner. The sun was streaming through the space as he opened the door, making it bright and inviting. There were few elements of note, but what was present was elegant and understated. He walked to the center of the room to a classic oak desk and dropped his keys in a Waterford ashtray. There were minimal supplies on the desktop and only one file folder. Reggie could see the name "Manchester" on the side, reminding her of the quiet escape Tucker had made from the U.S. while she searched for murderers in Florida.

"Have a seat," he said, waving his hand to a furniture grouping by the windows. A credenza, starkly situated against the opposite wall, sat sporting only a decanter, glasses, and a vinyl record player.

"A turntable," laughed Dulcy. "Does it work?"

"Of course. Any requests?"

"I don't see any records."

Tucker smiled and opened a bottom desk drawer to reveal a stack of vinyl records tucked inside.

"What's in the others?" asked Reggie, laughing. "Since I know how much you like your drawers."

"My 'desk' in America, such as it is, is a ridiculous piece of Lucite without a single cubby to even lodge a pencil. Great silly thing," he said, winking at Reggie.

The door glided slowly open, followed by a knock. In came Audrey, smiling brightly and waving at the group by the window.

"Miss Audrey! Come in, join us. We were on our way to Brooklands and thought a stop-in was needed. How is everything today?"

"Well, it's been quite the morning. The police were here, the employees are gossiping, there has been a steady stream of phone calls, and I heard that the tea gala has been rescheduled, unbeknownst to me. Imagine my surprise, sir."

"That would have to do with me. I instructed Reggie and Tolliver to take care of that as I was otherwise engaged. I was sure you'd be pleased as it would be one less thing for you to worry with on a day like today."

Audrey nodded and backed down immediately, as the rest of the room witnessed. Reggie was again reminded of why he was the boss and was impressed, if not a little aroused, by his command of the situation.

"Uh, yes, sir. May I have the details, please?"

"I don't actually have them. In between bailing my mother out of jail, followed by our Miss Winter here, I haven't really had the opportunity to negotiate the details. We'll get to those soon enough. On to other things. I understand you were interviewed this morning by DCI Campbell's men. How did that go?"

Reggie coughed quietly from her corner, intimating that he could go a little easier on the girl since it wasn't her fault the way things had progressed. She alone had made Tolliver drive out to Brooklands and usurped the company directive. Poor Miss Audrey had only gotten up and driven into a small hailstorm.

"The police were waiting for me when I arrived, sir. I was about to call Candace back when April reminded me they were waiting in the lobby."

What was it Tucker saw in her eyes? Was she irritated with the process, or was she glossing over something? Had she really thought about calling Candace?

"Just tell me what you've done since you walked in the door, Miss Ratliff. I need the details as close as you can get them if I'm going to keep my mother out of the nick. Brief, please."

Audrey looked as though she might choke. She knew about Tucker Elliott's blunt deliveries. This was how he got his information - no beating around the bush. He made you too caught off guard to tell anything but the truth. And he could smell a lie within an inch.

"Okay, April told me they were waiting in the lobby. I knew Candace had called, but I decided to wait to call her back. I went down to greet them and attempted to escort them to the office. They were going to conduct the interview right in the middle of the lobby. In front of everyone, sir. Which, well, in the end, they did anyway."

"They have their duty, Audrey; they don't really care how they carry it out. It's all about results."

Audrey wondered if he was talking solely about the constables or trying to send her a message.

"Right, sir. We went over everything that happened at Brooklands, including that awful Weatherford man, his horrible behavior, and then when he came back in after Mrs. Weatherford had told him to leave."

Tucker was instantly alert. What did she just say?

"Miss Audrey, please repeat that?"

"Oh, uh, we were talking to you and Miss Reggie," she said, nodding towards her, "with Candace and the other two. Then you both went into the kitchen, and we watched the crowd for a while. We had to be up to the podium for Mrs. Elliott, so we were waiting for our cue, so to speak."

"And then?" said Tucker, getting tired of waiting for the punchline.

"I was watching the royals talking with the Beatle gent when I saw him."

"What did you see, Audrey? Get to it, please."

"It was Mr. Weatherford. I thought he'd left, but he came back in the front door of the clubhouse and went over to the sampling table."

"What did he do, Audrey?" said Reggie, rising from her chair, sunlight backing her like a ghost.

"He poured something into one of the cups there. I didn't see what; I thought it was a tea sample. He was quite quick about it. A splash out of a pitcher sitting there, and then he was gone."

"Back out the front door?" asked Tucker.

"I don't know. I think so. No, wait! He went around that side area by the loos and back by where the kitchens are. Do you think that's important?"

"Only if you're trying to figure out who murdered him," said Tucker, staring at Laird, who was scribbling rapidly in his notebook.

###

"Uh, thank you, Audrey. I appreciate all the information you provided and all you do for us. I'm sorry it's been a bugger of a morning, but please don't worry about any of this. I'll be in touch as to what I need from you for the launch going forward. Thank you for being so understanding about us buttin' into your territory. I'm to blame for not letting you know we were moving so quickly," he said, glaring meaningfully at Regina Winter.

Reggie caught the inference and knew she was being reprimanded. She turned and stared at Tucker, but Tucker appeared to be moving on to the next order of business. He was dismissing the girl, but Audrey did not look to be leaving. She was gazing intently at him with questions that Reggie knew he wouldn't answer. She could see the girl was unhappy that he had stepped in and taken over. She felt like she should smooth things over when she stared out the window and caught sight of impending company. Hadn't the constables already questioned the Farthing's staff?

"Yes, I would also like to thank you for all you do, Audrey, but I'm afraid I have some bad news. Do these men look familiar?" asked Reggie.

They gathered by the window to see Campbell's men back on the premises, back on the job. What did they want now?

###

"Where are you going, dear?"

"I told you, Douglass, I'm going to pay a visit to Olivia."

"With Dame Abbington. Are you sure you know what you're doing, Alene? She could be useful, but then we could just as easily be rescuing you from the nick. Again. What do you plan to gain from this?"

"I plan to console a widow in her time of need, dear. What else do you think

I'm doing there?"

"God only knows, Alene. I take my leave, as Shakespeare says. That way, when they ask me if I knew what the hell you were up to, I can honestly say no. Do not involve me with this, Alene Farthing."

"Oh, there it is. Calling me by my maiden name. You only do that when you think I'm making a mistake. Do you think I'm making a mistake, Douglass?"

"I'm too much of a gentleman to say what I really think, Alene. Now go about your nosy business and keep me out of it. I'm sure I have some formulas to sift through."

Douglass Keenan Elliott turned on his heel and meandered back to the kitchen, where Myra would surely have something in which he was interested. Something that would at least keep his mind off what the rest of his family was doing.

"Bloody nosy woman," he said. "Hope she finds something useful, dammit."

With that, he smiled, rounded the corner, and called for Myra, sniffing what he thought could only be her cottage pie.

###

"Oh, Olivia, I'm so terribly sorry for your loss," said Alene, patting Olivia's hand and seating herself on the opposite cushion.

"Yes, my dear. Words cannot describe the pain you must be feeling," drawled Dame Abbington. "Please tell us everything about poor Winston."

A deferential, feathery-looking older gent glided into the room with a heavily-laden tray stacked with silver from end to end.

"Please put the refreshments on the table, thank you. What is that, Simmons, tea?"

"Yes, ma'am. Would you prefer something else, then?"

"No, Simmons, the tea is fine. Thank you. Now, with regards to Winston, my husband was a foolish, impetuous bother. Oh, don't get me wrong; I will be utterly bereft without him, but he could be one of the most boorish prats I've ever laid eyes on. So embarrassing at your lovely gala. Sorrier than I can say, Alene."

The women gave her a moment while Olivia wiped a small, leaking tear from her cheek and took a deep breath.

"Olivia, I don't want to be indelicate, but your husband was sending ... communications. Do you know anything about them?"

Alene watched Olivia for any motion that might give her away. Was she a part of this, or wasn't she? Olivia dropped her handkerchief and stiffened her back. Alene now had someone to play with. This was going to be fun.

"Well, now that you mention it..."

"Oh, Olivia, tell us all about it," said Flora.

Dame Olivia Chesterton Weatherford was no fool.

"I'm sorry, Flora. How do you come to be a part of this?"

The air was stifling. The three women pulled up like they were in a corset fitting and faced off. Alene was no stranger to confrontation.

"Ladies, please, let's not forget why we're here," she said.

"Why are we here?" asked Olivia, staring between the two women.

"Well, to figure out what happened to Winston, of course," said Alene.

The room grew quiet. The ladies contemplated the next move as Simmons stepped in and replaced the tea urn with a bottle of brandy.

"Simmons? Did I ask for that?" demanded Olivia.

"No, ma'am," drawled the lanky man. "It just seemed necessary," he said, slithering away, an impertinent smirk slapped firmly on his face.

"Well, I never," said Olivia.

"Of course you have, dear," said Alene. "May we get back to the subject at hand, please?"

"Oh, yes. You're here, why, Flora?"

"Because I'm your good friend, I'm concerned, and I wish to help in any way I can."

"Pardon my french, but bullshit, Flora, you're here for gossip, and Alene, I'll give you more of the benefit of the doubt. What do you really want?"

Alene Elliott was the first to be conciliatory in matters of life and death, but this was the death of a worm of a man, the life of her company, and the honor of her family—it was time to move to the main point.

"I came here to offer my condolences, my friendship, and my help. And when I say my help, I mean to help find out who murdered your husband, despicable as he may have been. No offense, Olivia dear."

"Oh, Alene, none taken. Do go on."

"This has made quite an impact on my company and my launch. Winston was threatening us with letters stating we had stolen his research and his formulas. This is utterly preposterous, Olivia, and I will not stand for it. What shall we do about this?"

"Nothing. He was a total fraud. And I have proof," she said, patting a stack of papers in a folder tucked safely by her side.

Dame Abbington swallowed her tea and choked till Alene thought they would have to call for Simmons. She eyed Olivia Weatherford carefully, not sure whether to believe her. Her proof was nestled next to her on the sofa. Alene had hers hidden in the depths of her bag. She would not produce anything unless necessary.

"Do explain, please."

"Well, Alene, I would think it would be obvious. I have his research papers and his lab results. I have contacted the team members at the company facilities. They were reluctant to speak with me until I reminded them of their contractual obligation to the firm and their 'positive' work recommendations should they wish to seek opportunities elsewhere."

"Ah, very devious of you, Olivia. And did they cooperate?"

"Of course. Far be it from me to interfere with a person's livelihood, but once they understood how important the information and their cooperation were, they were more than happy to help."

Alene was cut out of the same cloth. If money or job security were on the line, she knew how to use them to her advantage. She was sure the lab crew and any other crew in the Weatherford lineup would not cause trouble.

"Olivia, I'm a bottom-line kind of gal, so let's get to the point, shall we? What did the papers show, dear?"

"Without going into a mess of unnecessary detail, the 'bottom line,' as you say, is that none of the results, research, or formulas were his."

Alene and Flora shot a look at each other, then back at Olivia. She was pouring small measures of brandy from the snifter Simmons had left. She passed one to Alene and one to Flora.

"Thank you, Olivia, but then whose research was it?"

"Well, again, Alene, I would think it would be obvious. It was yours, dear!"

13

Chapter 13

Here's another one of those self-satisfied doors.
-The Hitchhiker's Guide to the Galaxy

Simmons appeared like an apparition. Out of nowhere, a crystal glass of water was handed to Dame Abbington, who had not taken the news, as well as the other two, who looked on with impatient silence.

"Feeling better, Flora?" asked Olivia.

"I'd like to get back to our, uh, discussion?" said Alene, pulling a large sheaf of papers from the bottom of her bag.

Olivia raised an eyebrow at the documents. Flora leaned so far forward that she almost spilled herself onto the floor.

"Do right yourself, Flora; you're tipping the legs of my Gainesborough.

"Alright, Alene, what are those, please?"

"These are the 'communications' of which I spoke earlier. One of the reasons for our visit."

The two women slowly pulled the papers to their ample chests and staring at each other through narrow slits. Dame Abbington grabbed the snifter and knocked it straight back. Olivia handed her a napkin while Alene regretted her decision to bring the meddlesome woman along in the first place.

"Well, I suppose we should see what they say," said Olivia, holding out her file to Alene.

The women switched their precious cargo in a quick, fluid gesture. Dame Flora folded into the recesses of her chair and let the effects of the brandy wash over her. Before diving into the proofs of her husband's transgressions, Olivia rang the small bell next to her, summoning Simmons into the room to hover protectively in the wings. As the two scrutinized the documents, Flora occupied herself by assessing her surroundings with the eye of an appraiser. Simmons stood by, secretly assessing Flora.

"What lovely things," murmured Flora.

"Excuse me?"

"Oh, nothing, Olivia. Just relaxing a bit."

Olivia glanced at Alene and then at Simmons with a knowing nod. Simmons gave a slight nod and continued his vigil. Dame Flora had a regrettable habit of helping herself to things that did not belong to her.

Flora was feeling the effects of the brandy. She relaxed even further while she took in the contents of the room. There was a gathering of Gainsborough chairs, the mahogany inlaid breakfast table upon which the silver tea service had been resting, a Sheraton mahogany sideboard, and the centerpiece of the room, as far as she was concerned, a George III mahogany library step ladder. Flora strained to get a better view of the tabletop structure. It was poised in front of the floor-to-ceiling library filled with leather-bound classics and rare editions of authors she had read as a child. She was zeroing in on a volume of Beatrix Potter's The Tale of Peter Rabbit, wondering if it was an original 1902, when the clearing of a throat across the way brought her back to the present.

"Switch, please."

Alene gave her papers to Olivia, who reciprocated with her set. Both women sighed and rolled their eyes as they absorbed the whole meaning of what they had read.

"Well, now what?" asked Olivia.

"Now that I know the details of what he was up to, we have two choices, Olivia."

"And those are?"

Flora moved slightly in her chair, trying not to draw attention to herself. She knew she was about to hear some of the juiciest gossip to hit the county in years.

"We can turn these over to the CID, the crass Campbell man," said Alene, "or we can put them in a safe and keep a stiff upper lip."

A startled hiccup from the opposite Gainsborough caught their attention, though they did not break their gaze upon each other.

"Be quiet, Flora," stated Olivia.

"But isn't that withholding things? Evidence, I think?" gasped Flora.

"Be quiet, Flora," said Alene.

"But, I don't think..."

"Be quiet, Flora!" said Olivia and Alene in unison.

"No one is asking you to think," said Olivia.

"Well?"

Both women sat silent for a moment, never taking their eyes off each other. They then stuffed the papers back into the depths from which they had come. A slight cough near the library entrance made all three jump, having forgotten that Simmons was still standing guard.

"Yes, Simmons. What is it?"

"Miss Cora has just informed me that Mrs. Elliott's presence has been requested at her office."

"Thank you, Simmons."

"Just a couple of things still," said Alene, darting a glance at Flora. "We shall need to reconvene. There's still the matter of what happened to Winston and who did this horrible deed."

"I have a question," stated Flora. "What does the 'J' stand for?"

"Oh. James. Should have stood for jackass, but there you have it. And the other?"

"Not a word of this conversation is to leave this room. Is that clear, Flora?" said Alene as she and Olivia turned icy gazes on the slumping woman.

"Because we shall know if this gets out, shan't we?"

Flora hiccuped and had the grace to zip her mouth shut as she picked up the brandy snifter and splashed a large dollop into her glass.

###

"Why are they here again?" asked Audrey petulantly, staring at the incoming constables. "I answered their questions earlier; now what do they want?"

They joined Reggie at the windows, watching as the officers marched to the entrance of the classic Farthing's building and disappeared inside.

"Miss Ratliff?" said April, sticking her head in the door.

"Yes, yes, April, I see them. Stick them in the outer office until I call for them, please."

"There's no good in putting them off, Audrey; it'll just make it worse," said Reggie. "Trust me; I was just sprung from there, and they don't take waiting well. Not the most patient of men."

April lingered in the doorway, hoping for direction. When none came, she quietly backed out with a grimace and accepted her fate of having to deter the constabulary until Audrey called for them.

"We'll stay with you while they bully you, Audrey," stated Reggie.

"They won't bully me," said the girl, eyes on fire. "I think if I were you, I'd make a clean getaway. There's no good in them finding all of you here right now. There's that nice set of stairs right over by your office, Mr. Elliott. Please give Candace my regards and let her know that I will return her call as soon as I can get the bloody police out of my hair!"

Tucker felt like a heel, but he knew she was right. Their presence would only prompt more conjecture from the constables and would be quickly reported back to Campbell. And the longer they stayed, the longer it would take to get to Brooklands and sort out the confusion of the moving body. Tucker couldn't let his mother go to jail. The inmates would never survive it.

"I feel like a cad running out on you like this, Audrey, but I do think you're right; we can only do more harm than good by staying. If you don't mind, I'll use this exit here."

"What exit, sir? There's no exit there."

But in true Tucker Elliott fashion, he moved a book and pressed something recessed within. Shelf and all gave way to a person-sized opening as the group gazed on in astonishment. The only one not surprised was Tolliver.

"But, but..."

"This was my office before I took over Mother's. I love my jib doors, you know. This is how I escaped when she would come looking for me. I know, a bit shocking, but functional."

"Of all the crazy ass things," said Laird.

"That's utterly fantastic," said Dulcy.

"I don't believe it," said Reggie.

"I do," sighed Tolliver, who ushered the ladies before him and grudgingly followed.

14

Chapter 14

What's your record for consecutive questions asked?
-Uncle Buck (1989)

"That was fun!" exclaimed Reggie. "How did you do that?"

"I grew up with those doors all through the house. Something to do with the servants' quarters. Green baize door and all that. Since this was an old country house, of course, there would be one somewhere. There are several, actually. Works well as a means of escape if you're trapped. Brilliant idea, really."

Tolliver, you knew about this?" asked Reggie.

"Yes, Miss. It has to do with Las Vegas and the... incidents there. I would be more than happy to discuss them. At a time in the way distant future, please."

"Of course, Tolliver, whatever you like. They were before my time, but I'm dying to hear more about the scandalous events that happened there anyway. For now, I really do feel awful leaving Audrey to handle the police. They're such tenacious men. Thank you, Tucker. I really didn't feel like dealing with them again."

"Let's just get out of here," said Laird, looking up at the stately face of Farthing's. "I'm not sure we should go to Brooklands either, though."

"You're welcome to check on the homestead, mate," said Tucker. "I'm sure my father would love a bit of company. You two can talk formulas, galas, gardening..."

"Alright, you've made your point. And I want to make mine that I do not condone this activity. When you're staring at a train ticket out, don't say I didn't warn you."

"I'm glad we got that settled," said Dulcy. "I'm starved. Let's go."

"You know, for a tiny thing, you sure do put away the food," said Reggie. "But I'm with her; I'm starving. And I can't wait to see what's happened since we left. Maybe Campbell's men found the cup!"

Tucker watched as she turned on her heel and headed for the car. She threw a glance over her shoulder and winked. He did not like the twinkle in her eye. It was mischievous and slightly dangerous. And that, he had found, was always followed by trouble.

###

When they arrived at Brooklands, the police were still inspecting parts of the clubhouse. They drove up to the constable they had seen earlier, who greeted them with a courteous tip of his hat and an expectant stare.

"Welcome back, Miss Winter. I see you have brought reinforcements. Will you be wanting to see Miss Corbyn, or do you need Mr. Alex? They are both inside from the last I saw."

"That's so nice of you to remember me," gushed Reggie. "Actually, we're here to have lunch at the adorable little Sunbeam Cafe around back."

The constable checked his watch and reassured them that luncheon was still being served. They would be able to find a lovely table if they just went round by the Concorde and proceeded to the back of the hall.

"I suppose I really should check on Candace and let her know that we've met with Audrey, and she has no worries about re-booking the gala. Is she in her office?" she asked as she headed for the door, the remaining police tape still stretched over the "friendship bench."

"If you'll wait, Miss, I'll see if I can locate her. I shan't be a moment."

This was just what Reggie was hoping for. As soon as the constable disappeared, she grabbed Tucker by the arm and led him to the doorway. Laird, Dulcy, and Tolliver followed uneasily, watching for the constable to return.

"Right up there," she said. "See the eave there? Now, see the indentation and the floral accents? Those are the cameras. I would guess that they look like that all around the clubhouse. We'll find out when we have lunch."

Constable Givens popped out of the front entrance and bid them into the foyer. The group trailed after him like initiates being dared into a haunted house.

"Wait here, then. Miss Corbyn will be out in half a tick. And mind the police tape. We don't want to be getting into any more trouble now, do we?"

They stood in a clump in the middle of the entrance. Reggie glanced over at the cordoned-off sampling table and gave Tolliver an elbow in the ribs.

"Look at it now. They're getting ready to take it all away, I should think."

Tucker turned a baleful gaze on Reggie and Tolliver and stepped in their path to the table.

"I know what you're thinking about doing, and I wouldn't if I were you."

"Oh? What am I thinking then?"

"That you are going to get a closer look at everything before it all goes. I won't have it, you know. I won't bail you out a second time today."

"I was thinking nothing of the sort. I just noticed that it's packed up as though it's going somewhere. Look, Tucker, there's the pitcher Audrey mentioned. Honestly, I don't remember that last night. I must have overlooked it."

"That's what she said he used to pour the drink into the cup he had," said Laird. "I'm sure we'll find out what's in it as soon as they get all this to the lab. Does anything look different to you? Tolliver?"

Tolliver was gazing intently at the pitcher, the bagged urns, and the stack of cups at the other end. Once again, something was bothering him. The cups. This time, there wasn't one sitting askew atop the stack. They looked different somehow.

"I can't say exactly, Agent Laird, but I would swear that the cup I took the picture of this morning is gone."

"Are you sure?"

"There's only one way to find out," said Reggie, turning to the confused man.

Tolliver scrolled down his phone till he came to the pictures taken earlier that morning.

"This one here," he said, pointing to the still from the video. "The cup. It's definitely gone. How can that be?"

As they gawked at the picture and then the display table, the clicking of heels made them jump like thieves caught red-handed. They steadied themselves as Candace came bustling around the corner.

"Oh, dear, it is a bit sad, isn't it? It was such a lovely display. And now it'll all be tossed like yesterday's fish. Awful, you know. Is there anything wrong? You look a bit odd," she said, inching closer and viewing them through her strong spectacles.

"We were just thinking," said Reggie. "It seems like there's something different about the setup. It doesn't look like it did this morning."

"Oh, well, that could be because they were mucking about here a bit ago. I sneaked a peek," she said, grinning. "They were doing their testing process. You know, they had equipment and beakers and syringes and such. They were getting things off to the lab to start analyzing. I heard them say they would bring along the containers when they were finished with everything else. I guess that's why all the industrial packaging."

"Well, that certainly does seem to explain it," said Tucker.

Reggie wasn't so sure, and she darted a glance at Tolliver, who looked like he agreed. He shifted in his stance and shot another glance at the table as if he expected it to rearrange itself.

"Anyway," she said, giving them a once-over, "what can I help you with? I was actually just in a meeting with Alex, and he's thrilled that you've decided to go ahead with the launch again. We're all just confounded over the whole incident. So glad you're going to give it another go. Mr. Tolliver, is there a question?"

Sydney Tolliver felt caught out. Staring at the cups and the other table contents, he couldn't reconcile the missing piece. He had a photographic memory, and this sudden change in scenery did not sit well with him.

"I'm so sorry, Miss. It's just that..."

"What Tolliver is trying to say, Candace, is that he thought he saw something earlier, and now the scene seems to have changed. I'm sure it's all just part of the investigative process."

Candace stared past them at the sad spectacle of what was their debut, not only of new taste treats but also a new design concept.

"Oh, well, I'm sure I don't know what you mean. What is it you wanted?" she said, turning abruptly on her heel. They could do nothing but follow.

"What just happened?" whispered Dulcy to Laird, who remained silent, watching Candace with a keen eye.

"To be honest, we just came for lunch," said Tucker, flashing his charming smile. "We've begun the relaunch, and you and Audrey can work out any minor details that should come up. We're famished, and the cafe sounds like the perfect solution."

Candace listened with interest, even managing a smile. But she didn't believe they were happily lunching without a care in the world or an underlying motive. She must move them along. It had been a hectic, stressful morning, and she no more wanted them to know what she had done than she did the police.

"Well, right this way. The Sunbeam Cafe is a most enjoyable spot, especially this time of day when it's a bit quieter. Let me walk you in and make sure you get a lovely table. Or would you rather eat up in the member bar? I can arrange a table for you. It shouldn't be too crowded at this hour."

"Oh, thank you, but maybe another time, I think," said Reggie before Tucker could butt in. She wanted to search for cameras in the cafe.

The group trailed behind, wondering what was going on behind those specs, when Candace rounded a corner and ran straight into DCI Campbell.

"Oh! Hello, Mr. Campbell. Back so soon? Anything I can do to help?"

"It's DCI Campbell, and what the hell are you lot doing here? Back to the scene of the crime? Again?"

"Oh, no! We're starving and thought we'd take advantage of the cafe out back. And I don't know about you all, but I wanted to see the Concorde," said Dulcy.

"You're hungry. That's brilliant. Don't you have homes? If I catch you meddling in even one thing here, you'll all be behind bars. Isn't one of you missing?" he said, eyeing the group from one to the other.

"Oh, you mean Miss Porter," said Tucker. "She was nursing a sick headache, but she should be charged up and ready to go by now."

"Since you mention it, Dulcy, I wanted to see the actual racing track, but we didn't get that far this morning," Reggie said, leveling a rather nasty gaze on DCI Campbell. "Still looking for your cup, constable?"

"It's still missing. But then you knew that, didn't you? Oh, never mind. Remember what I told you all. Miss Corbyn," he said, tipping his hat and brushing past the group with a huff.

Candace was pressed up against the wall, white as a sheet, her pale eyes like tea saucers behind the magnifying lenses.

"Perhaps you should have a bite to eat with us," said Reggie. "You look a little odd yourself."

"Oh, no, no, I'll just take you along this way. Still so much to do today," she said, glancing at her watch and avoiding their eyes.

She rounded a corner and stepped outside into the brisk English air and the warmth of the country sun. She approached a tall, long-faced woman hovering about the courtyard and motioned for them to follow.

"Victoria will take care of you. Now, if you'll excuse me, I must be getting back. Still taking calls from clients, you know. Find me if you need anything," and she was bustling off before any of them could utter a word.

They followed Victoria to a bright corner with a view of the grounds, situated under an oversized model of a biplane hanging from the ceiling. Dulcy stared openly at the granite counter tops near the front, which were loaded with cake platters, brownies on stone blocks, sandwiches, and other confections. Reggie followed her eyes and let out a sigh. She was hungrier than she thought and was thinking back to her abandoned breakfast hours before.

"I think I'm about to drool," she said.

Tucker was leaning on his elbow, scratching his thinking scar. This was never a good sign. It always led to things, things that usually meant trouble. Without a word, he popped up and approached the counter. He meandered back to the table, sat down, and slumped into an uncomfortable position in the misshapen wooden chair.

"What's on your mind, Elliott? You're beginning to look like him," said Laird, pointing his elbow at Tolliver.

"Thank you, sir. I think."

"There's something wrong. Why is he back here? Did he follow us?"

"I would think Campbell's just tying up loose ends so they can get on with it," said Reggie. "What do you think is wrong?"

"Why isn't there any usable camera evidence? Where could the body have been before the bench? And where is that bloody cup?"

Reggie shifted uncomfortably in her chair and sighed heavily as she raised her gaze and studied the ceiling.

"Oh, dear," she said.

The rest of the table shifted as well, all eyes on her. Laird shook his head, and Tucker groaned. Dulcy looked confused, and Tolliver stared at the table, wishing he could disappear.

"Alright, alright. I took the cup. I knew it was one of ours. It was just sitting there under the odious little man, and the attendants were about to come and take him away. You and Laird were talking about something..."

"The cup!" said Tucker and Laird together.

"I just didn't want it to be a problem, so I leaned down like I was fixing my dress, picked it up, and put it in my pocket. Who knew it would be such a big thing?"

"We did!" said Tucker and Laird together.

"May I ask a question?"

"Yes, Tolliver, what is it, mate?"

"So this morning, when we went into the venue, the cup was where?"

"In my purse," said Reggie.

"And later, when you were being... detained... and there was a cup sitting crooked on top of the stack, that was..."

"Me, plopping it back on there when I excused myself to go to the ladies' room."

Tolliver nodded and digested the information. It was sitting in his stomach like a heavy meal.

"So, why did you want a picture of it when you left your purse?"

"So we could prove that I didn't take it."

"But you did take it!" snapped Tucker.

"I was thinking I was being helpful, and now they will certainly find it."

"Yes, helpful, wasn't it? Quite. Mother off to the nick, Audrey in a state, DCI Campbell apoplectic, coppers running in circles, and something definitely off with Candace. I'd say you had a full morning, Reg. Well done."

“I have another question,” said Tolliver.

“Let’s have it.”

“So, if you put it back, then where is the cup now?”

15

Chapter 15

Clever girl, Clover.
-Batman and Robin, 1997

"Jennings! Where is everyone? How long have I been sleeping?"

"You have been resting for a good portion of the day, Miss Dahlia. I hope you're feeling a bit better."

"Oh, yes, finally. Where is everyone? Have I missed anything interesting?"

Jennings coughed and handed a tea tray to Dahlia as she propped herself up on her pillows and straightened her covers.

"Well, Miss, there has been quite a lot of activity today. I can give you a recap if you wish."

"Oh, yes, please, Jennings. Hope I haven't missed anything too exciting," she said, pouring herself a cup of actual tea rather than the usual scotch for that hour of the day.

"Miss Dulcy and Agent Laird were off early this morning as Mrs. Elliott had been taken into the local station for questioning as the lead suspect in Mr. Weatherford's murder. Mr. Tucker and the senior Elliott followed for moral support, having alerted Attorney Chalmers to meet them there, along with Miss Dulcy and Agent Laird. Miss Reggie and Mr. Tolliver decided to assist by driving out to Brooklands to investigate the security cameras and reschedule the launch gala. Unfortunately, Miss Reggie managed to get taken down to headquarters as well after apparently incensing DCI Campbell by insulting his character and intelligence. Actually, it's not surprising given the man's brash and coarse nature. Mr. Elliott had to again go to the station to, uh, 'spring' Miss Reggie while the others waited. They visited the Farthing's offices to make sure all was well with the launch rescheduling, while Mrs. Elliott paid a personal visit to the widow Weatherford. The five of them then 'raced' back to Brooklands," said Jennings with a short laugh at his own joke, "where they were going to have lunch at the cafe and try to get things, well, back on track, if I may say," he said, chuckling again at his joke.

"Well, bollocks! And I've been lying around all day feeling sorry for myself with this ridiculous headache. I must find them and help however I can."

"If I may interject, Miss Dahlia, all they've really managed to do is upset the general order of things and the DCI's investigation. If I may, your presence has been requested at the Elliott Manor this evening for cocktails and dinner, where you will be updated on everything. They will let you know how you can help. Please relax for now. I've laid out your wool travel suit since it's turned chilly. Is there anything else with which I may assist?"

"Good Lord, no, Jennings. I have some time before I have to be there, yes?"

"Yes, Miss. Your presence is requested at seven p.m. That does give you time to relax and refresh yourself before your departure. Would you like me to drive you, or would you prefer I put a car out front for you?"

"I'll let you know in a bit, Jennings. Thank you so much. What a day it's been, then. What are Mum and Dad up to?"

"Yes, Miss, it most certainly has been. Your parents have already departed for the Elliott house. Mrs. Elliott was updating your mother after recently returning from her offices, and, of course, as we know, Mr. Elliott always enjoys cocktails with your father. I'm sure there will be quite a few spirited discussions this evening, making for great entertainment. If I may say, Mrs. Elliott will have some new facts from her visit with Mrs. Weatherford. I'm sure it was quite fascinating, especially since she had Dame Abbington in tow."

On hearing this bit of news, Dahlia nearly choked on her tea and biscuit. She was most grateful for the large napkin Jennings whisked out of thin air for her.

"She took Dame Flora to the Weatherfords? What was she hoping to accomplish with that, other than possibly getting thrown out for lifting the silver? Flora does have such a tedious habit of taking things that don't belong to her."

"Yes, Miss. It is a regrettable quirk, of course. Dame Abbington was in attendance at the gala, and Mrs. Elliott was hoping for some insight into what happened from her point of view. She is quite well versed in the 'news of the day,' shall we say?"

"She's the biggest gossip in the county, Jennings. I'm sorry to have missed that little chat. Well, as you say, it should be great entertainment. Is there anything else?"

"No, Miss. I should think my update would have been enough for now. Please let me know your transportation needs."

"Of course. I do know where to find you, dear."

Jennings exited quietly while Dahlia refreshed her tea.

"Now. Where the hell did I put my address book? It might be time to put in a few calls of my own..."

###

Alene Elliott was proud of her progress on a day that looked as though she would be dining in a jail cell rather than in the comfort of her own home. Myra's cooking was bound to be better than what was provided in the nick, though how much better was a debate that was ongoing in the Elliott household. She had dropped off Flora Abbington with the reiteration of the "no gossip" rule they had put in place. Unless she wanted to visit Alene in prison, it was a policy she felt would be honored, at least until they discovered what had really happened to Winston. Flora could then blab all she wanted, as Alene was sure she would do. She pulled up to her reserved spot only to find an official-looking vehicle parked there as though its name was on the space rather than hers.

"Gillian! Find those... policemen... and tell them to move their car immediately or I shall have it towed."

"Yes, Mrs. Elliott, right away. Mrs. Elliott," Gillian said gingerly, "Roswyn and Bella are waiting for you in Audrey's office. I'll let them know you're on your way up."

"Brilliant. Thank you so much. Just who I wanted to see."

Alene glanced at her watch as she waited for the elevator. She was proud of this relic. She had found it in a sale from a business closing and was thrilled when they were able to install it in the ancient manor house. As she waited patiently, the door slid noiselessly open, and two local constables moved to step over the threshold.

"Good afternoon, gentlemen," she said with a frosty glare that wished them anything but.

"Gillian, I've found the constables. Please move my car the instant they leave my space. I'm double-parked."

Gillian grabbed the keys and headed for the front door. She couldn't help but giggle when she reached the sidewalk and saw the constables' car boxed in by Mrs. Elliott's large, classic Mercedes. She swallowed her giggle as she turned to see the policemen staring at the scene with an acidic look that spelled trouble.

"You may tell Mrs. Elliott that we can ticket her for that park job there," said the taller of the two gents.

"Oh, I really wouldn't do that if I were you," she said thoughtfully. "And if you do, I never saw it, and that I'll swear to."

The men climbed in from the driver's side and started the car. A window rolled down, and Gillian was called over to it.

"Move the car, Miss, or we'll ticket it."

"Yes, sir."

Gillian backed up Mrs. Elliott's car and waited for the men to leave.

"I'd like to see them give her *that* ticket," she said, laughing as she pulled the massive car into its rightful place, locked the doors, and skipped back to her desk.

###

"Why, Roswyn, Bella, how nice to see you. Everything alright here then, Audrey?"

"It's been a bit of a morning," she said and then remembered how Alene Elliott had spent hers. "Nothing like yours, ma'am, I'm sure. Roswyn and Bella had something they wished to discuss with you," she said, changing the subject with lightning speed.

Alene ushered them to the door and swept through it with a flourish. This conversation would be better served without the help overhearing it.

"We'll be in my office, Audrey. Please let me know if there's anything else I need to tend to."

Audrey knew a dismissal when she heard one. It was fine; the less she knew, the better.

"Back to work!" she said, relaxing into her chair.

Alene, Roswyn, and Bella were seated in the comfy grouping near the window, much like Tucker's office. Alene had an idea what this discussion might be about, but decided to let the women introduce the topic.

"Now. How can I help you, ladies?"

The two exchanged glances of encouragement and, without preamble, dove straight into the deep end.

"Is what he was saying true? The dead man? Weatherford? About the formulas and the research?"

"Well, right into it then, I see."

The two stared back, knowing neither would gain anything by speaking first. Roswyn knew the merits of digging for answers with a closed mouth. Bella, although much younger, knew to follow her associate's lead and remained quiet but poised.

"As you both know, he was telling everyone that I specifically had stolen his research and formulas. I am here to tell you that this is not true in the least."

"How can you be sure, ma'am?" asked Bella as Roswyn looked on.

"Because I know for a fact that he had neither research nor formulas of his own."

The two women stared openly as she smiled serenely and relaxed into the deep folds of her chair.

"How do you come to know this, ma'am?" asked Roswyn.

"I have just had a very productive meeting with Olivia Weatherford. I have seen the papers and read through the information along with Olivia."

"I don't quite understand. What did the papers contain?" asked Roswyn.

"Theorems, formulas, research findings, and such."

"But then, if you say he didn't have research or formulas of his own, then whose information was it?"

"Why, yours, ladies. I didn't steal anything from him; he stole from us. Now. I have a question for both of you."

“Yes,” said Roswyn, narrowing her eyes at Alene.

“Which one of you leaked my information?”

16

Chapter 16

I wish I could tell you that I know precisely where it is, but I can't.
-Battlestar Gallactica, 1978

After her cup-stealing confession, Reggie settled back in her chair and reviewed her Sunbeam Cafe lunch. Tucker had properly admonished her, and Laird gave her a most graphic legal dissertation on cup stealing. Tolliver looked like he was warding off yet another headache, and Dulcy was hiding behind her hand, trying desperately not to laugh.

"This lunch is quite good, you know," said Tucker.

"Yes, it is," said Laird. "We should come here more often."

Dulcy, finding that she could no longer hold it in, laughed so hard she nearly choked. Even Tolliver managed a smile till they all slumped in their chairs and were still.

"Actually Tolliver, it's a good question," said Laird. "If you took the cup and then put it back, where is it now? Campbell said they didn't have it. I think we're back to our original question: was it someone from here, and if so, who, when, and not least of all, why?"

"The ever-popular disappearing cup. You know, whatever it was that killed him is still in that sampler. Why would anyone here take it? It's a bit of a reprieve for us, though," said Tucker. "Gives us a chance to do a little more poking about, doesn't it?"

"Why would they be so anxious to help us?" asked Reggie. "I can see why we would be suspected; it only makes sense. But why would someone here take a chance like this?"

"The real question is, does it really matter?" said Laird.

"I would think it would matter some," said Tolliver, finally speaking. "Correct me if I'm wrong, sir, but won't the results of the postmortem tell us what was in the cup?"

"Yes, of course, but they want to match the results with the cup, so they know for sure that it was the vehicle that killed him. And that still leaves the remaining question."

"Where was he killed?" said Reggie.

"Exactly," said Tucker, "which still makes the cup important but not priority number one."

Tolliver's eyes had been roaming the room as they finished their lunch and were deciding their next move. He had zeroed in on a spot behind the lunch counter where there appeared to be a recess, surrounded by decorative hanging kitchen gadgets. Tucker was pondering all these questions when he noticed Tolliver eyeing the upper reaches.

"What is it, Tolliver? You look like the dog that's found the rabbit. What are you looking at?" he said, following Tolliver's line of sight.

"If I'm not mistaken, there is at least one of the cameras, sir. Right there between those kitchen utensils," he said with a slight nod of his head.

"Hmmm. But it's inside. The cafe was closed for the gala. Would it even be of any use?"

"I think we should ask Candace. She might know what kind of range it has."

Reggie was trying to follow the lens's line, hoping it might show what had happened outside the night before. She was glancing at the molding for signs of additional units when Candace came bounding around the corner.

"There you are. You're still here. Mr. Campbell is on a rampage, and I think he's looking for you lot."

"*DCI* Campbell," said Laird and Tucker.

"Oh, who gives a flying ..."

As she was about to insert her favorite expletive, Campbell stormed around the corner like he was invading a country and stopped up short at their table.

"Still here? Brilliant. I just wanted you to know that we've found the cup. You've been so concerned about it, I thought you should know right away. You seem to have been eating when it happened, although you seem to be here quite often. I'm not inclined to take you off my list just yet."

"When what happened?" asked Dulcy innocently.

"When we found the bloody cup!"

The few remaining lunch guests stopped to stare at the garrulous man ranting among normal members of society. Campbell paused to glare at the onlookers, prompting them to turn back to their meals and roll their eyes. Why couldn't people behave properly in decent company?

"Well? So where was it?" asked Reggie. "You seem to think we've had it all along, so where did you finally find it, Constable?"

He glared at her, and she waved him off with a toss of her hand. The man needed to adopt a shorter title.

"It was where I knew we'd looked last night and this morning. Sitting right out in plain sight, the cursed thing."

"And where was that?" asked Laird.

"Back on the bloody sample table, of course. Now, if you don't mind, I'll be on my way. Behave yourselves. That includes you, Miss Corbyn."

"Ugh. That man. He's completely derailed my day. If it's not the bench, it's the cameras and if not those, that damned cup. I hope he's finally going. I know they've run off guests and members alike today. So irritating."

"Well, at least he got what he wanted," said Dulcy.

"And now maybe he'll leave us alone," seconded Reggie.

"I wouldn't bet on that," said Laird.

"And why not?" asked Dulcy.

"He'll keep picking away at it until he finds out who took that cup in the first place, you mark my words. Now he can match it to the other lab results, and then he'll be back to find out where it was. It's still a murder investigation, after all."

"So, only Weatherford's prints were on it?" said Tucker, giving Reggie a sidelong glance.

"Yes, but I used a napkin last night. I'm not that stupid."

Candace leaned in, mouth open, eyes wide.

"You took the cup??"

"Yes, but you can keep that to yourself. What I don't understand is how it disappeared again and then was back like a bad penny."

Candace turned a violent shade of red, then paled to the color of a new bed sheet as she watched them look at her in turn.

"Well, what could I do? I saw it this morning and knew it wasn't there before, so..."

"So..."

"I took the cup!"

###

"Well, that tears it," said Tucker. "We'll all be for it when he pieces it together, as he most certainly will."

"Not if we get there first," said Reggie.

"What do you mean?" asked Candace.

"We've got to find out what happened and now. When and where did he die, and who moved him to the bench?" asked Reggie. "We've got to get moving. It'll be dark soon, and we have to get back. We can distract him from the cup if we give him something else to occupy his time."

"Candace, if you hear anything else, please let us know. Other than that, do you know where each and every camera is here?"

"Well, there's a diagram. You know, like the blueprints to the place. With the remodel of the Edwardian Club, they uncovered ancient documents showing all the different upgrades and renovations that had been done over the years. I know where they're kept."

"That would be wonderful," said Tucker. "By the way, do you have any jib doors here?"

"I'm sorry, any what?"

Reggie rolled her eyes, Tolliver shook his head, and Dulcy and Laird tried not to laugh while Candace looked on in bewilderment.

"Oh, Tucker, no more jib doors for today," said Reggie.

Candace shrugged her shoulders and ran off to find the blueprints.

* * *

The staff at the Sunbeam Cafe were gracious and friendly, but had had their fill of the Farthing family. The brushes with the law over the past few hours had left a bad taste in their mouths that even the sweetest of the Sunbeam Cafe confections could not remedy. It was with heartfelt thanks and a generous sprinkling of compliments on the cuisine that the group was finally escorted to the exit. With stiff smiles, the staff turned them out and locked the doors behind them. They were wandering the courtyard when Candace came around the corner looking like she'd robbed the National Trust.

"Oh dear, you've got turned out, haven't you? Sorry, it was well past their closing time, though. But, if it makes you feel any better, look what I found," she said, holding up a tatty, discolored roll of papers.

Glancing around the patio, Reggie saw only a few straggling guests roaming through on their way to their cars. She looked at her watch and then at her brochure. The museum was officially closed, and unless there were more interruptions from DCI Campbell and his men, they had the place to themselves.

"Let's see what we've got," said Tucker.

Candace spread the old, yellowed papers on a picnic table and smoothed out the curves. Some of the darker areas were covered with recent diagrams, and as she straightened the edges, a sheaf of newer drawings dropped onto the table.

"What are these?" asked Dulcy.

"That's what I'm looking for," replied Candace. "Those are the plans that correspond with the scriblings on these blueprints. It's the camera positions for the upgraded system!"

They bent their heads over the papers of angles, geometrics, and measurements, unsure of what they were viewing, when a sound from behind stopped them cold.

"And what are we all doing this fine evening?" said a voice from the darkening corners of the yard.

They froze, caught in the act, and desperately afraid to turn and face the disembodied voice. As the man emerged into the glow of the spotlights, Candace clutched and then relaxed. This could be a good thing, hopefully.

Alex Aldeworth, museum director, was visiting his own museum after hours, like the rest of them.

"Candace? What is all this?" he said, advancing on the group as they moved aside to allow him to see the papers.

"Alex, these are the museum blueprints. We're looking to see where all the cameras are positioned so that maybe we can see if the police missed anything during their investigations."

"Ah. Good idea. I'd forgotten about these. They'll be most helpful. Hello, Mr. Tolliver, bearing up, I hope?"

"Uh, yes, sir, managing well."

"So, let's get cracking. The sooner we find something to figure out what happened, the sooner we can get that lot off our grounds. They're costing us donations!"

Tolliver took more pictures of each camera setting. They discounted the positions that wouldn't be useful and concentrated on the possibilities. They covered approximately half the locations in and around the buildings.

"What do you think?" asked Laird, deferring to the administrator, who would be able to pinpoint their best options.

"All of these," he said, pointing, "along with these cameras here. And we can't dismiss the ones that show the museum and the exhibition halls. Who knows where the man wandered before he showed up on the bench?"

"There are more than I thought," said Laird. "Where are the corresponding videos for these?"

"We can view them in the old security offices. I have a key. It won't take a minute to pull the ones from last night. You'll need to come with me. I'll have to let you out anyhow, seeing as how the gates are locked now."

They trooped past the Concorde and headed to the side area, avoiding the main cameras and the remaining security guards. It took a bit, but after twenty minutes of tedious screen staring, something jumped out at them.

"What was that?" asked Reggie. "Was that a person? I can't quite tell."

They zoomed in on the figure barely visible in the shadows by the collection garages. The area was dark, and the movement stopped. They leaned in and waited. In just a minute, a hand pulled on the side door, and in the blink of an eye, a person slipped into the building.

"Was that a man or a woman?" asked Laird.

"Can't tell. What time was that?"

They found a video stamp of seven p.m. How did that fit in with the timetable they had so far? And why hadn't anyone else seemed to have seen this?

"Well, I guess it gives us a place to start," said Laird.

17

Chapter 17

From there, the poison goes to work on the central nervous system, causing severe muscle spasms, followed by the inevitable drooling.
-Airplane, 1980

"Hello, darlings. So nice to see you. What in the hell did you think you were doing today?"

Alene Farthing Elliott was not really angry; she was having fun. She relished torturing her children.

"Hullo, Mother, sorry it's been a rough day. I hope we didn't add to it."

Alene had a disgusted look on her face. No person in their right mind would mess with this woman, much less on a day where she had been accused of murder, hauled into jail, and had to avoid a scandal with a dead man's wife. It was a lot to get done, and all before teatime.

The group sat before her like students waiting to be expelled by the dean.

"I'm going to pour myself a brandy and sit next to your father while you tell us what you've been up to because I'm sure it's well worth listening to," she said, resembling a cat with its paw on a mouse.

"Well, it has been a day, Mum, let's say that."

Tucker had learned well from his mother. If she thought he was going to roll over, she was devastatingly mistaken. As they were all getting comfortable, the study door opened, and Dahlia came in, looking well-rested and bright, unlike the rest of them.

"Oh, Dahlia, when did you get here? We were missing you."

"Yes," said Mrs. Porter. "Did Jennings bring you?"

"Hello, all. Yes, Mum, Jennings is in the kitchen with Myra."

"Thank goodness," said Alene. "She can use all the help she can get. Oh, God love her, but she's getting on and not as spry as she used to be. And Henry is blessedly lost anywhere but in the garage or the garden. Any help is much appreciated."

"Well, dear, we're all just glad you're not eating dinner with the other felons in the local jail," said the senior Elliott.

"That thought has not gone unnoticed, Douglass. I certainly believed that's where I could be right now at one point today. As luck would have it, Chalmers actually came through, the old windbag. At least he finally earned his pay. So, back to you all sitting in front of me like you're hoping for parole. What did you learn today?"

Tucker grinned and sat back in his uncomfortable chair. It seemed like his whole day had been made up of uncomfortable seating arrangements. Maybe this was his punishment for his transgressions.

"Well, Mother, I think you know what we did today. You've had a nice update from DCI Campbell and one from Jennings, the old character. What gaps may we fill in for you?"

"Why, all of them, dear. Start from the beginning, please."

"Does that include your invitation to the station, or shall I take it from there? Ah, from then going forward, I see," he said, hoping her expression didn't freeze his drink.

Tucker detailed the events after she had been "sprung" from the confines of Constable Downs' office to when they had arrived for dinner and cocktails. He did not, however, go into detail regarding Reggie's purloining the murder cup. Or Candace doing the same thing. Or the jib door escape from the Farthing's offices. He did mention they had a nice lunch at Brooklands and that everyone was looking forward to a successful tea relaunch.

"How nice, Tucker. That's a wonderfully PG-rated recap; only I was hoping for something with a bit more substance. And truth. Care to try again and actually tell me something worth hearing? Something helpful, perhaps? Something to keep me from receiving another invitation to the High Street police station?"

"If I may, Mrs. Elliott, I can fill in a few details for you," said Laird.

"Yes, I would appreciate that as well since I seem to have missed everything," groused Dahlia.

All eyes turned to Laird as Dulcy, Tolliver, and Reggie tried to shrink into their respective spaces. Tucker was anxious to hear this, too, since there was more than one instance that should be left out of the tale for the moment.

"I think you have a clear idea of the highlights. To go a bit further, we have found blueprints for Brooklands with the help of the director and Candace. These led us to the security camera videos, which were boring for the most part but did, in the end, give us one clue."

"And that was?"

"Someone was roaming the grounds close to the time of Weatherford's, uh, departure. The only thing is, we couldn't tell who it was or if it was a man or a woman," finished Laird.

"There are more videos to review, but we've left that up to Alex Aldeworth, the museum director. No one would question him going through the tapes. If we show up there one more time, we'll all go to the nick," said Tucker.

Alene sat back in her chair, still discontented. These short offerings were precisely that: no detail, no depth, no dice. She sighed and glanced at Douglass, who took a large gulp of his scotch and pretended not to see her. She would have to be satisfied with this paltry offering.

"So, what happens next? And be specific."

"We'll need to see what Candace finds. We should also get Audrey out there. She could be quite helpful in finding out more than we could. We can then follow up on it while we 'sightsee'," said Tucker.

A slight knock on the door ushered in Myra, who was followed by Jennings, who was bearing gifts. There were lovely hors d'oeuvres, a new decanter of cocktails, and a short description of dinner to follow.

"Will there be anything else, madam?" asked Jennings.

"No, not at the moment, Jennings; thank you so much."

Jennings bowed and held the door for Myra, who was dragging her feet, hoping to hear something of interest. With a clearing of his throat, she grudgingly turned and plodded through the door.

"So, Mother, you paid a visit to the widow Weatherford. That must have been arresting. No pun intended. Did you learn anything?"

"Did Flora steal anything?" laughed Dahlia.

"No, Flora was being 'observed' by Simmons, the old statue," she said, chuckling. "She did, however, come close to snorting down the entire contents of the brandy decanter. I thought she might be of some use, but if she had seen anything at the gala, she didn't mention it. Such a bother. But then again, I was a bit distracted."

"By what, dear?" asked Douglass.

"The research materials in Olivia's possession."

"Oh, so you were able to get a look at them?" asked Tucker hopefully.

"Oh, yes. Quite a lot of material, you know. Stacks of figures and formulas and diagrams."

"So, what was the old man working on?" asked Laird.

"Oh, he wasn't working on anything."

"I'm not following, Mother. What were the documents then?"

"They were research papers, formulas, and findings."

"But if they weren't what he was working on, then what were they?"

"They were plans and details of new flavors, new labeling, and new promotional programs."

"Still not following," replied Tucker.

"They were yours," said Laird.

"Why, yes! There you are. Now, there's a clever chap. They were all our proprietary details. All of our year's work in a tidy bundle sitting right next to Olivia on her Chesterfield. Very good, Agent Laird."

###

Dinner had been a smashing success. With Jennings's help, Myra had managed a lovely meal fit for a king. At least, that's what it seemed like to Alene, who was still having flashbacks to a jail cell and cardboard food served on a battered tin tray. They were again seated in the library, having coffee and port and still discussing how the odious little man had managed to pilfer their most guarded secrets.

"You're leaving something out, Mother. I see that nasty little grin; you've been up to something."

"As we were discussing what to do about our 'situation', Simmons informed me that I was wanted at the office. Luckily, by the time I got there, DCI Campbell's men were just leaving. They actually had the nerve to park in my reserved spot."

"Oh, Lord, that can't have ended well," said Tucker.

"I boxed them in by double parking. Gillian had to let them out."

Reggie stifled a small snort and cleared her throat. That was a show she would have liked to have seen.

"Roswyn and Bella requested my presence. They wanted to know if what Weatherford had been saying was true. You know, the part about us stealing his formulas."

"Oh, and what did you tell them?" asked Dahlia.

"I said, of course it wasn't true, and asked them which one of them had the audacity to leak my information to the old reptile."

This time, Reggie choked on her port as Tucker gave her a sharp rap between the shoulder blades in a clumsy effort to help. Laird was shaking his head while Dulcy remained quiet and watched the proceedings.

"Well, I guess you chose to cut to the chase, Mum."

"But what did they say?" gasped Reggie.

"Oh, dear, of course they denied it. What else could they do? 'Oh, yes, I did it. Desperately sorry about the corporate betrayal thing. Cheers! We'll just pop off back to the lab now.'"

"What I want to know is what the constables were doing back there," asked Laird. "What were they looking for now?"

"Audrey said something about Winston having come back in after Olivia dismissed him and poured himself a drink. I neither saw nor heard that. They were going to go back to Brooklands after more details on that. Something about a missing cup."

Reggie had the good graces to look guilty and averted Alene's eyes. She would have to own up to her larcenous activities if someone didn't speak up.

"The errant cup has been found," said Tucker. "Now they can match up the autopsy findings and the cup and be satisfied that everything is documented."

"Even with finding out what was in the body and the cup, we still don't have any idea where he actually died. I'm hoping those tapes give us something we can use," said Laird, staring at his phone. "Excuse me, I have to take this."

All eyes were on John Laird as he headed to the hall with the device glued to his ear, head shaking, listening intently. The room was dead silent as they looked uncomfortably from one to the other. When the door opened, an inscrutable Agent Laird entered the room.

"Well?" asked Tucker.

"That was the FME. They have analyzed the contents of the cup and compared them to the stomach contents. Both match, so now we know how he died, even if we don't know where. I can tell you one thing: it was a quick death."

"What was it, John?" asked Dulcy.

"Botulinum toxin."

"You mean he had botulism?" asked Alene.

"No, this was the neurotoxin, the pure powder used in labs for testing, some therapies, and some cosmetic procedures. This was not a food-borne issue. Botulinum toxin is odorless, colorless, tasteless, and deadly. It'll kill in a matter of minutes. Whoever put it in his drink definitely meant it for him and meant for it to kill him."

18

Chapter 18

Goodness me, what a time we're having.
-Fist of Fury (The Chinese Connection), 1972

The silence was broken only by the gulping of a few scotches. Someone had to ask, and Alene decided she would tackle the touchy subject.

"So, what is this 'toxin' you say was the culprit here? I thought it only had to do with food."

"It's a hazardous chemical compound. It's used in some manufacturing but mainly in the medical and cosmetic industries for controlling muscle spasms, migraines, and various other spasticity issues. It's uncommon to find it in its pure form, as it is extremely dangerous. As you say, you know it in its other form, botulism, the food-borne strain. That's more common and comes from contents being improperly canned or processed. It can also be found in fruits, vegetables, and fish. Spores can be present on any number of things, which can make someone dangerously ill."

"But this couldn't have been in anything we had at the gala," said Tucker. "Everything was fresh. Whoever did this had access to something from somewhere else. I'm fairly certain we don't use anything like that in our labs, manufacturing plants, or anywhere else in our business. Isn't that right, Mother?"

Alene looked thoughtful while trying to take an inventory of the various ingredients used in their business processes, but try as she might, there wasn't anything she could think of that would fit this description.

"No, I'm fairly certain there wouldn't be anything of the sort in our labs or plants. And it wouldn't be in any food we had offered because it wasn't *our* food. It would be the food provided by the Brooklands people and Chef Dumont. The only thing we contributed was the tea."

"This isn't going to be so easy," said Laird. "Botulism takes time to kill someone. This was very quick and was introduced into whatever he drank. As I mentioned, in its pure form, the toxin is odorless, colorless, and tasteless and can kill quickly if ingested. I cannot fathom where someone would get such a compound without having a license or some form of access to such a deadly ingredient."

"Then that's where you two shall start tomorrow," said Alene. "Tucker, you and Dahlia visit the labs and make sure we don't have any reason to have that type of poison in our possession. Make a show of it, love. You're giving your dear friend a tour of our inner workings."

"I'm going to see the FME," said Laird. "He's a good man, and I think he'll be cooperative. I'll just poke around as a fellow lawman scouting out the techniques across the pond."

"Tolliver, how about some more sightseeing?" asked Reggie. "You can drive Dulcy and me out to Brooklands. We'll have Candace show us the Concorde and the racing track. Maybe Alex will have found something else on the tapes by then."

"Yes, Miss. I would be happy to accompany you back to the museum."

Tolliver looked anything but happy. Tucker thought he was the exact picture of a man who had bitten into something sour and couldn't get the taste out of his mouth.

"What will you be doing, Mother?"

"Douglass and I will be going over the papers we have and those I took from Roswyn this afternoon. Maybe we can come up with something there. We need to find some answers here because what comes next will be even less pleasant than it already is if we have no direction."

"Why? What comes next?" asked Dulcy.

Alene glanced at Douglass and then at the group. They had not been informed about upcoming events.

"Next, my dears, is the three-ring circus of the formal funeral for the late J. Winston Weatherford. May God have mercy on his soul."

###

The next day dawned bright and sunny, with a chill in the air that comes with late fall in the English countryside. Tucker escorted Reggie to breakfast, where a crisp-looking Alene Elliott was already enjoying her second cup of tea and her second scone. Myra had offered kippers; however, the botulism conversation of the night before floated in her mind's eye like a belly-up fish in the back forty pond. She had opted for the safe delicacies of the local bakery.

"Good morning, Mum," said Tucker, dropping a kiss on the top of her head. "Digging into something tasty?"

"I went the safe route—scones from Whitlock's bakery. Myra offered kippers, but I'm afraid after the conversation last night, I'll be off fish for a while. Set for your sightseeing excursion, Regina?"

"Oh, yes," said Reggie, scooping a mass of eggs, bacon, tomatoes, and toast onto her plate. "I have an idea I'd like to think through. Maybe talk to Candace about it while we're there. Something she mentioned the other day, which might be quite fun. Not to mention a way to see more of the property."

She nibbled daintily on a charred piece of bacon, one of Myra's crunchier offerings, as she sat opposite Alene and Tucker. The two had familiar looks on their faces, and she knew their disapproval was coming shortly.

"What? You haven't even heard it yet."

"You're right, Reg. We haven't. We're being bloody unfair."

Alene leaned sideways and glared at Tucker, who knew she disapproved of his language. It was a shame he didn't care.

"Go ahead, Regina. I, for one, would love to hear it. We could use a nice diversion, and if it helps with any of this mess, that would be an even bigger bonus."

"I haven't thought it all out yet, Alene, but I know Candace will be able to tell us if and when we can do this. Just let Tolliver and me sort it out, and we'll have a nice surprise for you later on."

"There you go. Let Tolliver help. If anyone can lend a solid, steady hand, it's that bloke. He'll have it sorted out in no time. Brilliant idea, Reg."

Both Alene and Reggie were staring at Tucker with narrowed eyes and silent tongues. Tucker had made a sexist blunder that even he couldn't ignore. He hadn't meant to do it, but out there it was. He had totally discounted his lovely assistant in one fell swoop.

"Please let us know how everything goes, Reg. Must run; can't keep our Dahlia waiting for our adventures today. Bye, Mum, love you," he said, running from the room to the safety of the great outdoors.

"Cheeky little shit," sniffed Alene. "Remind me to raise your pay, Regina."

###

Once again, Dulcy woke to find herself alone in bed, with no FBI agent, no breakfast, and no idea.

"John Laird! Where did you get to this time?"

A hairdryer at full force told her she was once again behind on the start of the day. She sneaked out of bed, pushed open the bathroom door, and expected to surprise the agent in all his naked glory. Instead, he was nowhere in sight.

"Hey! Where are you?"

"Alright, Miss. Spread 'em. I'll have to pat you down. You've been a naughty girl," he said, holding her at gunpoint with the hairdryer.

"I haven't even begun to be bad, Agent. Are you going to frisk me or just handcuff me?"

"You'd like that, wouldn't you? C'mon, get moving."

"Wait, what are we doing? I thought you were going to frisk me, you know, in the other room," she said, nodding at the empty bed.

"That will have to wait."

He pulled her close to his still-wet, naked body and kissed her with a long, slow exhale. He wanted to give in, but timing wouldn't let him. She clung to his neck as he tried to pry her hands apart and scoot her to the shower.

"I have to circumvent Campbell. Tucker is on his way here to get Dahlia, and Tolliver is on his way to collect Reggie and then you. Play time will have to wait, I'm afraid."

He kissed her again and smacked her bare bottom as he gently shoved her into the shower.

"See there; that's how you deal with that," he said proudly.

"Uh, huh, and how do you propose to deal with that?" she said, staring down at his privates.

Dulcy flounced full into the shower stream and slammed the door in his face.

###

Tolliver had been humming a mindless tune as he traversed the back roads toward the Elliotts. It was a beautiful day, if not a bit chilly, and he was in no particular hurry to get this outing started. More time at the Brooklands Museum and race course was not high on his list. He would rather be involved in the search through the labs with Tucker than go back to the venue with its hidden secrets and suspect staff. He did not know what Miss Reggie had in mind, and he would be happier staying that way.

Pulling up to the Brooklands gate was a much better experience than it had been the previous days. The sentinels and crime tape were gone, and things looked back to normal. Tolliver parked in a designated spot, and he and Reggie followed the stream of visitors into the grounds.

"Alright, Tolliver, where to first?"

"I believe, Miss Reggie, that this is your expedition, so maybe you should take the lead."

"Then, the first stop is to visit Candace. And then to Alex to see if he's found any other evidence on those tapes."

Tolliver followed in silence as Reggie peeked in the security center and then veered off to Candace's office. He glanced at the space where the tea table had stood. It looked barren and sad, but it was always only just an event space.

"Good morning, Candace! How are things today?"

"Better since we're now lawless, so to speak. No more constables running around the place, poking here and there, and looking at you like you're guilty."

"But we are guilty, Candace," laughed Reggie.

"Okay, true. We're bonded by 'the cup'. Hopefully, they won't track that little tidbit down."

"I'm surprised they aren't here. It's still a murder investigation."

"Yes, and we're in the dark. We don't even know what he died of, or where, or worse yet, when they'll be back."

"We-e-e-llll, that's not exactly true," said Reggie.

Candace straightened and peered out of her robust spectacles at Reggie and then Tolliver.

"What's happened, then? What have you found out?"

"Miss Candace, we now know what killed Weatherford, and it was quick-acting. It's called botulinum toxin."

"That means it was in the food," her voice rising in panic.

"That's botulism. It's doubtful. Apparently, that strain takes longer to kill - hours, days. This was something that acted instantly. From what Agent Laird was told, it's a toxin at its deadliest: odorless, colorless, and tasteless when in its pure form. When introduced into something ingested, it only takes a matter of minutes."

"Which then..."

"Turns it back on us since it was supposedly in the tea."

Candace seemed to relax, but anyone would have if the burden had been taken off them.

"What do we do now?"

"Well, I think we take a tour... and throw a party!"

19

Chapter 19

Yoo- hoo! Where are you?
-The Three Amigos, 1986

"Bye, Mum, bye, Dad!"

"Dahlia, please, you two, try to find something helpful. Tucker, I know you'll fix this. Is there anything we can do to help?"

"Have a large scotch waiting when we get back."

"Done, sir!" came an energetic reply from the cupboard.

"You can always count on Jennings, can't you? Thanks, mate. Alright, Dahl. Let's go. Time to find the needle in the haystack."

Tucker and Dahlia's first stop was to the Farthing's offices, where Tucker had a list of locations tucked in his oak desk, the one with the drawers. There was no lab on site, but it was only a short walk away in a newer, more secure structure.

"Right. This building here, Dahlia. Shall we?"

"Is this the one Roswyn and Bella work in?" she said, her steps faltering.

"You're a quick one, you are. C'mon."
Dahlia took a deep breath and followed Tucker through the main entrance. She was hoping he had a plan and vowed to keep her mouth shut.

"Good morning, Mr. Elliott. How are you today?"

A young female with somewhat frizzy orange hair smiled up at them through even orangier lipstick and stood to offer her hand.

"Hello, Miss Dahlia. We've been expecting you. So nice to see you. I'm Lizzie. Can I get you anything before your tour?"

"No, thank you, Lizzie. I've just come from breakfast, but thanks so much for asking. Busy morning?"

Lizzie grinned and shook her head, indicating a hectic morning in full swing. Tucker watched Dahlia as she met Lizzie's hand. She smiled broadly, greeting her like a long-lost friend. Tucker stood wondering at what point he had lost control of the situation.

"Come along then, Miss Dahlia, Mr. Elliott, and I'll take you to the labs. That's where you're going, yes?"

"Uh, yes. That is where we're going, correct, Tucker?"

"Yes, love. Lead on, Lizzie. Mother called ahead," he said to Dahlia.

"Right-o. Follow me, please."

Tucker looked on as Lizzie used her key card, typed in a code, and pressed a fingerprint onto a separate pad. The door slid open, and she let Tucker and Dahlia pass.

"Quite a lot of security, Miss Dahlia. You know how competitive this tea game can be, right, Mr. Elliott?"

"Yes, of course. Sinister business, really," he said, looking up at the hall camera.

Lizzie let out a light laugh and led them through several other doors till they were in an office with no windows, a computer, two chairs, and a beat-up file cabinet—a relatively sparse, derelict space to serve as a confidential area.

"Alright, sir, I'll just go fetch Miss Walsh and Miss Fielding for you."

"Uh, wait a tick, Lizzie. I don't want to bother them just yet; I know they're busy. I want to scribble down a few things so I don't waste their valuable time, you understand."

"Of course, Mr. Elliott. I'll be back shortly, and you can let me know."

Lizzie backed herself out of the door, leaving Tucker and Dahlia watching her intently.

"So, now what?"

"I would rather work on the element of surprise. They don't need to know we're here and what we want."

"But the girl, Lizzie, won't she tell them?"

"Not if she wants to keep her job. I'm known for two things here: what I tell them to do and what happens if they don't do it. I also don't pretend to know everything. Keeps them in the dark as to what I'm up to at any given moment."

"You are an evil one. I love that about you. So, what are you up to at this given moment?"

Tucker walked over to an ancient computer and entered his credentials. Dahlia leaned against the desk and watched with curiosity. He then pulled a small drive from his pocket, entered commands, and waited. The machine hummed and buzzed, but after several minutes, it subsided. Tucker then pulled the portable drive, shoved it in his pocket, and winked at Dahlia.

"Let's go."

"So, we're not going to question anyone, are we?"

"Not at this time. We have things to do first."

Dahlia leaned around Tucker and glanced at the computer. The screensaver featured a decorative teapot, cups, and saucers with a plate of biscuits placed before them. She watched as Tucker peeked out the door. He glided over to the decrepit file cabinet shoved tightly against the wall. There was a picture of the English countryside above it in mixed media showing hills, fences, livestock, and a stile with an actual brass padlock. Tucker smiled back at Dahlia, slowly pressed the lock, and stepped aside.

"Oh, my gosh!" exclaimed Dahlia.

The battered old filing cabinet swung easily away from the wall to reveal an opening of the same size.

"Come along, Dahl. Time to go!"

"Oh, geez. You and your bloody jib doors, Tucker," she said, rolling her eyes.

###

John Laird breezed into the High Street police station and smiled at the young lady at the screening device. He flashed his badge and waited while she reviewed his credentials and eyed him carefully. She passed him through, and he took a sharp right to the FME's area. He found the man sitting behind his desk, bent over a sheaf of papers, scratching notes.

"Good morning, McCallum. How are you today?"

"Ah, Agent Laird. Nice to see you. Good of you to come by. This one has me a bit buggered. I mean, it's easy to see how he died; he obviously drank it, but we may never know where it came from. A right awful way to die, you know."

"There can't be that many places where you can get that kind of strength, can there?"

"Oh, on the contrary, Laird. There are many places to get that sort of thing, such as surgeries, eye doctors, and clinics that treat spasticity issues. You could run 'round the countryside and never pinpoint exactly where it came from."

"Don't you have to have some sort of license for it?"

"Oh, yes, right. And most places have rather strict methods of accountability. You can't just wander into the meds cabinet and borrow a vial of botulinum toxin like it's a cup of sugar. There are safeguards and sign-outs, keys, and someone counting the inventory at every turn. All that rubbish, you know."

"But if someone did steal it, would you know about it?"

"Not necessarily. I mean, if it were a recurring problem, it would be reported. I couldn't imagine it would go on for long, though, you know. Someone always gets caught, and they don't always come to us. Want to keep it out of the press. Handle it themselves without the bad publicity. Reporting that sort of thing has to become public record."

Laird sat back and thought about what the man was saying as he watched him scan the papers. He jotted a note or two and then signed an attached form.

"So, are you calling it? What's going to be the official cause, McCallum?"

"Well, it wasn't botulism due to food, as we know. He could have been saved if it were that. The anti-toxin would have been administered, and he would have been ill for a bit, but he would have come 'round after a while. Of course, the older the victim, the longer it takes to recover."

"What was the actual time of death?"

"As near as we can say, between seven-fifteen and seven-thirty. He was seen inside taking a drink by the two women around that time, when he left out the back by the loos. And he was found ... just after eight o'clock," he said, referring to an earlier page.

"It really must have been quick if he was given the toxin and then moved to the bench in front."

"Oh yes, absolutely. It attacks the central nervous system, starting in the cranial area. It works so fast that even if he wanted to, he more than likely wouldn't have been able to call out. It progresses from there, causing muscle paralysis, eyesight failure, and breathing difficulties. If he died and was moved as has been suggested, it would have had to have been a good-sized bloke to get him to the bench. Otherwise, anyone could have done it by helping him along as soon as he took it."

"So it could be a man or a woman, then?"

"Either, mate. It all depends on where he was when he took it, how far he had to go, and who assisted him to his great reward. Doesn't help much, does it, Agent Laird?"

"No, not really. Sounds like we're back where we started."

"Yes, it does. Cause of death: death by homicide. Bloody hell; the papers are going to have a field day with this one."

The press. John Laird had forgotten about the media. They had managed to keep them at bay for the time being. Everyone had been waiting for the result. Now that it would be out there, he needed to get back to the Elliotts. It was time to circle the wagons.

20

Chapter 20

Men love women, but even more than that, men love cars.
-Rush, 2013

"Well, of course, we'll do your tour. And a party? Are we talking the relaunch or something else?" Candace said with hopeful eyes.

Tolliver was lagging behind, but quickened his pace to catch up so as not to miss anything.

"Oh, I just have a little idea. Actually, you put me on to it, Candace, and I think it would be great for your business and everyone's spirits. You can even invite the press, and they can get some good news to report about you for a change."

"Oooo, I'm intrigued."

"So am I, Miss," added Tolliver.

"Double for me," said Dulcy.

Reggie gave Tolliver a prize smile and reached back to take his arm. He succumbed to her bidding and joined her, Dulcy, and Candace as they walked out the back to the Concorde exhibit.

"If I'm not mistaken, Miss Dulcy, this was what you wanted to see especially, yes?"

"Oh, absolutely! I'm so interested in its mechanics. I've been reading up on it. This is the Concorde B-DDBG, correct? The very first Concorde produced from the prototypes?"

"Yes, correct. It really is a great tour. Such a fascinating ship with such history. The restoration work on G-BBDG was an amazing achievement by our team here. They had to acquire parts from British Airways, which included some interior fittings and other items, such as flight deck instruments. They were also able to acquire the full forward passenger cabin fittings, which had been removed from Concorde G-BOAB at Heathrow by BA sometime earlier while they were carrying out work for Project Rocket."

"I read all about it. I can't wait to see it."

"And the perfect introduction to my idea!" said Reggie.

The three turned to see her gazing up at the monument, just like a starstruck fan would look at a movie idol.

"Ah," said Candace. "I get it. Let's have a special soiree to show them that we're just fine and there's nothing awful happening here."

"Exactly. There are a couple of ways you can do it; my offering is that we show everyone that Farthing's Fine Teas isn't jinxed and invite some of the main characters from the tea gala. We'll show them that we can have a party that doesn't include murder."

"And the other?"

"Open it up to a charity function. Have people bid on items at a silent auction and make it a big party, sponsored by Farthing's, with proceeds going to the museum!"

"Why not do both?" said Candace.

"That's a great idea," said Dulcy.

"We can talk about it after we take a look. I think you're going to love this. It's brilliant!"

Even Tolliver was impressed as they scooted around the sleek machine and climbed the narrow staircase into the cabin. Reggie could imagine being a passenger in this fantastic vehicle, with its stylish interior and high-tech instruments. It made her long for a time when they could have actually traveled in such luxury. She could imagine hosting a posh party aboard her with all the trimmings to take everyone's mind off the incidents of the past couple of days.

"It's just the thing. We can get Audrey involved and plan it for... when? I don't know your schedule and don't want to intrude on your bookings."

"I know what we have going on, and I can shift some things around. How about in the next week or so? It'll give you time to make special invitations for your guests, and we can get everything ready. I know Alex will be ecstatic. He's been so worried about everything. Oh! Speaking of, we have a lovely offering available. It's a driving experience where guests can run the track as if they're racing. They can choose from several prestige cars, such as Aston Martins and the Jaguar E-type, or classics like the Austin-Healey or MG. Alex is actually out there now working on the route changes. I'll show you the old race course, or what's left of it, and then you can talk to him.

Let's go have a look."

They hiked past the exhibition buildings and collections, and out to the sections of the track that were still in existence. Parts were overgrown and sad-looking from the ravages of WWII bombs and the installation of aerodrome hangars. But there was still a vestige of track left that beckoned to those with the racing spirit. Those who still believed in rubber meeting road and speed enough to make your face blur.

They were trudging up a narrow hill when Candace stopped them at a point where overgrown brush met uncoated concrete. Though worn and rough, Test Hill still held an allure that captured all four of them.

"This is amazing," said Dulcy softly. "You can almost feel the history. I'm so glad we got to do this today."

"Now we'll just wait over here to see Alex coming."

The four walked out to the edge of the turf, navigating the pitted surface. Reggie thought it would be an incredible treat to drive one of their classic cars.

"You're right, Candace. You can even feel the vibration of the earth as if they're racing like back in the day."

"And you can hear the sound," said Tolliver. "I think we need to back away a minute, ladies. That sounds quite close."

They were rooted to their spots, straining to find the direction of the engine. It was close, closer than they knew.

"Look out!" yelled Dulcy, pushing Reggie and Candace away as Tolliver threw himself in front of them.

A speeding Aston Martin spun out of control and slid by them as if in a movie scene. With a bang and a whine, the machine crashed into a haystack barrier, jolted to a halt, and sat steaming and still. Before they had a chance to move, they heard a moan near the wreckage. Alex Aldeworth lay motionless and half-hidden in the sheared grass.

###

They raced toward the sound of the moan, the steaming car hissing as they passed.

"Look! Just there! Oh, Gawd, please let him be all right," yelled Candace.

Just yards from the car, Alex was lying in a crumpled heap. Technicians, visitors, and personnel were streaming out of buildings toward the accident scene. Tolliver was dialing 999 as Reggie and Candace leaned over Alex, checking for injuries and breathing. A man on his own phone was running towards them, barking instructions and directions. He moved Reggie and Candace gently aside and checked Alex according to the disjointed voice on the other end.

"He's breathing! He's breathing but unconscious. I'm putting my jacket under his head. Wait! He's coming to. Alex, don't move. We don't know the extent of your injuries."

Tolliver guided Reggie, Candace, and Dulcy away from the wreckage as men in hazmat suits sprayed down the car. Reggie and Dulcy clung to Candace, who was shaking to the point of loosening her teeth.

"Mr. Elliott, it's Tolliver, sir. There's been an accident here at Brooklands. No, sir, the women are fine; they are just a bit shaken. Call DCI Campbell right away, please."

The three stood off to the side with Tolliver, observing the tangled Aston Martin and the man attending to Alex.

"I'm not leaving him," said Candace. "There's an ambulance coming, I think. I can hear something in the distance."

Reggie was concerned for Alex, but she was more concerned about what caused such a horrific crash. Glancing around the track, she strained to view the activity with the injured museum director.

"Something had to have happened," said Candace. "People have been doing this without incident for months now. Something's not right here."

Reggie walked past Tolliver, who fell in step with her, watching silently. They walked out to the section of the track where Alex had come into view, staring down at the marks on the rugged concrete.

"You must be thinking what I'm thinking, Miss."

"You betcha, Tolliver. This was not a normal accident. Look at those marks. I don't know what those things are. Where are the tread marks?"

They gazed down the stretch of pavement but saw nothing related to the crash. A rise of voices drew their attention back to the scene, as constables corralled bystanders and made room for an ambulance rolling into the crowd. A lone figure came toward them with a disgusted expression.

"I might have known. Dirty great surprise, you two. What the bloody hell are you doing back here?" said DCI Campbell.

"We came here for our tour from Candace. Is there a law against that, Campbell?" snapped Reggie.

"No law, just trying to understand why every time you set foot on these here premises, some bloody cock up happens. What do you have to say about that?"

"Nothing. We came out here so Candace could show us the track. Alex was out here running the visitors' experience route. When we heard him coming, he almost hit us. He was so out of control. I'd like to know why that was, Detective Inspector."

As she turned to face Campbell, she saw familiar figures observing the accident scene. Tucker Elliott and Dahlia Porter had arrived. Dahlia was enveloping Dulcy and then Candace in tight hugs while Tucker searched the crowd. She saw him straighten and make a beeline for her.

"Thank God," she murmured.

"What?" said Campbell, following her gaze. "Ah, brilliant. Now we're complete. Wouldn't be an investigation without the rest of the club."

Tucker was speeding toward Reggie, covering ground like a thoroughbred. Dahlia stood with Candace and Dulcy, monitoring the accident crew.

"Glad you could make it, Elliott. Wouldn't be a party without you."

"DCI, I've missed you. Wouldn't be a visit to Brooklands without *you.*"

"Stuff your bloody sarcasm, Elliott. We have a situation here. Again."

"Obviously. Reggie, Tolliver, what happened?"

"We were just explaining to DCI Campbell here, sir, that we don't know. One minute he was driving, and the next, he was bang out of control. You see the result just there," he said, nodding his head toward the attendants.

They looked over in time to see Alex Aldeworth lifted carefully onto a gurney. Rather than being dazed, the man was waving wildly, pointing, and yelling. Reggie took off like a shot before either Tucker or Campbell could stop her.

"Bollocks," said Tucker and Campbell at the same time.

"What is it, Alex? What happened? Tell me. Please!"

The man swallowed hard and pulled her to him.

"He's been sedated, Miss; I'm not sure he'll be of any help."

"He doesn't look sedate to me, and he's got something to say. I know it's important."

"Miss Winter! The car!" he said, rolling his head to the charred vehicle. "No brakes! No brakes! Couldn't stop, wouldn't stop. Nothing! Nothing!"

And with that, Alex Aldeworth lay back on the stretcher and passed out.

21

Chapter 21

"That's it. I want out of this family.

-Ferris Bueller's Day Off, 1986

"Nobody move. I want a word with all of you. You can either wait here or go to the cafe; I don't care which. But no one leaves until I've done with you."

The group huddled on the side as the mechanics were removing the wreckage to one of the outbuildings, with DCI Campbell on their heels.

"Whatcher think?" asked Tucker.

"Staying here won't help anything," said Reggie. "Let's go to the cafe. Candace, are you okay? Let's get you something to drink. We can talk there."

Candace nodded and let Tolliver guide her away from the cratered grass, which was now almost clear of the remnants of the crash. Only the forensic men were studying the area for clues. Dahlia and Dulcy followed behind Tucker and Reggie. Dulcy desperately wished she knew where John Laird was, but she didn't want to call and sound like the hysterical female.

Once they were seated, Tucker nodded to Reggie and rose with his phone. He turned his back, but not before Dulcy heard him say Laird's name. She was grateful to Tucker for calling him; she had wanted to, but hadn't felt she should. She wasn't sure if she had any nerves left. Tucker pulled up a chair between Dulcy and Reggie and stretched out his long legs.

"John's on his way. He had just finished with the FME when I called."

"Any news?" asked Reggie hopefully.

"I didn't really ask. We'll find out soon enough."

Reggie had gone to the counter and returned with Fanta sodas for everyone.

"Sorry, wish these could be something stronger. You could do with a brandy shot right about now, Candace."

"I've a flask in my office. I'm really alright. The shock is starting to wear off. Poor Alex."

"He's going to be fine," said a voice behind them.

They turned to find DCI Campbell standing alone, hands in pockets, observing them casually but carefully.

"Detective. Pull up a chair. It's been a busy day already, I know."

"It has. This whole bloody week, especially since you lot came to town. You're leaving when?"

"Very funny," said Tucker.

"Wasn't meant to be."

"What's going on out there?" asked Dulcy.

"We've got forensics going over the vehicle with a fine-tooth comb, and then we'll be examining it even further in the garages. We'll see if we can find any clues as to why he crashed."

"He said he had no brakes. He said there was nothing," said Reggie.

DCI Campbell took out his notebook and yanked a chair over from the next table. Reggie could hear the scratching of pencil on paper and waited for the next question. Campbell looked up at the faces glued to his and continued to write.

"You said Alex was going to be okay. How do you know?" asked Candace.

"I asked if they would stay till I came back from the outbuilding. They were treating him in the ambulance when I came back. They said he was stable and would be fine. He's got a dirty great bruise on his head where he landed when he was tossed and a few other injuries, but overall, he's a lucky bloke. We'll know more once they get him to hospital."

"Oh, I'm so glad," said Candace. "This project has meant a lot to him, and I'd hate to see it shut down. Visitors have had such a lovely time with it."

"How did all this start today?"

"Well, Alex had been talking with the race experts who felt that some adjustments should be made to the route. Alex loves the classic cars and offers to help out whenever he can. He told them this morning that he'd run the Aston Martin through the course to see where they could change a few turns. He's an ace driver and knows the track well. He must have just taken it a bit too far on the speed."

"We'll find that out when we take it apart. Hopefully, there'll be some evidence if anything was done to the vehicle. All I can say is he's lucky it was a full tank."

"He is?" asked Dahlia.

"Yes, if it wasn't a full tank, the vapors are much more likely to catch fire. Your friend Alex is a fortunate lad, my dear."

###

"Glum faces all around, I see," said John Laird, advancing on the cafe table.

"Ah, Agent Laird out of his jurisdiction once again. How are you, sir?"

"I'm well, Campbell, but it looks like things could be better here. How's Alex?"

"He'll make it. He's lucky; it was a full tank, and he was thrown. But he was going on about not having brakes. So there's something to start with, at least. If we can get anything out of the vehicle, we may be able to corroborate that. And if that's the case, we need to sort out who wanted to see him dead. And why."

Candace shook and began to cry. Reggie and Dahlia leaned in and shielded her from the abrupt copper.

"Come with us," said Reggie, lifting Candace and leading her away.

She threw a nod over her head as she and Dahlia walked her anywhere but where she was.

"Really, mate, do you have to be such a wanker? Can't you just give it a rest for five minutes? What's the good in making her so miserable? C'mon, give me your best."

"I needed to know."

"You needed to know what?"

"I needed to see her reaction."

"You think she was in on this?" said Laird.

"I don't know," said Campbell. "But it's my job to find out. You lot would have done the same to get to the truth."

"Not bloody likely," said Tucker. "Not bloody likely."

###

"What in the name of all that's holy were you all doing today?"

"Mother, calm," said Tucker.

"Go sit and be quiet. And do not irritate me. Now, what did you do today? I couldn't imagine how things could get worse, but thank you for disabusing me of that notion. Explain yourselves."

"Well...

"Mother Elliott, please let me explain," said Reggie.

She counted on her special bond with Alene, which would allow her to remedy this situation, and all would be well.

"You have two minutes," said Alene, setting her watch.

"All we did was go to Brooklands to take our tour of the Concorde and the track. How were we to know that the museum director would crash an expensive automobile and almost die?"

"What?? I was talking about the offices. You went to the offices and drew ridiculous attention to yourselves without finding a thing, correct?"

"Oh, that would be Dahlia and me, Mum. We did go to the labs today, but we didn't interview anyone. How did you know?"

"I know everything, Tucker Farthing Elliott. When will you learn?"

"Shit. She used my whole name," whispered Tucker to Dahlia.

"I'm not deaf, you twit. And you dragged me into this, and now I'm in trouble too. Ass."

"You can't go to the labs, sign in, and then disappear without a trace. When you didn't come back out, they figured you had decided to leave without seeing Roswyn or Bella. The only problem is, son of mine, is you never came out of the room, according to the hall camera."

"I confess. We left, but the camera just didn't catch us. I decided not to question those two because I suspect they're up to no good. I didn't want any trouble, so we made a quick exit."

Alene Elliott did not take well to smoke being blown up her skirt, tweed, or taffeta.

"If I go in that confidential room and find a jib door, you've had it, my son."

With that, she poured a ridiculous measure of port into her tiny glass and downed it.

"Reg, love. Please take a memo: one jib door will be removed from the lab offices on Balfour Street. Thank you."

22

Chapter 22

On behalf of the body, I'd like to thank you for a lovely funeral.
-A Funny Thing Happened on the Way to the Forum, 1966

They were bumping along a back road toward St. Mary the Virgin Church. It had been a relatively quiet ride, with only Tucker trying to make light conversation. Dulcy was staring out at the countryside through the spitting rain while Laird held her hand. Reggie was flanking Tucker on one side while Dahlia flanked the other. What would you really talk about on your way to the funeral of a man most people detested and who had tried to steal your corporate identity? Tucker was secretly envious of Henry, who only had to drive the car and come back later to collect them.

"So, what are we expecting here, Tucker?" asked Dahlia.

"Lord, I don't know. Mum would know better than I. And I don't even think she knows. She's been pretty tight-lipped ever since her meeting with Olivia. Those two are up to something, and sooner or later, I hope she'll tell us."

"Who do you think will be here?" asked Reggie.

"That I did find out. Curiosity seekers, family, competition, that would be us, press, and friends? If he had any. I would imagine those present are coming to support Olivia. Winston managed to alienate just about everyone he came in contact with."

"Odious little man," murmured Reggie.

Henry maneuvered the car onto the church grounds and parked near the graveyard. The obligatory tent had been erected, and chairs were lined in neat rows under a canopy that stretched yards down the grass to accommodate the gatherers. They walked slowly up the muddy lane towards the church, watching as cars dropped off umbrella-bearing passengers. Reporters were gathering in the front, pushing in on mourners with cameras and microphones. A familiar figure stood waiting near the door, hands folded in front, hat dripping with rain.

"Ugh," said Dulcy. "What's he doing here?"

"You didn't think he'd miss this, did you, love? Of course, he's here. He's hoping to smoke out his murderer. You know what he says: they always return to the scene of the crime. I think you can expect just about anyone to be here, so I wouldn't be too surprised at anything you see or hear today."

"Well, if it isn't the amateur sleuths club. Nice to see you."

"DCI Campbell, what an expected surprise. You wouldn't miss this for the world, would you?" said Tucker.

"Of course not. Silly git. How do you think I'll catch my man if I don't get out in the world?"

"Or woman," threw in Reggie.

"Yaass, could be, couldn't it, my dear."

"And who have you picked for your victims today?" asked Dulcy.

"No victims, just perpetrators," he said, a steely glint in his eyes.

Reggie thought he looked like a wolf baring his teeth at his prey. A shiver ran down her spine. It had nothing to do with the rain. As she eyed him from under her umbrella, she caught sight of Candace and Audrey waiting together outside the church. Behind them were Roswyn and Bella, and another shiver traveled down her back. Not far from them was Tolliver, hovering as usual. Reggie smiled, knowing he was eavesdropping for all he was worth. She nudged Tucker, who followed her eyes to the two women waiting for the family. Alex was conspicuously absent, still in hospital.

"Shall we? Sorry, Campbell, time to mingle. Lovely to see you again. Call on us anytime."

Dulcy, Laird, and Dahlia fell in behind him and made their way to the front, where the crowd was building. He searched the throng for his mother, father, and the Porters as Tolliver joined them. The group was sprinkled with other competitors, along with many of the higher-society women, including Dame Abbington.

"Keep your eye on her," said Dahlia. "Make sure she doesn't make off with the church candlesticks."

"Or the sacramental wine," said a voice from behind them.

"Oh, hullo, Mother, Dad. Didn't see you just there. Quite a showing, eh?"

"Who is she with?" asked Alene, craning her neck to see the company Dame Abbington was keeping. "Ah, I see. Looks like the rest of the county set.

This should be interesting."

From inside the church, organ music could be heard signaling the imminent start of the service. Tucker turned to see the pallbearers loaded down with the Weatherford casket making their way to the entrance. The attendees were parting to either side as the men marched through, followed by the family, Olivia Weatherford in the lead.

"Who's that with her?" asked Reggie.

"Those are her children, along with their children."

"I never even thought about them having offspring. Can't imagine anyone breeding with him. Odious little man."

Tucker gently shoved her into the crowd, closer to Dulcy, Laird, and Dahlia. Alene Elliott had a slight smirk on her face, and Tucker could see she agreed with Reggie.

"Remind me to brush you up on your funeral etiquette, Regina. That was bang out of order. You're standing in front of a church with a grieving family, love."

"Do you really think they're grieving him? Oh, well, sorry."

"No, you're not in the least. Please show a little decorum and behave accordingly while we're here. You can cut up later at the wake."

"Oooo, there's a wake?"

"Of course, but that depends on how well you behave here."

Reggie shot a glance at Dulcy, who was snickering under her umbrella and trying to hide her smile. Tucker ushered Reggie before him, joining the throng entering St. Mary's.

"Are we ready for this?" asked Dahlia.

"As we'll ever be," said Laird.

They followed respectfully and were placed in a row three-quarters of the way up the aisle. They scooted together and observed the guests and activity at the altar. DCI Campbell slid into the row directly behind them.

"Going to keep an eye on us in case we try something else?" asked Tucker.

"Ah, so you admit you were involved. Naw, just the luck of the draw, Elliott. Just the luck of the draw."

"Do me a favor, then - try not to sing."

Tucker adjusted to face forward, missing the scowl firmly planted on DCI Campbell's face.

###

The funeral attendees had paid their respects, hugged, witnessed the graveside blessing, and promised to meet at the Weatherford home for the wake, which was sure to be the event of the season. The dead man was quickly forgotten.

"That was quite the service," said the senior Elliott. "Wish I knew what the hell the reverend was going on about."

"What do you mean, Douglass?"

"Well, love, to whom was he really speaking?"

The rest of them looked as though he had slipped a cylinder.

"I don't understand, Douglass. What are you talking about?"

"The reverend was trying to tell us something. I have to think about it, but there were some key words in his sermon that made me think he was trying to make a point. Didn't you think so, Tucker?"

Tolliver was reflecting on the minister's words when a light went on. There were a few references that seemed a bit out of sync, but he didn't think much about them at the time.

"I agree with you, sir. I think I know what you're saying, but I need to think on it as well. Yes, I think you might just be right."

They were watching the guests mill about the Weatherford estate, dressed in various shades of black and trying to look demure and respectful. Laird noted that many just looked like they were waiting for something interesting to happen that could be shared with the gossip chain.

Olivia Weatherford had spared no expense, mainly because she didn't have to. What had already been a wealthy existence had become even more so, according to the rumors floating through the attendees. The detestable J. Winston had left quite a legacy, with Olivia benefiting more than most. Tucker wondered if Campbell would jump on that and put her at the head of the suspect list. Anything to take the focus off Alene Elliott. He spotted the detective inspector leaning against the wall, nibbling on cheese and watching the guests like a rat waiting for the next morsel.

"Oh, Alene! How are you? So nice to see you again. Thank you so much for bringing me with you to Olivia's the other day. I do so hope she's well. Such a tragic thing," said Dame Abbington.

Alene took the shot she had missed on that day with the nosy woman.

"You're welcome, dear. Oh, Flora, I was just wondering. Since you were at the tea gala, did you notice anything out of the ordinary that night? I realize a lot was going on, but you must know how important any little piece of information you might have could be."

"I see," said Dame Abbington, reviewing events in her mind. "I'm not sure I could say. I must think about it, Alene. Why don't I do that and let you know? Nothing comes to mind at the moment, but that doesn't mean there isn't anything there."

Alene gave her a look that said she was indeed sure there was nothing there, but decided to take the high road.

"You let me know, Flora. Anything would be helpful at this point."

Alene glided toward Tucker and Reggie, trying not to roll her eyes. Reggie couldn't help but grin as she watched her make her way through the mingling guests, greeting a friend here and a colleague there. Simmons was offering a tray throughout the crowd and watching the hired help. Reggie was trying to decide if the sour look on his face was due to his disapproval of the staff, gas, or if he always looked that way. As he swung past them, Tucker nabbed two glasses of champagne and handed one to her.

"I'm going to do my family duty and make the rounds. The receiving line has dwindled somewhat. Care to come along?"

"Oh, Lord, I wouldn't miss it. Did you even need to ask?"

Tucker and Reggie queued up, leaving Dulcy, Laird, and Tolliver to observe the other guests. Dahlia was across the way, having been grabbed by Mrs. Benson, her neighbor. The woman's character had been assaulted when Dahlia was last home, hiding out while pretending to be dead. Mrs. Benson had been painted as the town drunk, along with her staff, and Dahlia knew it was only a matter of time before she would have some explaining to do. One can't allegedly be dead, yet driving the family car into town and calling the neighbor a lush.

"Here's the end of the line. I'll take you through and introduce you."

"Oh, thank you, Tucker. And how will you introduce me? Am I your assistant, friend, lover, concubine, marketing executive, partner in crime?"

"How many of those have you had?" asked Tucker, staring at her half-empty glass. "Concubine? Stop reading trashy novels before bed, darling."

"But I like my trashy novels. Wait, here we go. First victim."

"Not funny. Regina, my executive assistant and right-hand woman, this is James Weatherford, Winston's son. And those must be your little ones. Not so little anymore, eh?"

"So sorry for your loss," said Reggie, stepping to the next family member.

The line moved slowly but steadily, and they found they didn't need to stand on ceremony too long with any one person. The last, of course, was Olivia. She was standing erect with sad eyes, a gracious nod, and a correct smile for each person she greeted.

"Olivia. Please let me say how sorry I am. Ours has been mostly a business relationship, but no one wishes this on anyone. If there is anything we can do, please let me know."

"Thank you, Tucker. I appreciate you, dear. And yes, there is something. Please come to see me tomorrow. I need you to do something for me. Please don't mention this to your mother; she'll find out soon enough."

Tucker smiled and patted Olivia's hand as he held it in his. What was she up to? And what was he to do? He would show up promptly tomorrow, that's what.

###

Meanwhile, the crowd was growing in the lower level of the estate. Tucker thought it would have been thinning out by now. The noise level reached a crescendo, with each person trying to talk over the next. He had a fleeting thought that J. Winston Weatherford would have liked this gathering and was probably smiling somewhere. Tucker didn't like to think about "where" that might actually be.

"Look, Tucker, over there. One of them has managed to infiltrate. I wonder if Olivia knows."

Tucker followed Reggie's gaze to a conspicuous member of the press cornering a woman who had been at the tea gala. The man was scribbling for all he was worth on a tatty notepad. Tolliver and Laird were keeping an eye on him in addition to some of the county set who seemed to be enjoying the wake. It definitely was the social event of the year.

"I see you've noticed what crawled in," said Dahlia. "He's been making the rounds. Mother Elliott is rather sure-footed. I've seen her side-step him several times. Very graceful, she is."

"Mum finds the press tedious at best. Years of them twisting her words have only sharpened her sense of flight as well as her tongue. On a different subject, Olivia has asked me to stop in tomorrow, but wouldn't say why. She also said not to mention it to Alene. Whaddya reckon?"

"Ooo, touchy, that. And you have no idea what it's about, then?"

"No, and I don't want to be blindsided. Plus, if Mum finds out I've visited and didn't tell her, I'll be fired."

"And written out of the will," replied Dahlia.

"Most likely, love."

Reggie could see Alene across the room talking to an elderly gentleman. Dame Abbington cozied up next to her, hanging on her every word. From time to time, Alene would get a bead on the press and adjust accordingly, using her friends as human shields.

"Maybe I can sidestep her like she's sidestepping the smarmy journalist, if you can call him that. I'm bloody curious, so it's not likely I'll give it a miss. If it's nothing, we can chalk it up as part of the investigation and not even mention it. Ever."

"What if it's important?" asked Reggie.

"How about we jump off that building when the time comes?"

"Fine with me."

"Me as well," chimed Dahlia.

The consistent Simmons glided toward them once more, and Tucker grabbed two glasses. So did Dahlia. Tucker gave her an amused stare.

"Who knows when I'll see him again. Don't judge," she said.

They sipped their champagne and observed the crowd, finally relaxing into the scene. The relaxation did not last long. As they stood watching the mourners, they caught sight of Dame Abbington bending her frail frame to the floor, right behind Olivia.

"What is she doing, the barmy old thing?" asked Dahlia.

"She's picking something up. What is it?"

"What is *this*, Olivia?" Flora said loudly.

It was a vial of indeterminate color and relatively small in size. Olivia turned to stare at the woman, then at the vial in her hand. Others began to stare as well. Reggie noticed Audrey and Candace sipping champagne against the opposite wall and watching the women intently.

"I have no blessed idea, Flora. Where did you get it?"

"It fell from your pocket, Olivia. You dropped it."

"I most certainly did not. Give that to me."

"I'll take that," said DCI Campbell, swooping in and grabbing the vial with a handkerchief. "Now, what do we have here? Looks like a vial with some sort of substance in it. And it's only half full. Dodgy-looking stuff, yes? And you don't know what this is?"

"I most certainly do not!" said Olivia.

"Well, there, Mrs. Weatherford, I have a guess," he said, turning the vial around in the handkerchief.

"What are you insinuating?"

"We've been looking for this. And here we find it on you. Shocking."

"What is the meaning of this?" asked Alene as she shouldered her way through to stand next to Olivia.

"I think we just found our murder weapon, lads," said Campbell to several constables who mysteriously appeared at his side. "Party's over, for you anyway, Mrs. Weatherford. You'll have to come with me."

"But I..."

"Say no more, Olivia," said Alene. "Tolliver! Call Chalmers!"

And with that, Campbell led Olivia Weatherford through the guests of her husband's wake and out the front door.

23

Chapter 23

Well, do you know where she is? Do you know when she'll be back? Do you know anything?
-Ferris Bueller's Day Off, 1986

"Well, I'm thinking my appointment with Olivia may be canceled for tomorrow," said Tucker.

They were sitting in the unusual gloom of the Porter's sun room, Jennings presiding as usual. It seemed appropriate; it was anything but sunny on this depressing day. The rain trickled down the glass in a steady stream, blurring the views of the gardens and the drive. Tucker was sipping his scotch when he realized he'd made a tactical error.

"Excuse me, but what meeting with Olivia?"

"I don't quite know, Mother," said Tucker, reddening. He had promised himself he wouldn't say anything, and then stepped right in it.

"What the devil does that mean?"

"Before she was so ceremoniously hauled off to the nick, she asked that I stop by and see her tomorrow. She wouldn't say what it was about."

"And she asked him not to tell you about it either," added Reggie.

"Why, thank you, Regina, for reminding me of that small detail."

Tucker looked at her like a child whose sibling had just ratted him out. If he had been seven, he would have stuck his tongue out at her.

"You're welcome!"

"Hmmm. Why would she want to see you and not tell me about it?"

"We thought we'd see why and then let you know if it was anything important. Now I don't think I'll be going."

"Why not? By now, Chalmers has sprung her, and she's probably on her way home for a stiff brandy," said Alene, looking at her watch.

"Possibly. I'm still not sure about it."

"I'm going to check. Maybe the guests have cleared out, although I wouldn't count on it—not with that lot."

"Don't ask for trouble, Alene. We've already stuck ourselves in too far where we don't belong," said the senior Elliott.

"I don't know; I say do it," said Delia Porter.

"I agree," said Dahlia.

"Sticking together, eh?" said Rodger Porter.

Delia politely ignored her husband as she watched Alene dial the Weatherford home. The only sound in the room was the rain pelting the glass.

"Oh, yes, Simmons, Alene Elliott. Has Olivia returned from the... Ah, brilliant. Tell her Jennings is coming 'round to fetch her and Tolliver. I think she could use a break. Yes. Thank you!"

"Jennings!"

But Jennings was already dressed in a mac, holding an umbrella in the conservatory doorway. His wellies squeaked on the floor as he entered and waited for further instructions.

"Thank you, Jennings. I appreciate you running out in this appalling weather."

"My pleasure, ma'am."

"Now, why would you go and do that?" asked Tucker.

"Let's take care of this right now. I didn't get where I am by letting people run around me. Oh, and Jennings, make sure Dame Abbington stays put if she's still there."

"Of course, ma'am."

By the time Jennings returned with Olivia Weatherford and Tolliver, the group had relaxed, and the rain was slowing down. Tucker was sorry for that as he rather liked the sound of the drops on the glass. It took his mind off the noise on the inside. Jennings settled the widow into a comfortable chair near Alene and handed her a snifter with a generous "smidge" of brandy. She looked neither feisty nor flustered as she leaned back in the seat and smiled at the group.

"I said not to tell Alene, Tucker. There's a naughty boy, then."

Tucker reddened, bringing the total for the year up to two, both on the same day and in the same room.

"Alright, Olivia? Stressful thing being hauled down there. Trust me, I know."

"Me too," said Reggie.

"What happened, Olivia?"

"I haven't the slightest idea. One minute, I was enjoying my guests, and the next, Flora was holding that horrible vial in my face. She was so loud that I do believe even the neighbors down the road heard her. Crazy old biddy needs to wear her hearing devices, don't you know. Thank you for Chalmers, by the way. He is efficient when it comes to this. And you, Tolliver, I appreciate you holding my hand."

"My pleasure, ma'am."

"Well, Attorney Chalmers is getting a lot of practice," said Laird.

"Do they know what was in the vial?" asked Alene.

"Yes! The botulinum toxin. What was in Winston's drink. I believe they think it's the very same vial."

"It's unlikely there are two floating around," said Laird. "How do you think it came to be in your pocket?"

"Someone put it there. I had no idea until it fell to the floor. I had taken out my hanky, and there it was right at my feet. Flora seems to see better than she hears."

"So, now what?"

"Well, it puts me in an awful light, then, doesn't it? They want to know how it came to be there, but in the end, they don't *think* I killed Winston. Of course I didn't, you know, even though I would have liked to on many an occasion. They were only making it look like they suspected me. Hopefully, it will make the real murderer relax and make a mistake. Who knew?"

"Now that you're here, Olivia, what did you want to see me about?" asked Tucker.

"Alright. Here it is - that toxin came from somewhere, but where? And with what happened today, it's even worse-looking for me. They told me what it was, and I know you were looking around the labs. It's what I would have done. The question is, did you find anything?"

"Not really. I'm still running through my list."

"If I may," interjected Laird, "the FME said that it was quite easily obtained. I wouldn't have thought so, but if you have a research background, a license of any medical kind, or connections to those who do, it's an easy task to get your hands on it, according to McCallum."

"That's not too helpful, then, is it?"

"He said it could be all around the countryside between the medical offices and the industries."

"That doesn't leave us many avenues to run down. I was hoping for more of a narrowed answer, Tucker."

"We're not done just yet, Olivia. I still have a trick or two up my sleeve."

"And they would be?"

"One would be this," he said, holding up a small object in front of her."

"The stick!" said Dahlia.

"Yes, from the lab offices yesterday. I did accomplish something at least before I ran out of there, Mother."

"And what was that, dear?"

"Files, Mother."

"Must I drag it out of you? What files?"

"Personnel, love."

"Ahhh. Brilliant."

"So that was what you were doing," said Dahlia. "Find anything?"

"Not yet, but I will. And then we can narrow the field a bit?"

"Yes. I knew you'd do it. Thank you, Tucker. Well done."

Tucker shoved the stick back in his pocket as Alene looked on with parental pride. If she were a cat, she'd be purring.

###

The day dawned with angry skies and a brisk breeze. Reggie was lazing in bed with the covers drawn to her chin while Tucker was stretching in front of her.

"This is a switch. I'm lying around in bed, and you're doing the yoga stretches. Is this a different dimension we're in?"

"No, love, but the morning activity we just did gets me revved up. I need to keep the blood flowing," he said with a wink.

"I was hoping you'd stay in bed a little longer."

She sounded disappointed and forlorn. Tucker rolled across the sheets and nestled next to her. He began nibbling her ear and tickling her neck.

"Don't start something you can't finish."

"Not to worry. We'll finish later. Hungry?"

"Yes. Ravenous. That last round was quite athletic, and I could use a few good carbs. Wonder what Myra has cooked up for breakfast? Something smells good through the halls of the Elliott estate."

"Let's run find out. Then we can decide how we want to tackle our day."

"Oh, Tucker, about that."

"Oh, Lord, here it comes. What has that gorgeous, devious head thought up now?"

"Well, I don't think I actually had a chance to tell you what we talked about when we were out at Brooklands. I think it's a wonderful idea and will not only help them out but will help Farthing's as well."

"I've got the hard sell. Now, the bottom line, love."

"Oooo, a bottom-line kind of man. I like that. Okay, we do a mini pre-launch gathering with champagne on the Concorde with a Chef Dumont dinner, proceeds going to Brooklands and underwritten by Farthing's."

"You know, Reg, you may actually have something. Let's head out there and see Candace. We'll stop and see Alex at the hospital on the way. We can also let Audrey in on it as she can help you and Candace plan it."

"What are you going to do?"

"Why supervise, of course!"

"I had to ask," she said, rolling out of bed and shutting the bathroom door in his face.

###

"Where are you miscreants off to?" asked Alene, nabbing Tucker and Reggie bolting out the door from a quick breakfast.

"Didn't we tell you?" said Tucker.

"How could we have told her since I just told you?" said Reggie.

"Sit, please."

The two turned on a dime and sat obediently at the long table.

"Kipper?" she asked.

"No, I thought you were off kippers, Mum."

"I have no willpower. Now, what are you two up to?"

"Regina?" said Tucker. "You do the honors as it is your idea and plan."

"This is what we were doing at Brooklands the other day."

Reggie detailed the plan and deferred to Tucker once she was finished. When Alene only silently sipped her tea, Reggie thought they would have to start from scratch.

"I think it's a brilliant idea. Be off with you and get it done. Oh, and Tucker, where is that stick?"

"Right here, love. Do you mean to start doing a little poking around while we're gone?"

"Not I, but I'll put someone on it. Like your father or Tolliver, if he has time. I can't just leave Olivia to the likes of Campbell. That won't get anyone anywhere now, will it?"

"Not bloody likely."

"Language, Tucker. See you for tea."

"Tea. Right, Mum."

They were parking in Alene's spot in front of the office when two constables turned into the entrance as if someone had lit a match under their uniform.

"Whaddya reckon?" said Tucker.

"I don't know. What is it now? I'm starting to sound like Audrey."

When they entered the lobby, the constables were squared up at Gillian's desk, demanding entrance to the labs. Reggie stood by as Tolliver rounded the corner and hovered in the background. This was something they hadn't seen coming, and Tucker moved quickly before Gillian had to answer their demands.

"Search warrant, mates?"

"We were thinking that you'd allow the search of the premises since you keep insisting you have nothing to hide. Sir."

"Well, you thought wrong. If DCI Campbell wants to search the labs, he'll have to produce paperwork. No one enters proprietary areas without the proper credentials and orders. Be off, thank you."

The disgruntled constables groaned and turned back to the door.

"We'll be back."

"And that's your prerogative, gentlemen. Ta for now."

"Oh, Lor, Mr. Elliott. Thank Gawd you came when you did. I wasn't sure what to do."

"There never has been and never will be a search of any of our offices, labs, or storages without approval and a designated officer of the company to escort them."

"Is that per company policy, Mr. Elliott?" asked Reggie.

"That's per Alene, and God help the one who doesn't follow it. Including me. We'll be up with Audrey, Gillian."

"Mr. Elliott, I don't think she's here."

Tucker looked at his watch and then at the massive wooden timepiece on the back wall. It wasn't like Audrey to be late to work.

"Tolliver, have you seen her this morning?"

"No, sir. I've been here for a bit, but when I passed her office, it was empty. No sign of her."

"Did she call? Where is she?"

"I'm not sure. I was monitoring the tea shop for a time. Maybe April knows. I'll call her."

April bounced down to the front desk with a large smile and excited eyes.

"Have you seen Audrey this morning?" asked Tucker.

"Why, no. I thought maybe she'd been here before I was because her office was unlocked, but I haven't seen her since yesterday at the Weatherford wake. Is anything wrong?"

"I don't know. Call her, Gillian."
Gillian reached for the phone and dialed with a panic-stricken look. Something was wrong; she could feel it. They watched as she waited and then waited some more. After a minute, she hung up the phone, shaking her head.

"No answer, sir."

"I gathered. What's her address?"

Gillian wrote quickly and handed Tucker a scratch sheet with Audrey's address and directions.

"We'll be in touch," he said, wheeling Reggie around and racing for the front door, with Tolliver on their heels. Gillian and April could only stare.

When they reached Audrey's apartment, her car was in its parking slot, and the lights were on. They knocked, and when there was no answer, they tried the doorknob. It easily gave way to a surprised Tucker, Reggie, and Tolliver.

"Audrey! "Yelled Tucker. "Are you here? Are you alright?"

A low moaning came from the back of the house, and Reggie brushed past Tucker and ran through the kitchen with him on her heels. She pulled up in front of a door where she heard another low moan.

"Audrey! We're coming in!"

"Wait! What if she's naked or has a... guest?"

"Stop it, Tucker. Let's go."

Reggie burst through the door to see Audrey half in and half out of bed, eyes fluttering with rapid blinks and shallow breathing.
"Call 999," said Tucker to Tolliver, who already had his phone out.
Tucker felt her weak pulse and listened to her irregular heartbeat. The EMTs were quick. Audrey was lifted onto a gurney and given fluids and oxygen within minutes. The paramedics looked concerned but professional, and the three followed them out to the ambulance as if they were under a gravitational pull.

"Will she be alright?" asked Reggie.

"It's close. It's lucky you got here when you did. Are you family?"

"No, I'm her employer. We were concerned when she didn't show up to work this morning. It's not like her. What's happened?"

"It's hard to say, but it has all the looks of an overdose, sir. We'll know more when we get her to hospital. Will you be following?"

"Yes, of course."

The team loaded her into the ambulance while the three headed for their car. The doors shut on Audrey as a lone siren blared.

"Tucker, an overdose?"

"I can't believe it; in fact, I don't. Something's dead wrong here, Reg."

"I agree, sir. She is not a drug user," said Tolliver.

Reggie had a visual of Candace and Audrey watching as Dame Flora Abbington picked up a small vial at Olivia Weatherford's feet. A vial only half full. Could it possibly be?

"Tucker..."

"Don't say it, Reg, but yes, I agree. We have to find out where that vial came from and how it ended up with Olivia. And if it's the same stuff, how did Audrey get it if Campbell had the vial?

"Don't lose them, Tucker. They're speeding up."

Tucker ground to a screeching halt behind the ambulance and ran after them. Reggie had a violent recollection of trailing after Dahlia in Florida when she was taken to the hospital after collapsing at her tearoom grand opening. It was a horrible vision.

They ran through the electronic doors, trying to follow the team, only to be caught straight in the arms of DCI Campbell.

###

"What a shocker. We have a coding patient headed in, followed by..." he said, throwing his arms wide. "Why is it that where there's trouble, there's always you?"

"She's coding?" asked Reggie breathlessly.

"She was starting to. We'll just have to watch and wait. Have a seat and tell me what happened."

"After yesterday, we thought it might be a good diversion to do a private charity function at Brooklands, supported by Farthing's. One of their champagne experiences for those who would like to invest in the museum. Would be good for Brooklands and hopefully for us as well."

"Go on."

"We went to the office to check in with Audrey, but no one had seen her. When we got to her home, we found her in the back, delirious and very ill. When the ambulance arrived, they thought she might have taken an overdose."

"Have you ever known her to use drugs?" he said, scribbling in the ever-present notebook.

"No, sir," offered Tolliver. "I can't say as I have. She's always been a responsible thing. This has been a bit of a shock."

Reggie was thinking back to their visit to Dahlia's tearoom in Florida and how someone had slipped a drug in her drink. It was a disturbing experience. The most frustrating part had been watching people look at her differently afterwards, thinking she was an addict. She hoped Audrey would come around and be able to tell them what had happened.

"So, as usual, Elliott, you have no idea what's gone on, how she got the drugs, and how she ended up taking them."

It was more of a statement than a question, and Tucker felt like he was in an endless loop of incidents, inquiries, and investigations. It was becoming tedious.

"You know I don't. But that doesn't mean we won't try to find out."

"Stay out of my investigation, or I'll arrest you myself."

"Why shouldn't you? You've taken everyone else in."

Reggie was sure that DCI Campbell was on the verge of reading Tucker his rights when she noticed a man in scrubs heading their way. She ran to meet him as Tucker and Campbell were about to face off.

"Well, Doctor? Will she be all right?"

"It's touch and go. She's under strict observation, and the next twenty-four hours are critical. Can you tell me how she came to be in contact with such a virulent poison?"

"If we knew that, we'd know who killed Weatherford the other night. I'm putting a guard on her door. No one allowed in or out other than hospital staff or unless ordered by me," said Campbell.

Tucker and Tolliver silently stared at each other while Reggie headed for the desk. Obviously, Campbell felt the culprit could come back to finish the job. She wished that Audrey had been able to answer just one question: What had she consumed since the wake, and who had given it to her?

24

Chapter 24

If my calculations are correct, when this baby hits 88 miles per hour, you're gonna see some serious shit.
-Back to the Future, 1985

The staff and Campbell had scattered quickly, leaving the three alone in the hall.

"Now what?" asked Tucker.

"Hey! Isn't this the hospital where they brought Alex? I bet there's no guard on *his* door."

"Let's get up there before they install one."

They found the room number and ran for the stairs. This way, they could stay out of Campbell's sight. They traversed the hallways, hunting down the odd-numbered rooms.

"Here it is, sir," said Tolliver. "One eleven. Look at all the directives on the wall. Let's see if he's awake."

Tucker pushed open the door and poked his head in. It was a private room with Alex planted in the center. He was surrounded by bags and machines that hummed, beeped, lit up, and spat paper. He looked like a corpse lying flat on his back, tucked up and folded into a hospital cocoon. Reggie scanned his monitors and noticed that his vital signs were strong and stable.

"I think he's asleep," said Tucker. "Maybe we should come back another time."

"Look," whispered Reggie. "His eyes are fluttering. I think he's waking up."

"Miss Reggie? How are you?" he asked weakly.

"Oh, geez, forget about me. How are you feeling?"

"Like I was run over by a car."

"Close, mate," said Tucker. "Looks like you'll be just fine. A few scratches, though."

"And broken ribs, burns, a concussion, and a twisted ankle. And all because... "

They watched as Alex's eyes grew wide, and he winced with pain. He was remembering something, hopefully something useful.

"What is it, Alex? Have you remembered something?"

"There were no brakes at the turn. None at all. I was having a bit of a lark, running it up to speed, but when I tried to round the corner and press the fool things, there was nothing. They just went straight to the floor. I tried turning the wheel, but it wasn't enough. That's when I lost control. I wrecked an Aston Martin V8 Vantage," he said in a choked voice.

"I'm thinking they're insured, sir. Can you remember anything else?" asked Tolliver.

They watched as Alex's eyes glazed over in an effort to recall a memory. Finally, he blinked and stared at them.

"Something. A smell in the cabin. An unlikely smell."

"Like what? Fluid, gas, filters?"

"Like something burning, but not a burning smell exactly. We've got to find out what happened. We've got to find out who did this. You must help. For the sake of the museum."

"Alex, please don't agitate yourself. We're working on it, and Campbell's men have salvaged everything from the accident and are going over it piece by piece. I'm sure they'll turn up something," said Reggie.

"Yes, mate, please get some rest."

"I so hate to bother you with this now, but were you able to find any other evidence on the surveillance tapes?" asked Reggie.

"I had set them up and then was called to the track. I was going to continue checking them when I came back. I never got to do it."

"We'll see what we can do. You rest and try not to worry. If we find anything, we'll let you know," Tucker said, giving Tolliver a silent order.

"Thank you for coming to see me. They say I can be released soon. I'm anxious to get back there and sort this out."

"Yes, I'm sure you are. We'll see you soon," said Reggie, giving his hand a squeeze.

They slowly walked to the stairwell and pushed the door. Then, they exited the ER again and sat in the waiting area. No one said a word until Reggie broke the silence.

"He was set up to crash, Olivia was set up with a planted vial of botulinum toxin, and Audrey was set up to take that same toxin, but by whom, and how?"

"That's not the biggest question, Reg. The biggest question of all is why?"

###

The ride to Brooklands was silent. Reggie was enveloped in her thoughts, as was Tucker in his, while Tolliver was devising a plan to infiltrate the security center. What were they to say to Candace?

"Tucker, let's not tell Candace about Audrey. Should we tell her about seeing Alex?"

"I agree, but I see no reason to keep our seeing Alex from her," said Tolliver. "But why would... I see. Maybe you're right. Are we saying we can't even trust Candace?"

"Who do you think we can trust at this point?"

"You trust me, don't you, Reg?" grinned Tucker.

"Don't be silly. Can I?" she said coyly.

"I wouldn't trust myself alone with you, but other than that..."

Reggie reached over and pinched him while Tolliver blushed in the back seat. Tucker grinned, and she felt a sense of comfort. Things had gotten so out of hand for what was supposed to be a happy trip. The entrance to Brooklands was beginning to look like home now, with the Concorde model greeting them at the gates and the winding path up to the museum.

"Looks alright," said Tucker. "No coppers here today. That's a stretch in the right direction."

But he was wrong. As they walked towards the outbuildings, they could see police cars by the race course. They were just yards from where the torn grass lay as an eerie reminder of recent events. Personnel from both the High Street station and the Brooklands race team were intermingling between the accident site and the outbuilding where the remains of the Aston Martin were in autopsy mode.

"I know what you're thinking, but let's go find Candace. Maybe we can get a pass for Tolliver to view the security tapes," said Reggie.

They entered the Edwardian Club, stopping in front of the "Friendship Bench" with a solemn glance and a short prayer. The scene sent a chill up their spines as if it were still fresh.

"Hello there," said Reggie to a young man passing by. "Have you seen Candace?"

"Um, yes, she was here, but I think she went back to her office."

"We'll just pop in and find her. And then we wanted to go over to the building; you know, the one where they have Mr. Alex's car," said Tucker.

The man regarded him silently, blinked, nodded, and went on his way.

“Ugh, that was weird,” said Reggie.

“What about any of this isn’t? Do you think these people aren’t either desperately intrigued or ready to turn in their resignations? Wait, Tolliver, is there anyone in the security area?”

They looked about, then casually walked over to the room and tried the door.

“Can I help?” said a bulky man with a stern glare and a bright badge.

“Wasn’t expecting that,” said Reggie in Tucker’s ear.

“Oh, sorry, I was looking for the loo.”

“Around the corner, first door inside on the right for you, sir.”

“Thank you so much,” said Tucker with one of his most ingratiating smiles.

“Didn’t work,” muttered Reggie.

As they headed to the loo they weren’t looking for, they glanced over their shoulder to see the man observing them with the trust of a chicken watching the fox guard the hen house.

“So much for that,” said Reggie, throwing the man a pretty smile.

“Don’t even try. They’re onto us.”

“I know. What now?”

“To go where we were going in the first place, I believe, sir?”

“To find Candace and then go to the outbuilding.”

"Yes."

"Oy! Please come to my office. I need to speak to you."

Candace was antsy and white, with a pleading look. She waved them into her space and quickly shut the door.

"What are you doing here, and what's going on? No one will tell me anything."

"Then you don't know what's going on out there, Miss?" asked Tolliver.

"No, and I'm losing my mind. What are they finding? I can't get any information. No one will tell me anything."

Tucker slipped Tolliver a glance. If she didn't know what was going on in the investigative areas, she didn't know what was going on anywhere else either.

"What? What was that look? What's happened?"

Candace was a bundle of nerves. Was it because this had escalated beyond her abilities, or was it something else?

"We just thought we'd come out and see what was happening and talk about our amazing charity function. Is this a good time?" asked Reggie.

"Oh, yes," said Candace, visibly decompressing.

She rounded her desk and sat heavily in her chair. They watched as she laid her heavy spectacles on the table and rubbed her eyes. She had no idea what had happened to Audrey, so it was a good decision not to tell her.

"We visited Alex on the way here," said Reggie. "He's a bit banged up, but he'll be just fine. He's looking forward to getting back here and sorting all this out."

"Yes, he sounded well this morning when I called. That's good. I'm glad he's better. I still don't understand all this."

"That's what they're doing in the outbuilding. We came to see, but first, let's talk about the Concorde fundraiser experience."

"Oh, yes. I looked at my book. We can do it this Saturday. We've got a small party we can accommodate in another space. The scheduled events all have to do with the motor clubs in the other areas. Chef Dumont is on call, and if you can get your guests together, we can do a nice party for you. We could do a couple of shifts and have a nice gathering."

"That would be brilliant," said Tucker. "We'd be happy to host the party and invite not only a few well-heeled donors but smooth things over with some of the important tea gala guests as well."

"It's a date," she said, entering it into her computer.

"Shall we venture to the outbuilding, sir, and see what they've found?" asked Tolliver.

"Yes, I would also like to see what's happening," said Candace. "I've sat here long enough being a good girl."

They passed the Sunbeam Cafe, where guests were warming themselves on the sunny patio in the chilly weather. Activity was as brisk as the breeze in the trees, and Reggie glanced at Tucker, wondering what he was thinking.

"Hello, Cyril. I was hoping we could take a look now," said Candace.

"I'm not sure I should let ya, Miss. They said to tell ya no. The coppers is millin' about, and they don't take too well to buttin' in."

"I'll take responsibility for that," said Tucker, stepping up with authority and handing the man a card. "If there are any questions, let me know."

They parted the flap and entered a bright area full of spotlights and extension cords. Car parts were strewn across the floor like a jigsaw puzzle and men were meandering in and around them, poking here and there. A lone familiar figure stood off to the side, examining a prominent wreckage piece and listening intently to what a small man next to him was saying. On sighting the group, he dropped his hands to his sides and turned to face them.

"Didn't I leave you in hospital? Hello, Miss Candace. What are you doing here, you lot?"

"We've come to schedule another party," announced Reggie. "Surely you can't deny us the opportunity to make it up to our guests."

"And our donors," smiled Candace.

"But why are you out *here*?"

"Oh, well, I guess we're just being nosy," said Tucker.

"More's the better because I have to question you anyway."

"You do?" asked Tucker.

"By all means. Why would I leave you out now when we've only just found something so very interesting?"

As they looked on, DCI Campbell held up a thin, slightly charred wire.

"What is that?" asked Reggie.

"That, my dear girl, is a brake line."

"Alright, it's a brake line. What does it mean?"

"Brake lines do not look like this. They have ends with parts that attach to things. They attach to other parts. They do not have severed areas in the middle of them."

The group leaned in and stared at the strand of rubber, then at each other.

"So, that means..." said Tucker.

"This, my children, is a major factor in the crash of Alex Aldeworth."

The three leaned in again and stared harder at the crispy part.

"That's a sharp edge there. Like it was clipped."

"Exactly. Cut clean off. Your Alex Aldeworth would never have been able to stop that car. Not with this," he said, holding the blunt end in front of their faces.

Tolliver lunged for Candace as she flickered and was heading for the floor.

###

They had managed to get Candace back to her office and settled at her desk. Reggie rummaged through the drawers, looking for the flask Candace had mentioned the other day. She found it hidden amongst an old pair of wool socks and a spare umbrella. She held out a massive measure of brandy, which Candace grabbed from her and tipped hard. The color began to return to her face, and she slouched back in her seat and coughed roughly.

"I'm glad you're feeling better, Candace. Now, why don't you let us in on what you're not telling us?"

The color drained from her face again, and she straightened in her chair.

"Why ever would you say such a thing? I'm not hiding anything. I'm not keeping anything from you."

Her indignant response only made Tucker even more suspicious. It seemed there was something else here. He beckoned to Tolliver, who lightly stepped to the desk.

"Would you please tell the security center that I have permission to review the tapes from the other night? We need to get through these before something happens to them, Miss."

"Why would anything happen to them?"

"One never knows; so many things have gone wrong here, and we don't want to lose one of our main hopes for evidence. I can get to work on that right away. I promised Alex I would take over for him."

"I'll see what I can do," she said, scurrying out the door. "I don't have my key with me today."

"I find that a bit strange," said Tucker. "She's hedging. You'd think she would want this cleaned up as soon as possible, as worried as she is about the museum's reputation."

"Sir, I think we should be wary here. What do we really know about her? It seems illogical that she would not want me to review the tapes."

"Yes, Tolliver, agreed. Something smells worse than the wreckage of Alex's Aston Martin. We need to be careful here. We can't give her any more information. Reg, do you feel safe with this Concorde idea of yours?"

"I was. You don't think she'd jeopardize the museum, do you?"

"She might for reasons we know nothing about. Still, I believe it to be a good way to flush someone out."

"Or another way for the killer to strike again, sir," added Tolliver.

Reggie looked thoughtful. Tucker peeked out the office door, shoved his hands in his pockets, and strolled back to his chair.

"If DCI Campbell were part of the guest list, no one would think to try anything while he was hovering about, sir."

"Yes, good point. Or even let him be in the background and have one of his men up front in the thick of it. Whaddya reckon?"

"I think we stop talking and see where it goes. I hear her coming," said Reggie.

"What ya got there, Reg? Bat ears? I hear nothing."

A quick click of the door and Candace was with them again. Tolliver gave Tucker a raised eyebrow while she breezed through and sat back down.

"All ready to go?" offered Tolliver.

"Oh, no, I wasn't able to find the guard. He was here earlier. I wonder if he took a break. The door is locked."

The three shot each other a look, and Reggie was elected to continue.

"So, I think Saturday sounds wonderful. We'll have our guests ready to go. What else do you need from us?"

"We have a set program including the menu for the appetizers during and after the shifts. I can just go ahead and put the orders in for everything. Reggie, I can send you the full details, and once you approve them, we'll be all set."

"That sounds wonderful. And we'll make sure Alex can attend. I know he wouldn't want to miss it."

A shadow passed over Candace's face, and she looked as if she was about to protest.

"I hope he'll be alright; it seems like he's so beat up."

"I'm sure he wouldn't miss it. He'll be fitted with a boot for his damaged ankle, and everything else is superficial. He's going to be just fine."

"So glad to hear," said Candace in a preoccupied way. "I'll just start working on everything now. You'll let me know if there's anything else you need?"

Tucker knew a dismissal when he heard one. He just couldn't understand why. Better not to stir the pot.

"This will be a grand step in the right direction. Once we make our splash with this, we can work on the details for the relaunch. Thank you for your time today, and I hope you're feeling much better."

"Better?"

"From your, uh, fainting spell."

"Oh, yes, much, thank you. Just a fleeting thing," she said, brushing her hand across her forehead.

They walked out to the car in deep thought.

"Quite a quick recovery, don't you think?" said Tucker.

"And the stall with the security tapes. What was that about?" asked Reggie.

Tolliver looked pensive and frustrated, which Tucker could always see. He knew the cogs in his brain were turning overtime.

"What is it, Tolliver?"

"Well, sir, again, it's like the camera angle. You know what I mean. Why didn't Campbell's men hop on those tapes? Why are we the ones reviewing them?"

"I'm sure they did. Like we said, maybe they didn't find anything. Maybe there isn't anything there. What are you getting at, Tolliver?"

"Let's go back and see Alex. We can tell him that Candace asked him to give us his key so we don't have to bother the security people."

"It'll never work."

"I have a feeling, sir, that getting her to cooperate won't either."

"Reg? Worth a shot?"

"Oh, I believe so. I have an idea."

The two men stopped in mid-stride, waiting for her to speak. A far-away look in her eyes came into focus, and she smiled an evil, slow grin. Tucker wanted to run away. So did Tolliver.

"She's harder to contain than you are, sir."

"I'll take that as a compliment, Tolliver."

And she uttered the phrase that always led to trouble.

"So, here's what we're going to do...

25

Chapter 25

It's the car, right? Chicks love the car.
-Batman Forever, 1995

They sprinted back to the hospital where Alex was being given his bending and stretching therapy options with a look that said he would rather take another beating in the defunct Aston Martin. Six of one, half dozen of the other.

Since DCI Campbell was occupied at Brooklands, the trio took the elevator to Alex's room rather than sneaking up the back stairs. They then waited outside while the last instructions were given.

"Well, hullo! I didn't expect you lot back so quickly. Why are you here?"

"We won't bore you with the details, but we couldn't get into the security room to view the tapes," said Reggie. "We've come to ask a favor."

"If I may, sir, I was hoping to make quick work of sorting through the video to save some time, but when we arrived, the security man was a bit...formidable," said Tolliver.

"Large man, whiskers, badge that I swear he spit shines every day?"

"Yes, sir, that's the man. After that, Candace was going to try to get us into the room, but she said he must have been on rounds because he had gone missing."

Alex shifted in his bed, looking confused.

"But Candace has her own key, and there's always someone there. Why wouldn't she have just given it to you to get on with it?"

Tucker jumped in before Tolliver or Reggie could move.

"I think she's just overwhelmed at this point, mate. Plus, she said she hadn't brought it today. Why don't we just help her out and get it done for her? She's planning two different parties, you know."

"She is? That's wonderful news. For your new launch?"

"It's better than that," said Reggie, jumping in. "We're going to do a charity function to raise money for Brooklands and appease some of our VIP guests. It's a private Concorde experience this Saturday. You will be one of the VIPs, Alex."

Alex brightened and then crumpled before their eyes. It was like watching a balloon being blown up and then let loose.

"I think I'll still be here. I'm not sure the warden will pardon me from this hell hole in time."

"We'll take care of it," said Tucker. "Not to worry, mate. We'll get DCI Campbell in on it, and between the lot of us, I'm sure we can get you freed. Now, do you actually have a key we may use?"

Alex gestured to the drawer under the movable tray, where a god-awful-looking lunch lay untouched and melting into the plastic. Reggie reached over and spooned a bit of the goo from one side to the other.

"Ugh. You poor thing. You didn't eat any of that, did you? I'll be right back."

And with that, she was gone in a flash, leaving the three staring after her. Tucker had taken the master key, and Tolliver had been given strict instructions when Reggie bounded back into the room with a bag that smelled heavenly.

"Oh, my Gawd, what is that, Reggie?"

"My dear Alex, this is from the bakery next door. No man should eat what I saw on that tray. Now, dig in, get rest, and we'll be back for you before the Concorde can take off on Saturday."

They said their goodbyes and were heading to the car when Tucker stopped the two with a withering glare.

"Wait, now just exactly are we going to do with that key?"

"Whatever do you mean?" asked Reggie innocently.

Tolliver blinked and tried to appear invisible, a trick that never works even when you're a child and still have magic in you.

"We're going to investigate and sort through the rest of the tapes."

"Alright, then. So, when, and how, and exactly what? And maybe I don't want to know."

"Of course you don't, Mr. Elliott," she said. "You know I adore you, but I need you to tend to Alene while Tolliver and I get our work done. Do that for me, please?"

"Tolliver?"

Sydney Tolliver looked green around the gills, but he was all in. Something he hoped he would not live to regret.

###

Tucker was on his way home as Reggie and Tolliver were seated on the patio of the member bar at Brooklands. The courtesy card from Alex gave them access to everything they wanted: grounds, the exhibits, the collections, and, best of all, the classic race cars.

"What can I get you, Miss, Sir?"

They turned to see a quintessential Englishman in tie and apron leaning graciously toward them, awaiting their order.

"Oh, uh, a glass of sauvignon blanc, please," said Reggie.

"And I'll just have a Cloudwater soda," said Tolliver.

"Any food, then?"

Tolliver deferred to Reggie, who, as usual, was starving.

"I'll have your lovely luxury artisan roll, and you Tolliver?"

"Your jacket potato, please."

Their server smiled, bowed, and was off like a shot, weaving through the tables to the art deco bar.

"I think we're going to like this member thing," smiled Reggie. "Uh, Tolliver?"

Something in the tone of Reggie's voice made the man steel himself.

"Yes, Miss?"

"I have a thought."

"Oh, please, Miss, must you think?"

"Tolliver, since we're here..."

"Yes?"

"And we have this lovely courtesy card..."

"Yes, Miss?" he said, wincing.

"I have a wonderful idea."

"I'm sure that you do, Miss, but I fear that Mr. Elliott would frown on investigating anything other than the security tapes. Remember his warning and the reason we came here. Please?"

Reggie tossed her hand and lightly laughed as the server deposited the wine and soda. She leaned across the table and engaged him with her dark green eyes. The man resembled a duck rolling on its side in the water.

"As long as we're here, let's have a little fun, shall we?"

"With all due respect, Miss, I'm not sure we share the same concept as to what constitutes fun."

"You're going to love this, Tolliver."

Sydney Tolliver did not look like a man who would be in love with many things, especially one of Regina Winter's hair-brained schemes.

"I think we should go to the track and drive the cars!"

"Miss??"

"You know, like a Porsche 911T? Or a Jaguar? How about an Austin Healey? Did you know, Tolliver, I learned to drive a stick in an Austin Healey Sprite?"

"No, Miss, I was not aware of your driver's training experiences."
"Have you ever driven a Mustang? You haven't lived until you've been behind the wheel of one of those."

"I don't see how this helps with our sorting out the security tapes."

"Well, it doesn't. It's just flat-out fun, son!"

Reggie couldn't tell which Tolliver disliked most - her driving idea or being called son. She decided it was probably both, then brightened when a thought came to her.

"Oh, Miss, just..."

"Listen, darling, there is a use for this idea, you know."

"And what could that possibly be?" he asked, looking stunned and forgetting his polite manners.

"We can get into the area, not as investigators, but as honored guests. We can see how it works, who's actually in charge, observe the personnel, and find out how accessible it all is. Whaddya think?"

"Um, what about the security tapes, Miss?"

"We can do that after. Do you really think we'll find anything else on them?"

"We found the first bit where the unknown person went into the side door, Miss."

"True," said Reggie, staring at the paddock area. "Do you remember where you left off with the tapes, Tolliver?"

"Why, yes, Miss. They were numbered. I know exactly where I was."

Reggie's face broke into a grin, a cross between an evil grin and a satisfied grin. Tolliver took a large gulp of his soda.

"We have the key; we'll just round up the ones left and watch them at the Elliott's. With popcorn!"

"I'd rather drive the cars into a deep ravine, Miss."

"Nonsense, Tolliver. We'll do both," she said, ignoring his comment. "Oh, bless you, sir. Lunch. It looks delicious. Let's eat."

Tolliver had suddenly lost his appetite.

26

Chapter 26

The ninjas are trying to get me.
-Talladega Nights: The Ballad of Ricky Bobby, 2006

Tolliver stood in the viewing area, admiring the classic and prestige automobiles. Reggie was walking arm in arm with a most bewildered-looking gentleman. Tolliver could see by her gestures that she was weaving some fantastic tale for the wide-eyed man. Who could resist an almost six-foot-tall woman with an engaging personality and eyes that reached down and grabbed onto your soul?

When Tolliver heard the name "Alex," he wanted to turn tail and run. Then, he noticed a man in coveralls watching Reggie with rapt attention. He discreetly snapped a shot with his phone and kept watch on the man, who continued to eye her in a most disturbing manner.

"Here then, you there, Jeffrey," said Reggie's new ally, reading the man's badge. Please do me a favor and bring up the Ford Mustang. This young lady and her companion will be taking it for a spin. They are guests of Mr. Alex."

The man nodded sullenly and wandered off toward the car park. Reggie made her way over to Tolliver with her new-found friend in tow.

"Tolliver, this is Sidney Barrow-Smith. Tolliver is also a Sidney, though we affectionately call him, well, Tolliver."

The men shook hands while Reggie beamed at them, leaving an uncomfortable silence in her wake.

"If you'll follow me, sir, the Miss has specified that you drive our Mustang. Have you ever had the opportunity to become acquainted, Mr. Tolliver?"

"Uh, no, sir. I have not, although Miss Winter here has sung its praises. I'm feeling fortunate to be able to have the experience."

Reggie clapped her hands in joy as they approached the custom candy-apple-red 1964 Mustang convertible. Tolliver had to admit - this was one fine motor car.

"Right, then, in you go," Mr. Barrow-Smith said, opening the passenger side door for Reggie. "You alright driving on this side, Mr. Tolliver, sir?"

"Oh, yes, I've had to do it in America. It's fine, sir."

Reggie wasn't sure, but she thought she saw a glint of excitement in Tolliver's eyes.

"Why, Tolliver. You're falling in love."

"It is a rather beautiful piece of machinery, Miss. I must say, this is quite extraordinary."

"Of course it is. You're welcome, Tolliver."

"Thank you, Miss."

After a strict set of instructions, Tolliver eased the car onto the track.

"Ready when you are," said Reggie.

Tolliver was off, easing the machine into each gear like a pro. Reggie was thrilled with not only the track but also Tolliver, who seemed to be enjoying himself. After a few turns around the course, he slowed the car back into the spot from which they had come.

"That was amazing, wasn't it?"

Tolliver was showing a rare smile while the other Sidney beamed brilliantly beside them.

"Excuse me, Mr. Barrow-Smith, would it be possible to see the garages before we take the Austin Healey out? You know, where they take care of these magnificent machines? It would make the day complete."

The man showed a slight hesitation, but Reggie looped an arm around him and chattered away, walking him straight to the mechanics area.

"This is where we take good loving care of our motor cars. We're specialists in all classic and antique and, of course, our prestige vehicles."

Reggie watched as the white clad mechanics operated on their prize cars, tuning an engine here and a carburetor there. Tolliver noted the constant activity and searched for the sullen man from earlier, but he was nowhere to be found. Reggie tucked her arm through Mr. Barrow Smith's and glided out into the bright sun and the waiting Austin Healey.

"Have you driven one of these before, Miss?"

"Oh, yes! This was the exact car in which I learned to drive a stick. It's even the same color - Old English White."

Mr. Barrow-Smith lowered her into the driver's seat while Tolliver made himself comfortable on the passenger side.

"Enjoy, now, Miss!"

Reggie and Tolliver were off with a roar of gear changes and squealing tires.

"This is amazing," yelled Reggie over the thunder of the Austin A-series 14 engine.

Tolliver gripped the door handle and hung on for dear life as Reggie stomped on the clutch and shifted into fourth gear.

"Hang on, Tolliver," shouted Reggie.

They were scooting down the straightaway towards the curve when Reggie downshifted to third to take the turn. As she leaned into the bend, there was a whooshing sound, and the car began to slide out of control, twirling like a baton.

"Hang on, Tolliver!"

"I'm fine, Miss," he yelled, holding the handle hard while Reggie turned the wheel into the slide again and again.

The car finally slowed and came to rest only yards from Alex Aldeworth's accident site. Men in coveralls were racing toward them as Reggie pulled the key from the ignition.

"What the bloody hell was that?" yelled Tolliver, staring at Reggie's oil-spattered face.

"I don't know, but it wasn't there before," she said, wiping her face with her scarf and staring at the oil-slicked track. "It damn well was not there before, Tolliver.

###

"Alright there, Miss?"

Sidney Barrow-Smith was panting as he approached Reggie and Tolliver. One look at her turned him white. He lifted her gently from the car and stared in astonishment.

"'Pon my word, Miss, I can't rightly say what happened."

He stared hard into her face and then at the track. Oil was spread over the course like mayonnaise on bread.

"I don't understand it. How did that get there? That wasn't there before. We're right careful about how we keep these lanes. All right there, sir?"

Tolliver was shaken but upright, blinking in the sunlight at the glistening swatch across the track. He would've seen that while driving the Mustang if it had been there. But he knew it wasn't.

"I'm fine, sir. Do you mind if I ask where all your men are? Your mechanics. Is there anyone missing, sir?"

Mr. Barrow-Smith scoured the grounds as the men in coveralls examined the Austin Healey. Tolliver watched as other men threw sawdust on the track, spreading it along with brooms. He was about to give up when the man from earlier was spotted toward the edge of the track, listlessly pushing a broom and keeping his head down. As Tolliver watched, the man glanced directly at him, turned his back, and continued to casually sweep the dust.

"Please don't fuss," he heard Reggie say. "I'm quite alright, and I don't believe there's any damage to the car. We have other business, so maybe it's best if we move along now. I want to thank you so much for allowing us to do this. It was wonderful being behind the wheel of one of these again. And I know Tolliver enjoyed it; you got to see a rare smile from the man."

Mr. Barrow-Smith was still ruffled and confused as to why there should be anything on his pristine driving course. It seemed a personal affront to him as he glared at the remains of the oil spill, but he smiled graciously and shook Reggie's hand.

"Thank you, sir," said Tolliver. "I'm sure you'll get to the bottom of it. If I may ask, do you have a list of your mechanics and their tenure here?"

The man looked surprised at the question but beckoned them to his offices so he could pull the information from the personnel files.

"I hate to bother you for it, sir, but it might be a good idea just to review the list. For your own edification."

"It's fine, Mr. Tolliver, sir. I imagine they'll be asking for it anyhow."

"Is that protocol?" asked Reggie.

"Oh, no, Miss, it's just that the detective inspector chap asked that we keep an eye on things, and if anything unusual were to happen, he was to be called right away."

Reggie turned a cool eye on Tolliver, who was reddening at the mention of the man's name. Her first thought was to run as fast as she could to the car and escape before he had the chance to get his hands on them. On second thought, that would make them look guilty, and they were already in enough trouble with the man.

"So you've called DCI Campbell?" she asked.

"Oh, yes, I had one of the men do it while the rest came out to help. Apparently, he was on his way here anyway when we called. I wouldn't be surprised to see him any minute, Miss."

Tolliver's complexion deepened to a burgeoning purple. Reggie truly felt sorry for making the man even more uncomfortable than usual. They were on their way back to the race offices in a deliberate manner. Reggie wished they would move more quickly. She wondered just how long it would be before the DCI descended on them like a vulture on roadkill.

"By the way, Mr. Barrow-Smith, are there any security cameras covering the track at the point where the oil was found?"

"Oh, yes, Miss. We have to do so for the safety of our drivers. Just like we saw what was happening to you right away, they cover all angles of the course. I'm sure DCI Campbell will want to see those as well."

"Yes, I shouldn't wonder. Are those down here, or are they kept up in the security center in the club?"

"They've upgraded the system, Miss. Personnel are able to view the goings on here 24/7 from that new central control room at the side of the museum."

"Thank you so much, Mr. Barrow-Smith. And thank you again for such an amazing experience. I'm sorry there was a bit of trouble. I'm glad no one was hurt and that the car is fine."

Reggie was confused. If all the track was covered, then why didn't anyone notice a swath of oil spread over it that hadn't been there minutes before?

"Will you be off, then? Did you want to see the names of the mechanics, Mr. Tolliver, sir?"

But before he could answer, a bellow came from the front of the garages and in blew DCI Campbell, motoring through the maze like one of the race machines. He pulled up short in front of Mr. Barrow-Smith, shook his hand, and planted himself between the man and Reggie and Tolliver.

"Why? Why is it always you?"

"DCI Campbell. How nice to see you again."

"Don't be buttering up me, my girl. Let's go."

"Where are we going now?" Reggie asked, confusion adding to her oil-spattered face.

"To the station, where else? I thought I told you to stay out of this, and here you are, right in the thick of it again. Do I have to lock you up for your safety and the good of the rest of the world?"

Reggie leveled a look at Campbell and then at Tolliver.

"Alright, lead on," she said, sighing.

"I'll call Mr. Elliott," said Tolliver, plucking his phone from his pocket.

The image that popped up was of the unknown garage man openly staring at Reggie as she conversed with Mr. Barrow-Smith. Tolliver slid the phone under Reggie's gaze before hitting Tucker Elliott's number.

"I'll make sure he alerts Chalmers, Miss."

"Alright, take us away, Mr. Campbell," said Reggie melodramatically as she held out her wrists to the detective inspector.

"That's DCI Campbell to you!"

The three trudged over the hill to the waiting car and another visit to the High Street station.

###

"Whatever were you thinking, Reg?" grilled Tucker as they awaited Chalmers in the police station.

Constables were throwing curious glances their way as they went about their duties.

"What did you tell Alene?" asked Reggie.

"Nothing. She doesn't know. I was hoping we wouldn't have to say anything to her, but I think that's just a sad and dismal dream of mine. She likes you; you tell her."

"She likes you too, Tucker. You're her son."

"Yes, but for how long?"

"If I may," said Tolliver, "we did see a man at the garages, sir, whom I think may be questionable."

He showed Tucker the picture and explained the suspicious activities while they were in the garages. He hoped to distract Tucker from the obvious breach of direction they had been given.

"You were supposed to be viewing the security tapes," he said.

Tolliver shot Reggie a look that did not go unnoticed by Tucker.

"Now what?"

"You sound like Candace," said Reggie, chuckling. "About those tapes..."

"About the entire system, sir," said Tolliver. "It appears they have recently upgraded their security setup, and where we screened the tapes isn't really used much now."

"Whatever do you mean? We watched them there. We saw a figure slipping into a building. I don't understand. Do you mean it's part of the scenery? Part of the exhibits?"

"No, I think it's maybe just an adjunct room where they can view things without disturbing the live broadcasts," said Reggie.

"Alright, out with it," said Campbell as he waltzed into the office and threw down his hat.

"Sorry?" asked Tucker.

"What are you trying to do to this investigation?"

"Nothing," said Reggie. "In fact, we're trying to see if we can get you some inside help, but the inside may be looking suspicious."

"You're talking about the oil on the track."

"Yes, and the sketchy personnel, and the double talk, and the fake security room inside the club. All of that," spouted Reggie.

"The security setup is outside the Edwardian Club. It's a state-of-the-art system that they put in last year. What the devil are you talking about?" asked Campbell.

They spilled the story of the tapes and the darkened figure skulking outside the building. Campbell flounced into his chair and took out his notebook.

"Something else we'll have to get to the bottom of. You know you create a lot of work for me, yes?"

The three looked like scolded school children while Campbell read through the scrawlings of his notebook.

"Listen, DCI Campbell," said Reggie. "We have something to offer you. No, wait, don't blow up just yet," she said, raising her hands as he looked about to launch from his chair.

"We've scheduled another event with Candace for this Saturday. It's to be a charitable experience on the Concorde and a peace offering to the important customers of Farthing's Fine Teas. We want you to be in the wings and keep an eye on things. Maybe you could put a man undercover inside while you watch from the security area. You could observe everyone and everything from there. Maybe we can flush someone out."

"Or manage to get someone else killed," he groused.

Tucker shot Reggie a look of 'I told you so' while the detective inspector sat silently thinking.

"It could work," he said slowly. "Tell me everything you know. Leave nothing out."

As they sorted out the details, a bellow and a series of slamming doors echoed through the station as Chalmers blew in like the latest summer storm.

"What is the meaning of this?" he demanded.

"We're chatting," said DCI Campbell.

"What are they being charged with?"

"Nothing, Chalmers," said Tucker. "Thank you for coming, but false alarm. We're fine, so you may toddle off and tend to other matters."

"These unnecessary trips are costing you, Mr. Elliott, to be sure."

"You're on retainer, Chalmers. Now, thank you, and good day."

"Your mother will hear about this," he said, echoing down the station hall.

"Oh, I know she will," said Tucker. "Now, where were we?"

27

Chapter 27

Now tell me the truth. You're just out of a jail or a hospital. Which is it?
-Monsieur Verdoux, 1947

"Tucker! Again? How could you? And Regina Elizabeth Winter. Don't make me call your mother. And Sidney Tolliver, I expected more out of you."

Alene was in a fit, and there was nothing to be done about it. Chalmers had tattled on them like an eight-year-old, and all they could do was sit and take it. Dahlia and Dulcy were on the edge of the action pretending to be invisible.

"I didn't know your middle name was Elizabeth," whispered Tucker. "Rather regal sounding, isn't it? Sort of inspiring, really."

"Mrs. Elliott, if I may, please," began Tolliver.

"You may not. Please tell me one thing, one small snippet that redeems your actions."

"We've scheduled an event for Saturday night for our favorite patrons, murder suspects, and policemen," stated Reggie.

Alene was staring harshly at her before wandering over to the bookshelf and pulling out a large volume. She said nothing to Reggie's announcement but paged through the book while the group sat in uncomfortable silence. Not knowing what to do next, Reggie continued.

"Uh, it's a Concorde experience. Actually, DCI Campbell is all for it. He's going to participate in a security background way while stationing men inside to keep an eye on everyone. Would you like to hear a sampling of the guest list?"

"That's what I'm doing now," she said, without looking up from the volume. "This contains the lists from previous years and, of course, this last...attempt. If you want to double-check your guest list, this will be where you start. Of course, you'll want those most necessary to our... dilemma. I will help you there."

Reggie took the delicate volume and rested her arms on it, patiently waiting for Alene to continue. Tucker moved to take it from her, but she slapped his hand and watched Alene roam the study in silent contemplation.

"What do you hope to accomplish with this?" she asked, straightening and facing Reggie.

"We hope to uncover the murderer," stated Tucker flatly.

"Or leave another body in your wake?"

"Now you're beginning to sound like Campbell, Mother."

"I thought you said he was all for this."

"He is, but it doesn't come without strict rules and regulations."

"I imagine. Dahlia, I think you should be front and center on this. You know how to host an event. And this time, you won't have to be dead to enjoy it."

"That is a bit of a benefit, eh? I'll be happy to help. So much easier to plan something in plain sight rather than hiding in the wings in horrible street clothes."

Dahlia's entrance to her recent "memorial service" was quite the extravaganza. While supposedly dead, she blew onto the scene in horrific, smelly street clothes, accusing the head detective of murder. The attendees watched in shock as a local philanthropist was exposed and hauled away for his numerous crimes. As Tucker and Reggie detailed the arrangements for Alene, Laird's phone started to buzz, catching everyone's attention.

"Excuse me, I'll just take this out here."

The conversation continued in low tones for a few minutes as Tucker and Reggie completed the details of the Concorde experience. Laird hung up and waited while they finished their arrangements.

"Alright there, Laird?" asked Tucker.

"Yes. That was DCI Campbell."

"What's up, John?" asked Dulcy.

"It's Audrey. She's awake. Time to go."

###

They piled into the Mercedes where they raced to Audrey to find the answers to some rather important questions.

“They’ll not let us all in, you know,” stated Dahlia.

“I wouldn’t think so,” said Tucker. “I do have an idea.”

“I can’t wait,” said Laird. “Will this land us back at the police station or the train station?”

“You need to have a little faith, mate. Since it was Tolliver, Reggie, and I who found her, we’ll go in first, ask our questions, and then Laird, you follow in with Dulcy and Dahlia while they start reviewing the details of the Concorde experience and the tea launch. That is, if she can get a pass from the doctor to attend.”

“Well, that actually does give us a chance to shape Saturday’s event while we wait. She won’t know the difference if it isn’t perfect, right, Dulcy?”

“Oh, of course not. And she may be too loopy to care.”

Which gave Tucker an idea.

When they got to the hospital, DCI Campbell was in the hallway, speaking with the guard at the door. All was well; no attempts had been made to enter, either scheduled or of medical necessity.

“Thanks so much for calling,” said Tucker. “I appreciate the confidence you’re placing in us.”

“I’m not placing any bloody confidence in you; I’m keeping my eye on you. You’d find out soon enough, and then I’d have another mess to clean up,” he said, staring past them as if he was counting chickens. “One, two, three... you’re not all going in there at once. That nursey marm would have my ass."

"We're going to go in and see how she is first," said Tucker. "She is one of my employees, and she scared the bejesus out of us. I need to know that she's all right. Then, if she's up to it, they can go in and cheer her up with the party plans."

"How touching, Elliott. I'll be right there with you. You lot, wait out here."

He opened the door and took out his pen and notebook as he slammed the door in Laird, Dahlia, and Dulcy's faces.

The situation reminded them of Alex, machines buzzing, a computer humming, and Audrey tucked into a hospital cocoon tighter than a woven chrysalis. She looked bright and alert, a far cry from the condition in which they found her the day before.

"Oh, Audrey, you look so much better," said Reggie, reaching for her hand. "You gave us such a scare. What happened?"

"I... I don't know," she said with a faraway look in her eyes. "I just remember being at the wake, that awful scene with Mrs. Weatherford and that funny little woman, Dame ..."

"Abbington," supplied Tucker. "Yes, she is a bit of a pip, that one. But what happened when you went home?"

"Candace and I decided to go out to have a bite. I'm not very good at eating at those things. Always so awkward, plus, well, it just didn't feel right enjoying all that food and drink while he's... you know. It was like they tossed him in the ground, and he was just... forgotten."

"Where did you go to eat? Someplace close, local, I'm sure."

"We went to the Chequer Inn for something shareable and a pint. I didn't really feel like eating but knew I needed to. Candace couldn't stop talking about the funeral, and the wake, Dame Abbington, and that horrid little vial."

She stopped suddenly, and they could almost see the picture dancing in her head. It wasn't a very nice one.

"Well, then what, Miss?" asked Campbell.

"Not much that I can remember. Candace dropped me at the house. She came in for a minute just to make sure I was all right. I felt...sad and a little sick, actually. She sat with me for a bit, and I decided I needed to go to bed. She went in with me to make sure I wasn't really ill, made me a glass of hot milk, and sat it on my bedside table. I didn't want to drink it; it's awful without something in it like chocolate or a liqueur. I thanked her for her trouble, and she let herself out. That's all I know."

DCI Campbell was evidently questioning her story. He cleared his throat and looked at the girl sternly.

"That explains why we were able to just go marching right in when we did," said Tucker. "I mean how the door was open, you know, not locked."

"Alright, then, that clears up the entry. But with all due respect, Miss, you must have drunk the milk at some point. There was no glass in the bedroom. There were a few in the kitchen sink, so maybe it was one of those. We found nothing in them. They had been rinsed clean."

"I honestly don't know. That's all I can remember," she repeated, staring up at the DCI like a small child.

Reggie drew closer to Tucker and pinched him on the back of his thigh. The man skipped forward like a horse spooked by a snake. DCI Campbell noted the exchange, raised his eyebrows, and wrote in his notebook. Tucker took Reggie's hands in both of his, patting them in comfort.

"You'll excuse me for a moment while I make a call," said Campbell. "The others can come in when you three leave."

Yet another dismissal duly noted by Tucker, Reggie, and Tolliver. As soon as the door closed, Reggie swooped down on Audrey.

"Audrey, do you have the key to your house? It's important."

"Of course. It's in the bag with my clothes in that alcove," she said, pointing across the room.

Reggie flew to the shelf, tipped the bag sideways, and clamped her hand down on the key.

"Got it!" she said, holding it up for them to see, just as DCI Campbell waltzed back in the room, the other three on his heels.

"Out with ya," said Campbell, holding the door for them to exit.

"Of course," said Reggie sweetly. "Audrey, please get some rest. Dulcy and Dahlia are going to fill you in on the Concorde party Candace is setting up for Saturday. It'll be a special event with a pre-party before we do the launch again. They'll tell you all about it. We'll see you there, I know."

Campbell leered at them and watched them leave the room, making sure they actually went.

Once in the hall, Tucker grabbed Reggie's arm and pulled her into the waiting room.

"What do you think we're going to see there? They've already combed the place. What could we possibly find?"

"I don't know, but it's worth a look. She didn't seem to mind either. What do we have to lose, Tucker?"

"My family, my job, my dignity, my freedom. Do you suppose I'd do well in prison?"

"Stop it. No one's going to prison," she said, pushing him toward the car and throwing him the keys. "And yes, you'd be the beau of the ball. You'd have a boyfriend immediately. Now get going."

"Thank you? I think?"

Tucker caught the keys in mid-air and popped the lock. It was a sound he hoped he wouldn't be hearing from the inside of a jail cell anytime soon.

###

Laird pulled DCI Campbell aside outside Audrey's room as Dahlia and Dulcy were animatedly discussing every detail of the party on Saturday. He wondered how they could come up with such a string of events with little to no time to prepare. Then he remembered Florida, the tea room, their ability to improvise, and their built-in guest lists.

"What do you think happened, Campbell?"

"She's blocking something. She's either hiding the truth or just can't recall it. In my experience, as I'm sure in yours, mate, a little time helps a lot. Whaddyer reckon?"

"I think you're right. A little rest, and hopefully, something will surface.

Let's hope she remembers it and tells you. And not them," he said, jerking his head toward Dahlia and Dulcy.

"Right-o on that. How do you reckon to clear them out of here?"

"We're going back to Brooklands."

"Oh, bloody hell. Whatcha gotta go and do that for? Things were shaping up nicely now. Why can't you take them away and lock them up?"

"Right back at you, DCI," he said, rapping on the door with a chuckle and a smirk.

###

Dahlia, Dulcy, and Laird were driving the familiar path to Brooklands in a getaway car provided by Jennings. After Tucker and Reggie had absconded with the Mercedes, it was, of course, Jennings who came to the rescue. Laird glanced at his watch, wondering if Candace would still be there.

"I hope Candace hasn't left," said Dulcy, echoing his thoughts.

Laird snorted, made the neat turn into Brooklands, and parked near the front. They piled out of the car, craning their necks to where Reggie had slid through the oil spill. How had she managed to keep her composure?

They rounded a corner only to find an empty hall and a set of stairs.

"Maybe we can still catch her," said Dahlia as they passed her office.

She was nowhere to be seen. They ventured further to another empty hall and the stairs to the upper level.

"Member area," said Dahlia. "That's for me, now."

"We're not members," said Dulcy, reluctantly climbing the stairs behind Dahlia.

"We are now," she said as she held up the courtesy card Reggie had slipped her. "We're just going to go up and have a quiet drink and relax after a rough day."

"Translation," said Dulcy, "is we're going to poke our noses in where they don't belong. I like it!"

They sneaked a peek at Laird, who was hanging his head and quietly following them up the stairs. They meandered down a hall till they came to the end, which branched in two directions: one led into an art deco bar and the other into an elegant dining room.

"This is brilliant!" said Dahlia. "Why haven't I been here before?"

"May I help you?" asked a cherub-faced girl with an apron and a huge smile.

"We'd like to be seated for a cocktail, please?"

"Are you a member, Miss?" she said, the smile never wavering.

Dahlia flashed Alex's card, and the girl smiled even harder. Then, she walked them to a table in the center with a view of the patio and paddock. After they had given her their order, they relaxed and took a deep breath.

"What now?" asked Laird. "What's your bright idea from here?"

"You really need to relax, John," said Dahlia. "I'm in my element here."

"You're here by someone else's graces. What the hell are you up to?"

"What do you see in this man?" she asked Dulcy.

"It's what's under the raincoat," she answered.

"Focus, ladies. And not on that. I thought we were here for Candace. Now what?"

"Just listen."

"To the people around us, yes, I get it. What do you hope to learn?"

"I dunno, but people must be talking. Two accidents in a few days, along with a murder? Do you think these people have no curiosity?"

"No, I'd even be gossiping myself," said Laird.

"Excuse me, Miss. May we please have a drink list and a menu?" asked Dulcy.

"Of course. Right away."

The young girl scurried off amidst the scattered tables to retrieve the sheets. Dulcy leaned back in her chair, almost able to put her head on the man's shoulder in back of her. The conversation was in low tones and the accent so thick she couldn't get a thing from it.

"Here you go, Miss. Anyone know what they'd like for drinks? Some water and then something after that?"

"How about a stiff scotch?" said Dahlia.

"Oh, I'm afraid it's only beer and wine, Miss," she said apologetically.

Something about that stopped Dahlia in her tracks.

"What is it?" asked Dulcy. "You have that look in your eye."

"It's nothing. I'll have a red wine, Miss, thank you."

But Dulcy was not to be put off. She eyed her suspiciously and leaned in to capture her attention.

"Give it, woman. I know when you're plotting."

"Alright. The other day, when you all were out and about and I was lounging with my headache, I felt guilty when I heard everything you all had been up to when Jennings brought me my tea."

"You mean your scotch," said Dulcy.

"Oh, no, it was actually tea this time," said Dahlia. "You know..."

"Focus!" said Laird.

"Oh, right. I thought about making a few calls myself and took out my address book. I wasn't sure what I would do, but as I leafed through it, I found a name I hadn't thought about until recently. And then, as I went over the events from the tea launch, I remembered she had been at the gala. I even pointed her out to you. There she was, the whole time in plain sight."

"What are you talking about?" asked Laird.

"The woman scorned. She has a grudge against the family as much as anyone else could, I suppose."

"What *are* you talking about?" asked Dulcy.

"The girl Tucker snubbed. The girl who got away, or the girl he sent away, if it comes right to it."

"Are you saying this woman has it in for the family?"

Dahlia had a faraway look in her eyes, as though she was reliving something. Her face changed from curious to stern and then to realization.

"Could it possibly be?"

"Again, Dahlia, please tell us what you're talking about. You're starting to scare me."

"Let me think on it for a minute. I need to talk to DCI Campbell. We need him to do a little background check, loves. I wonder..."

28

Chapter 28

Don't give me that tone! That sarcastic, contemptuous tone that means you know everything because you're a man, and I know nothing because I'm a woman

-The Birdcage, 1996

Tucker passed by Audrey's drive and slid into a street spot. He shut off the car and stared at the house.

"What are we doing?"

I'm just making sure there's no one here, Reg. That should be or otherwise, you know."

"Why does it matter? We have her key. We can just say we're getting her a few things for the hospital."

"True, but I keep seeing Laird shaking his head."

"And DCI Campbell is next to him holding five train tickets."

"Something like that. C'mon, love, let's go. Looks clear to me."

"Oh, gracious" said Reggie as they walked into the foyer.

"I'll send in a cleaning crew," said Tucker.

The house had been sifted and sorted but still bore the telltale signs of fingerprint powder, a tricky mess to clean if you didn't use the correct agents. They glanced around the living and dining areas and made their way to the kitchen. Forensics had obviously been there, too, as the dish pad also showed signs of fingerprint powder. Still resting in the strainer was the cup that supposedly had held the hot milk.

"I have a question," said Reggie.

"Fire away."

Reggie winced and shot Tucker a look that he did not miss.

"Sorry, love, ask away."

"If Audrey didn't drink the hot milk Candace brought her, then why was the glass empty? And why was it in here? She left it on Audrey's nightstand."

"That is a damn good question, Reg. It means either Audrey did it herself or someone else was here."

"But she said she didn't, or she just doesn't remember. Do you really think there could have been someone else here?"

"That's what it points to. But who could it have been?"

"Well, it could be something else."

"And that would be?"

"That Miss Audrey is lying. But I can't figure out why."

"Yes. That occurred to me as well. We'll have to consider that possibility, you know."

Reggie shook her head and reached for the cup. She turned it around in her hands, then sniffed the inside. She wrinkled her nose in distaste and held the cup out to Tucker. He sniffed and made the same expression.

"What ya reckon, Reg?"

"When he said it had been cleaned, he wasn't kidding. This smells like bleach. Why would you rinse out a glass with bleach?"

"To hide some other smell. Or to hide an added ingredient."

"Do you think Campbell's men would've done this?" she asked, taking the cup from him and sniffing again.

"It's possible they used something that smells similar to it to test it."

"I'm going to ask Campbell. We need to find that out."

"So, we're telling him we came here."

It was more of a statement than a question.

"We had to pick up Audrey's things; you know - magazines, meds, jammies."

"Not believable," he said, shaking his head. "She has to stay in the fashionable gown they gave her, she has magazines, and they give her any meds she would need."

"Not her birth control," smiled Reggie.

"Ugh. You are evil, Reg. I love that about you," he said, giving her a quick peck.

They headed into the bedroom, where the scene was much the same as the other rooms.

"How do we find what we don't know we're looking for?"

"Bless me, I understood that. Methodically, Reg."

She walked the room, picking up articles that had been tossed like yesterday's press. She carefully folded a few pieces of clothing and set them on a chest across from the closet. The bed clothes were in the same disheveled, twisted tangle as when they found Audrey. Reggie bent down and draped the top sheet back over the bed and stared at the nightstand.

"What's this?" she asked.

"What?"

"This ring on her nightstand."

Tucker leaned in and glared at the empty space where she was looking.

"I don't see a ring. What are you looking at, Reg?"

"You're such a man," she said, pointing to a faint, round blotch on the furniture.

Tucker glared at the all-but-invisible spot. He switched on the light and looked again at eye level.

"There is something there, but it's horribly faint. Huh. I know what you're thinking. But would there be any trace of it still?"

"Only one way to find out."

She went back to the kitchen, where she had spotted a spray bottle for the plants. She spritzed a dry-looking fern in the window, and then her fingers tasting it to make sure it was water and only water. She parted the leaves and was spraying further down when her fingers touched a small, hard nodule.

"Hmmm. Let's take care of the ring and then come back and see whatever that is."

She yanked a paper towel from the roll and walked back to Audrey's bedroom.

"What ya doin'? You've been gone a bit, love."

"Watering the plants."

"Now? Whyever for, Reg?"

"I adore you, but you really must pay better attention," she said, cupping his face with her hands.

"I had to make sure it was just water. And the fern was dry."

"No tap water?"

"Chemicals. If this has been sitting, it's gone neutral. Nothing to interfere with the testing."

He watched while she painstakingly spritzed the tiniest amount of water on the stain and blotted it.

"Now, guard this with your life and follow me back to the kitchen."

"Why? Did you find something?"

"I'm not sure. We have to fish it out and see. C'mon."

Reggie grabbed another paper towel and held it up in Tucker's face.

"Our detective tool. Just push those fern leaves apart for me, if you would."

Tucker did as he was told while Reggie leaned in and gently pulled out a small, round object and rolled it into the middle of the paper towel.

"What is that?" she asked.

"That is a great, bloody clue! Reggie, my love, you are brilliant. If I am not mistaken, that could very well be the stopper to a certain vial."

"But didn't the vial have a stopper in it when they took it?"

"As you say, a plug, not a stopper."

Reggie broke into a wide grin and kissed Tucker on the lips. She kissed him again and lingered.

"I love that intrigue makes you randy, love, but shouldn't we be off with this tidbit?"

"Yes. Let's get out of here."

"Brilliant."

"Oh, Tucker, one last thing."

"What would that be, love?"

"Would you go in Audrey's bathroom and retrieve her birth control for me?"

Tucker's mouth fell open, and he stood in stunned silence.

"Just kidding. *I'm kidding.* I just wanted to see your face."

"One of these days, Regina. One of these days."

"Yeah, I've heard that before," she thought as she headed for the bedroom.

###

"Is she coming back?" asked Dulcy, as they waited for Dahlia in the member bar.

"She has a glass of wine, so, yes."

"Do you think she's onto something?"

"She sure seemed to think so. What that may be, I don't know. She has been gone a good minute, so maybe she found Campbell. Or maybe even Candace."

A bawdy laugh from the hall announced her return. The look on her face was troubled yet triumphant.

"What did you find out? I mean, what did you do? What the hell is going on, Dahlia?"

"I remembered something, but as it so happens, not everything."

"Did you talk to Campbell?" asked Laird.

"No, I gave him a miss for now. I called Alene. I needed background information, and Lord love a duck, I got it."

"Ooo, intriguing. Tell us."

"It was a while ago; it was after school, and I wasn't around so much. Alene looked her up in her big tome of gala invitations, and sure enough, there she was, lurking in the pages. Reminds me of her the other night at the gala. There, but blending into the scenery. Trying to be unobtrusive. She's been to a good many of these, according to Alene's book. I wonder if Tucker saw her? I still need to find that out."

"You mentioned she was the one that got away. Did she get away, or was she sent away as you said?" asked Laird.

"Ah, now that's the great question, eh? I'll have to back up," said Dahlia, obviously enjoying her story.

"Start with who she is," said Laird.

"Her name is Lydia Kent-Williams, and actually, I went to school with her at Great Walstead Prep. She was a bit of a wallflower, you know. A shy, diminutive type with great bloody glasses and orthodontic appliances."

"Ortho whatsies?" asked Dulcy.

"Braces, love. Teeth straighteners, and the most wiry, fiery, red hair. Skinny and gawky as well. Not the type you really notice, you know."

"Well, something changed if Tucker noticed her," said Laird. "He doesn't strike me as one who would pick the wallflower."

"Whoa! You made a joke, John Laird," cried Dulcy. "It's a miracle."

"Get him another ale, love. Anyway, we graduated, and she went her way, and the rest of us went ours. One thing, though: she was bloody brilliant—top of the class. She was accepted to Oxford. There was a bit of a scandal over it, actually. It's pricey, but she's brilliant, and she went on academic scholarship, even though her parents could afford it.

"So her parents are well off?" asked Dulcy.

"Oh, yes. That's why the Elliotts were pleased when she and Tucker became an item. Good English stock, smart, good match. All that rubbish."

"Where does the scandal come in?"

"Now here's where it gets tricky. Oxford is many things, including competitive, and it is most coveted when it comes to putting a school on your CV. She was a finalist getting ready to get her degree. Everyone just expected that she'd take a first, but when it was all sorted out, she was accused of plagiarism."

Laird and Dulcy exchanged glances and waited for Dahlia to continue.

"What was her field of study?" asked Laird.

"Eh, let's see. Something really technical. Oh, I remember now. She graduated with two chemistry degrees. The whole mess got straightened out, and she did indeed get her first, but it was testy for a bit there."

"What did she do when she left university?" asked Dulcy.

"Well, before she went to work for Farthing's, she worked for a drug company. Penders, that's it."

"What is Pender's specialty?" asked Laird.

"Oh, it's a big deal," she said. They supply the cosmetics industry."

"You mean like pure botulinum toxin," said a steely-eyed Laird.

"I think so. Oh, yes, I believe you're right. Oh, bollocks."

Laird grabbed his phone and covered the length to the patio in three strides.

"DCI Campbell, please."

###

The evening shadows were falling across the grounds of Brooklands as Dulcy, Laird, and Dahlia headed for the High Street station. Tucker and Reggie had called DCI Campbell about the nightstand blotch at about the same time Laird had called regarding the revelation about Lydia Kent-Williams. They were gathered in Campbell's office, looking like a group of junior detectives awaiting instructions.

"What, no Chalmers?" quipped the DCI.

"No, but for some reason, Mother will be joining us," said Tucker.

"What the bloody hell for?"

"Because why should he have all the fun?" said a voice from the hallway.

Alene Elliott marched in gracefully and waited while Tucker surrendered his seat directly in front of the inspector.

"You'll be needing some background from me, so rather than wait for your, uh, gumshoe to fall, I decided to save us all time."

She glared at DCI Campbell's shoes, looking as though she had stepped in something herself. Campbell was indifferent to her judgment and leaned back in his chair, feet on his desk, and notebook spread in his lap.

"Who wants to go first?"

Tucker approached the desk, hands in pockets, a smirk firmly in place. He pulled out his hand and held up a raggedy-looking, crumpled paper between his fingertips. Campbell turned up his nose and grimaced.

"What is that nasty bit of goods?"

Tucker dropped the towel on Campbell's desk and stood aside to reveal Reggie staring into space.

"Regina. Care to give the inspector your testimony?"

"What is this, a religious experience? Okay, not funny, but Mr... DCI Campbell, we have a couple of pieces of evidence that you need to have analyzed."

"Evidence? From where?"

"This is where DCI Campbell really does implode," thought Tucker.

Reggie also approached him and dropped the other, less assaulted paper towel next to Tucker's. She stood back, folded her hands, and waited respectfully. Tucker was impressed with her restraint.

"Well, out with it."

"We went to Audrey's on a mission for her."

"And what mission would that be?"

"We went to pick up her birth control," said Reggie evenly.

"Oh, really?"

Reggie was gratified. She truly believed she'd won.

"Do you expect me to believe that codswallop?"

The smile on Reggie's face faded like the sun before a cloudburst.

"Well, yes, you know that's quite a personal thing."

"Miss Audrey was provided adequate coverage for that yesterday. What were you really doing there?" spat Campbell.

"Uh, magazines?"

Campbell shook his head.

"Jammies?"

"Sit. Elliott, explain, and you have one minute to do so."

Tucker squeezed Reggie's arm and placed her back in her chair with the best reassuring smile he could muster.

"Look, Campbell, it's all my fault, really. I was the one who insisted on going back and taking a look."

"I don't give a flying... Just explain these," he said, checking himself in front of Alene, who was censoring him like a Sunday school teacher.

"She gave us her key. She was worried about the upheaval in her home, along with what really happened to her. She asked that we take a look. How could we refuse her, all small and pale in that hospital bed?"

"You're breaking my bleedin' heart. Get on with it."

"We were tidying her bedroom a bit when Regina spotted a faint mark on her nightstand. She went to the kitchen to get a towel when she found something else, but I'll get to that in a minute."

"What is this?" asked Campbell.

"That's what we wanted to know. That is residue from where the hot milk mug allegedly sat. But how did it get to the kitchen, who rinsed and cleaned it, and why did it smell like bleach?"

"One thing at a time, mate. So, on this towel is..."

"Some sort of remains that left a ring on the nightstand."

Campbell glared at the first paper like it was the guilty party and picked up the phone.

"Timmons, I have something to go to the lab. Get in here."

Alene Elliott gave him a sneer and cleared her throat.

"Please," he said, remembering his manners. "And this is?"

Tucker gingerly unwrapped the object from the folds of the second paper towel and held it up for Campbell to see.

"I'll be blowed. Where did you find this? Forensics was looking for it."

"I'm sure. Reg?"

"I was watering the fern in the kitchen and found it buried in the leaves."

"You found it in a house plant?"

"Accidentally, mind you. It's complicated."

"Ya. Usually is with you, girly."

As he turned the nodule in the paper, the door opened, and a willowy, pimpled boy entered and stood at attention.

"Ah, Timmons. Take these to the lab. Please."

The young man slipped each piece into a clear plastic bag and disappeared without a word.

"Is that all? Please tell me that's it."

"Of course," said Tucker with his best smile.

He backed up toward Reggie but gave his mother a bright wink before moving off.

"Mrs. Elliott, why are you here?"

"Well, my story begins with them," she said, smiling at Dulcy, Laird, and Dahlia. "I recommend you let them brief you before I add my part."

"Why do all of you insist on telling me how to do my job? Okay, you go," he said, eyeing Laird first.

"We may have a new suspect. Someone who's been in the background."

At this point, Alene turned to give Tucker a warning glance. The glance she used for bad news. He did not miss it. He stood up straight and stared at Laird. His gaze was stern and set. When Dahlia wouldn't meet his eye, he became alarmed but remained silent. No sense in panicking yet.

"If I may," offered Dahlia, "it was something the adorable little server at Brooklands said that jarred my memory. You know they don't serve liquor in the member bar there? Just beer and wine and I thought, 'What if you're allergic to beer and don't care for wine?'"

"I'm sure your drinking habits are fascinating. Get to the point."

"We won't go into my train of thought here, but I remembered someone who's allergic to beer. Someone who was at the gala, who has a chemistry first, and worked for Farthing's."

"And was a former lady friend of my son's. Lydia Kent-Williams. I'm sorry, Tucker."

29

Chapter 29

Protecting the Queen's safety is a task that is gladly accepted by Police Squad. No matter how silly the idea of having a queen might be to us, as Americans, we must be gracious and considerate hosts.
-The Naked Gun: From the Files of Police Squad, 1988

The dawn came again with brilliant blue skies and a chill in the air. There was lots for everyone to do before the Concorde experience. The shock had diminished a bit for Tucker after his mother's explosive announcement in Campbell's office.

Reggie had spent time with Alene, understanding the relationship between Lydia and Tucker and the business side of things. Alene had filled in the gaps, leaving Reggie concerned about how this woman fit into the current picture.

"You know she'll have to be at the Concorde experience," said Reggie.

"Yes, dear. It's already been taken care of. Would you like to see my portion of the final guest list? I didn't receive any regrets, you know. Says a lot for the family."

"Says a lot for the morbid curiosity of people in general," thought Reggie.

"Of course. And any background information on the guests would be invaluable."

Alene presented Reggie with a handwritten collection that read like a murder mystery party guest list. If you thought about it, that's actually what it was. Reggie dearly hoped there wouldn't be a body for everyone to guess whodunit at the end of the evening.

"Let's see. I'm curious about these people."

Tucker Elliott
Regina Winter
Dahlia Porter
Sidney Tolliver
John Laird
Dulcy Dandeneau
Alene Elliott
Douglass Elliott
Delia Porter
Rodger Porter
DCI Campbell
Constable Petry
Dame Flora Abbington
Olivia Weatherford
Audrey Ratliff
Candace Corbyn
Alex Aldeworth
Lydia Kent-Williams
Bella Fielding
Roswyn Walsh
Dame Eva Harrington

Lawson Harrington
Spencer Evans
Kenneth Stewart
Penny Ray Walters
Bimmi Beresford
Chester Oakford
Percival Jennings
Lady Lillian Tipton
Lord Tipton
Raleigh McMichael
James McHughes

"Interesting list. I'm so happy to see Jennings on it. How could you scope out a mystery without him? I'm assuming the people I don't know are more business associates. Are you concerned that Miss Kent-Williams will be suspicious with this invite?"

"Oh, no, she's quite thrilled, actually. She attends the galas. We don't exclude her. If anything, she left us because of what happened between her and Tucker, not because of her work."

But Reggie wasn't so sure and would be happier when it was over, and she had the opportunity to observe the woman herself.

"So, how is Tucker this morning?" asked Alene.

"You know your son; he's quite resilient. With most things."

"Is this one of those things?"

"Yes. Yes, I think so," said Reggie, convincing Alene and herself at the same time.

CHAPTER 29

"Good morning, ma'am, Miss Reggie. How is everyone today?"

"Tolliver! Sit and have a spot of breakfast. And tell us what you learned yesterday."

Tolliver seated himself across from Alene and Reggie and waited for Alene to prompt him. Reggie, unaware of his recent activities, was interested in the explanation.

"Can I get you a plate?" asked Alene.

Tolliver turned a bright magenta and shot from his chair to the sideboard before Reggie could blink. He would never let Mrs. Elliott wait on him, even though she would be happy to do so.

"What were you doing yesterday, Tolliver?" asked Reggie.

"Do you remember the personnel files Mr. Elliott purged from the lab computer, Miss?"

"Of course. Oh, did you find anything interesting?"

"I am still working through the information, but as to your most recent inquiry, Mrs. Elliott, I did print a copy for your perusal."

Tolliver pulled out a folded sheet and handed it to Alene, who read it silently while Reggie nibbled her bacon.

"This is quite interesting, Tolliver. I'm not sure I knew about this incident. Who handled this matter here?" she asked, pointing to a section of the paper.

"Your son, ma'am. It was his wish that you not be concerned with it."

"I can see why," she said sternly, passing the sheet to Reggie.

There was a mid-section highlighted in yellow. Reggie saw that it was a formal reprimand for the misallocation of resources and unapproved experiments that did not pertain to tea development.

"So, if I read this correctly, she was using your lab for her personal investigative purposes."

"Yes, dear. She did a nice job while she was there, but I think she was only there for Tucker, quite honestly, and now that I see this, I'm a bit more clear on what happened. It was an infatuation that ran its course. Plus a little more, I see. She bears watching."

"Anything else, Tolliver?" asked Reggie.

"Not really anything that stands out, Miss. I plan on spending a little more time on the lab personnel, and I don't see anything striking with any other employees yet, so I'll do another round on them."

"Do we know what Lydia is doing now?" asked Reggie.

Tolliver handed Alene a second sheet and continued eating his breakfast.

"She's retraced her steps, I see. She's back in the chemistry arena. As previously stated, Tolliver, she bears watching."

And Tolliver knew precisely what that meant.

###

It was to be a busier day than they thought. Audrey and Alex were being discharged from the hospital, and they would be able to help Candace put the finishing touches on the Concorde party.

Tucker had appeared as Tolliver was leaving. Reggie had finished with her breakfast and with Alene.

"Alright there, Tolliver?"

"Yes, sir, but I need to brief you on a small matter."

"Would this have to do with our surprise yesterday?"

"Yes, sir. In the study then, please?"

The study door closed as Reggie opened the dining room door. She headed straight for the upper regions to hurry Tucker along.

"You've been busy, Tolliver. Am I to understand that Alene now knows the full story on Lydia Kent-Williams?"

"Yes, sir. It put a completed picture together for her, which was not a surprise. I have been put on watch duty."

"Of course you have, mate. Not a better choice out there. So, what next?"

"I shall head back to the office to finish sorting out the personnel files, sir. Then whatever else you need me to do, I will be at your service."

"Brilliant, Tolliver. Say, have you seen Reggie this morning?"

"Yes, sir. She is presently in the dining room with your mother."

"Right then. Guess I'd better go and face the fire. You wouldn't have a blindfold on you, would you?"

"No, sir. And I don't envy you. Good luck, sir."

Tolliver was out the front door in a heartbeat, narrowly missing Reggie bounding down the stairs in search of Tucker, who had already disappeared. She threw open the dining room door only to find Alene pouring a second cup of tea and nibbling her toast.

"Where is that man?"

"I assume you mean my son. No sign of him yet. I do believe he may be hiding from me."

"I would be, too," thought Reggie.

"I'll keep looking. I'd like to get to the hospital before Audrey and Alex are released."

"Try the kitchen, dear. He often hides out there when he's in trouble."

"Is he in trouble?"

"No, dear, but I like to let him think so now and then. Makes the day more interesting."

As the kitchen door swung shut, the dining room door opened, and Tucker popped his head through.

"No good putting it off," he thought, as he went confidently into the midst to meet his fate.

"Ah, Tucker. How nice to see you. Miss Regina is looking for you."

"Really? I haven't seen her since she went dashing off early this morning.

Where is she?"

"In the kitchen, dear."

"Whatever is she doing in the kitchen, Mother?"

"Looking for you."

"Why would I be in the kitchen?"

"Because, love, that's where you go when you're in trouble and want to hide."

"Am I in trouble?" he said meekly.

"Not at the moment, but the day is young."

"Has anyone ever told you that you have an acid tongue?"

"Yes, dear, you on every occasion you've been afforded."

"Guess I deserved that," he said, pushing through the swinging door.

When one door closes, another opens, or something like that. As Tucker entered the kitchen, Reggie had just left by the hall door.

"Where's Regina, Myra?"

"Oh, Lawd, sir. She's just on to the study. I told her that's where I last saw ya. You was in there with that nice Mr. Tolliver."

"Do you miss anything that goes on around here, Myra?"

"Frequently, sir," she said and sighed as she returned to her casserole.

Reggie was becoming agitated as yet another room was Tuckerless. She smacked the door and strode back to the dining room as Tucker exited the kitchen. The study held no Reggie, and he backtracked to the dining room as Reggie tried the kitchen once more.

"Where is that woman?" he yelled.

"Try the kitchen, dear."

Just as Tucker was about to swing through what seemed like a revolving door, it flew open and whacked him on the head.

"Oh, my gosh! Tucker, are you okay? I'm so sorry."

The stars dancing before his eyes were stunning but not as stunning as the two women standing before him. They were beautiful even if it was just double vision.

"Hold still, lass."

"I'm not moving, Tucker."

"Then I must be."

"Sit down, you two, and tell me your plans for the day. Myra! Bring Tucker an ice pack, please."

"What are we doing? Ow!" said Tucker as Myra gently pressed cold, pillowed therapy to his forehead.

"Well, like I said, I'd like us to get to the hospital before Alex and Audrey leave, and then I think we should go to Brooklands and check on our arrangements. Tolliver seems to be occupied. What are the other three up to?"

"I've asked Dahlia and Dulcy to oversee the Brooklands details, so I'm guessing Laird will be with them. Let's hope he can prevent any fresh disasters."

Tucker winced while Reggie sneezed from trying not to chuckle.

"Bless you, dear. Next time, just go ahead and laugh. Much better on the constitution."

"What will you be doing, Mother?"

"Flora is all aflutter over this new party and has asked me to shop. You know I abhor shopping, but I may as well pick up an appropriate piece as well."

"Maybe if you talk about all this, she'll remember something useful," said Reggie.

"Yes, there is that hope. Anything to help with the tiresome task of shopping."

Reggie was standing to leave when Tucker's phone rang. She could see the screen, and her heart skipped a beat.

"Lydia Kent-Williams," he announced.

Not only was it a surprise, but why did Tucker still have her number in his phone?

###

It was a short conversation, and Reggie and Alene pretended not to listen.

"Thank you for not listening," he said.

"There is no need for sarcasm, dear. What did she want?"

A question Reggie was dying to ask but did not have the nerve.

"She wanted to personally thank me for the Concorde invitation. I also think she didn't want me to be shocked when I saw her there."

"Which answers that question," said Reggie.

"What question?"

"If you saw her at the tea gala, dear. She was there, you know."

"So, no, you didn't see her," said Reggie. "Dahlia thought you hadn't."

"But she saw her."

"Yes," said Reggie, tracing a line on the lace tablecloth.

"As much fun as this awkward silence is, I think you two had better push off to the hospital," said Alene. "Run along, now."

"Thank you for the polite dismissal, Mother."

"As I said before, there is no need for sarcasm, dear."

"Who's got the acid tongue again?"

But Alene just waved her fingers and shooed them out the door as she continued with her morning paper.

###

DCI Campbell reviewed Audrey's discharge papers as she packed her things. She looked a hundred times better than the other day, and the DCI wanted to ensure that she stayed that way. He patiently waited while she conferred with the doctor and signed her forms.

"All ready there, Miss?"

"Yes, Mr. Campbell. Thank you so much for all your consideration."

Campbell let the "Mr." part go and handed her bag to Constable Petry, standing eagerly to his right.

"This is Constable Petry, Miss. He'll be escorting you home and checking the house to make sure everything is secure. He'll also be escorting you to the party tomorrow evening."

"Oh, thank you, sir. Do you really think all this is necessary?"

"Yes, we do. Nothing else to be done with the killer still out there."

"Well, thank you again. It's nice to meet you, Constable Petry."

She shook hands with a handsome young man with wavy hair, green eyes, and an aquiline nose dotted with freckles. He was a tallish sort, and Audrey thought she might like Constable Petry protecting her. When she glanced at his hand, the absence of a ring sent a shiver through her spine.

"Good morning! Audrey, you look wonderful," said Reggie. "Hello. We haven't met. I'm Regina Winter, and this is Tucker Elliott."

"Nice to meet you. I'll be escorting Miss Audrey home. I'm Constable Petry."

"He's my protector," she said, batting her lashes so hard it looked as though there was something in her eye.

"And once again, you lot. Why?"

"We came to check on Audrey and Alex. We're thrilled that they're being released in time for the Concorde experience."

"Ah, yes. The Great Experiment."

"Why 'The Great Experiment'?"

"Because you seem to think that this is some scientific quest where you fill a room with rats and one of them will win out and be the rat king."

"Huh, I kinda like that," said Reggie. "Do you think it'll work?"

"We don't want to hear the answer to that, love," said Tucker. "So, Audrey, we'll see you tomorrow. Just relax, and we'll handle everything."

"Oh, isn't there anything I can do to help?"

"No, love," said Tucker. "Dahlia and Dulcy have gone to Brooklands to meet up with Candace. We'll be on our way there as soon as we spring Alex. You rest and relax."

"If only I could. There's such a mess at the house it'll take me till tomorrow night to put it right again."

"No worries. We sent in a cleaning crew. One that specializes in crime scene cleanup. Everything is straightened and tidy, and the fingerprint powder has been professionally cleaned. It's a bugger to fix if you don't have the right items."

"I don't know how to thank you!" she cried. "That's such a relief."

"My pleasure. We'll go see Alex now. DCI Campbell, it's been a treat. Miss me."

Campbell scowled at Tucker as he folded his arms across his chest and pointed to the door.

"C'mon, Reg, our work here is done."

"Oh, not quite," said Reggie, reddening. "Audrey, will you come with me for a minute, please?"

Reggie opened the door and stepped into the hall as Audrey stared after her in confusion.

"This is a bit embarrassing," said Reggie, "but here," she said, slipping a thin packet into Audrey's palm.

"My birth control? Do I want to know the story here?"

"No. No, you don't. You definitely do not. C'mon Tucker, let's go."

They ambled down the hall, leaving a laughing Audrey in their wake.

30

Chapter 30

First dead body I've ever seen. They look different in real life. They don't move.
-Saw, 2004

Tucker and Reggie rescued Alex from the thorough nurse who was explaining the discharge instructions for the third time. As Alex was teetering on his crutches, Tucker slipped a ten-pound note into the woman's apron. He then walked her to the door, thanked her profusely for her excellent care, and shoved her through it.

"You have been paroled, mate," he said to Alex. "How about a lift home?"

"If it's not too much trouble, would you mind awfully taking me to Brooklands? That's where my motor car is."

"Brilliant," said Tucker. "Just where we were going. Well, then we're off."

The trip was quick, and Alex was soon asking about his car, which had been garaged after the Aston Martin incident and his hasty departure to the hospital. They found Dulcy and Dahlia in the kitchen with Candace, working on starters for the party.

"Cheers! How's it going?"

"Lovely," said Candace, peering at them through steamy spectacles.

They were leaning over a boiling pot, stirring something that smelled heavenly with slow, even strokes.

"What ya got there?" asked Alex.

"Ah, I'm glad you asked," said Dahlia. "I'm sharing our lobster-stuffed ravioli with Candace. She was curious about what heavy starters work in an American tea room. These are just lovely, and everyone adores them, right Dulcy?"

"Oh, absolutely. They're a huge favorite at home."

"By the way, Dulcy, where is Laird?"

"He went out to the garages to poke around."

"That's our cue, Alex. We shall leave you to it, ladies. We'd only be underfoot anyway."

"Chicken," said Reggie.

"No, lobster," said Dahlia.

"No, chicken a la Tucker," said Reggie. "No stomach for the kitchen, so to speak."

"So, how is Audrey?" asked Candace.

"Oh, so much better. Color in her cheeks, her smile back in place, and an oh-so-gorgeous constable who will be in tow tomorrow. Campbell sent him with her for protection."

"Yes, but who will protect him?" asked Candace.

Reggie snickered and gazed around the kitchen.

"So, tell me how this will work tomorrow," she asked. "Lay of the land and all."

"It'll be sort of a hybrid Concorde experience. Since we're having two groups, one set will be here in the club while the others are on the plane. There will be champagne and hors d'oeuvres in here and out there. Guests can view classic pictures around the club and get a tour of the member area if interested. The museum will be closed to the public, so the exhibits won't be available. That's fine, really; discourages any unauthorized mucking about."

"Will there be a tea preview?" she asked as she eyed the ravioli. "Seems like a great opportunity to give them a sneak peek before the launch."

"Alene expressed her wish that there be something of the sort somewhere in the club. We'll do much the same as what was at the original launch. Well, minus the poison."

"Ugh - really, Candace?"

"Just a little joke. Sorry for the wry British humor."

"And what is the tour going to be like? I'm excited to see all this," said Reggie.

"So am I," said Dulcy. "I've been looking forward to this since we got here."

"Oh, you should. We have a grand program we present here," said Candace. "The attendees get a pre-flight briefing before they board, which is really just climbing up a flight of stairs. They'll present their boarding pass and proceed into the cabin. There's a lovely gallery of photos all around, and they'll also be able to go into the cockpit and view the controls. That's not usually part of this tour, but since we're designing something special, we can do anything we want."

"Sounds like a first-class experience so far," said Dahlia.

"Only the best for our guests and members. Once everyone is seated in their actual Concorde passenger seats, a brief film about the restoration project, completed in 2006, will be shown. The best part is that they get a virtual take-off and flight simulation. When it's all done, they get a flight completion certificate. At that point, they deplane, and the other group goes. All very professional and done by actual Concorde flight-trained pilots. It's brilliant."

Dahlia quickly stirred another pot on the stove, carefully dumped the ravioli into a colander, and poured the creamy contents into a gravy boat.

"Right then, ladies. The Sea Gables Tea Room presents lobster ravioli floating gently in a perfectly crafted garlic cream sauce. Bon appétit!"

"Oh my! This is delicious," said Candace.

"Do we smell food?" said a disembodied voice.

Tucker, Laird, and Alex rounded the corner and made a beeline for the counter where the ravioli were resting in peace.

"Here you are," said Candace, handing each of them a small plate.

"Did I eat today?" asked Tucker.

"No, you were too busy chasing me through the house till I knocked you senseless with the kitchen door," said Reggie.

"This is bloody marvelous, ladies. Is this for tomorrow?"

"Yes, I think I'll get Chef Dumont to add it to the menu. Excuse me while I get him up to speed."

"So, what did you see out there?" asked Reggie.

The three men exchanged glances, and Laird spoke up as Alex remained silent.

"We found Alex's cars; one neatly tucked away, and one still spread in an array of parts over the floor in the garage; pretty much status quo as to what we've already witnessed."

"Oh, right. I forgot you hadn't seen that, Alex. You alright there?"

"Yes. It's just sad for me. Such a beautiful piece of machinery scattered about like a broken toy. Makes one shudder."

"It was rather a close call, mate, but you heard the Smith chap. They'll put it right in no time."

"I hope so."

"And we didn't find any other information either. They're still baffled as to why Reggie spun through an oil slick on a previously clean track. Those who aren't tight-lipped have no clue as to how it could've happened."

"There was a man there that day that made Tolliver suspicious," said Reggie. "Now, what was his name? Jeffrey, that's it!"

"Do you think you'd recognize him if you saw him again?"

"Yes, but Tolliver took a picture. You can get him to send it to you."

"Bless that man," said Tucker, dialing his phone.

It was a quick conversation, and in a few minutes, they were looking at a picture of an ordinary man in coveralls standing near a wall, eyeing something across the room.

"He looks unexceptional, except that he's fixated on something in front of him."

"That would be me. Tolliver took the picture because the man was openly staring at me. It made him uncomfortable at the time," said Reggie, shrugging her shoulders.

"Let's go," said Laird.

Candace was still on the phone and waved distractedly as they passed her office. They covered the distance to the garages quickly and were standing in front of Sidney Barrow-Smith in no time.

"Back again, gents?"

"Yes, sir," said Laird.

"We were wondering if you could help," said Tucker. "Do you know of a mechanic named Jeffrey?"

"Doesn't ring a bell, sir. I don't believe we have anyone here by that name."

Tucker held out his phone and enlarged the picture of the man in the coveralls. Sidney leaned in and took a closer look.

"Ah. That bloke. I didn't quite remember. He wasn't here long. Not even long enough to do the proper forms. Strange thing about him, sir."

Tucker was feeling more uncomfortable by the moment.

"What would that be?" asked Laird.

"It was right after your incident, Miss. Never showed for work the next day. Not a call either. He just vanished."

Reggie blanched to the shade of Olde English White, the color of the Austin Healey in which she had spun out.

###

There was a hum of excitement in the air as everyone prepared for the exciting Concorde event. The family had gathered at the Porter house for a pre-Concorde aperitif and possibly a prayer. As ever, Jennings looked dashing in his tuxedo.

"So, back in the thick of things, eh, mate?" said Tucker.

Jennings had been revealed as more than the efficient genius butler while they had been closing out a cold case in Florida at Dahlia's tea room and bed and breakfast. The enigmatic man had been instrumental and a sure shot with a tea tray, just when it counted the most, capturing the culprit and bringing a supposedly dead Dahlia back to life. It was here that his brilliant government career had been uncovered. And the Porters had kept it a tightly guarded secret for years.

“Yes, sir. I do love the mystique of these experiences. And as usual, I shall just be doing my duties while keeping an eye on things and listening for revealing conversations.”

“And no one does it better. Well, except maybe James Bond. You know.”

“Of course, sir. May I get you another scotch, or would you like champagne?”

“Oh, I should probably stick to the program and have champagne like Miss Reggie. Where did she get to, that one?”

“I believe she is by the window with Miss Dahlia, discussing the event, sir.”

Tucker peered through Laird and Dulcy and landed on the tall, beautiful assistant whom his mother had assigned him. He hadn’t wanted an assistant, but he didn’t seem to have a choice, much like being assigned to Tolliver when going to Las Vegas. One babysitter was much like another, except for Regina Winter. She was only a shade taller than Dahlia, and as much alike as they looked, Reggie Winter should have been immortalized in paintings. Long chestnut hair, green eyes like emeralds in an almond-shaped setting, pouty lips that curled with expression when she was agitated, and two of the most enormous feet on a woman he had ever seen. She made his heart race at every turn.

Just as he reached her, a tap of a glass at the front of the room caught his attention. He could see Jennings herding the guests into pods and his mother standing on the hearth.

“Good evening, all, and happy Concorde Day! Thank you for coming to our pre-celebration. Jennings has organized us into travel groups, so just see him for transportation. Thank you again, happy landings, and enjoy yourselves this evening."

The ride was pleasant in the fall air. By the time they arrived at Brooklands, the sun had mellowed over the horizon, and the grounds were lit in a festive glow. The Concorde was majestic in its setting behind the Edwardian Club, and the soft music coming from the Barbara Cartland room foretold a magical experience.

"This is beautiful," exclaimed Dulcy. "So exciting."

They passed by the friendship bench without glancing its way and entered the reception area where a young woman was handing out name tags and directions should they decide to sit rather than mingle.

"And if you'd like to tour the member bar and patio, you are most welcome to do so. There will also be servers with hors d'oeuvres. Please enjoy the historical gallery of pictures throughout the building."

Dahlia had run off to the kitchen to meet Chef Dumont and thank him for including her special dish. Tucker and Reggie rounded a corner by the Sunbeam Cafe and ran into Olivia Weatherford standing with a brightly colored Dame Flora Abbington.

"Oh, Flora, what a beautiful gown," said Reggie. "Is this what you and Alene found shopping today?"

"Why, yes, dear, how lovely of you to notice."

Tucker thought Reggie could do no less. The woman was wearing a puffy-sleeved gown with a ruched bodice with pleats and folds that cascaded down the front in mountainous layers till they phased out altogether at the bottom. The most distinctive part of the dress was the color - the orange of a flaming sunset just as it sinks on a darkening horizon. If that wasn't enough, she had managed to find a lipstick in the exact shade as the gown. Reggie was afraid to look at her shoes or her purse.

"Hello, Olivia. So nice to see you," said Tucker. "Getting on alright, then?"

"Yes, Tucker, thank you so much for asking and for this lovely party, which takes all our minds off the horrible incidents of the past week. It couldn't have come at a better moment. You know, I've always wanted to see this full exhibit, but I could never get Winston to come to it."

"And this one is special since it's a combination of their two events with a little flair added just for the occasion."

The hors d'oeuvres were nothing short of spectacular. Dahlia's lobster ravioli flew off the trays like the Concorde itself. Ceviche, shrimp, cheeses of every kind, meatballs in a secret sauce, and miniature packs of peanuts, a nod to airline staples, were the highlights for the happy guests.

Dulcy and Laird had wandered over to the tea display, which looked eerily similar to the one from the gala. Dulcy slipped Laird a glance as they took stock of the items while Tolliver stepped in and shot a few images.

"Gathering your evidence before the event this time?" joked Laird.

"Something like that, sir," he said, nodding at the attendant behind the urns. Missing was the pitcher of water that had been the subject of confusion and alarm the last time.

"The guests seem to be enjoying the tea," said Dulcy. "I see quite a few demi cups out there."

Laird was watching the crowd as well as watching Jennings. The man was flitting through the guests like a cardinal, meeting and greeting and taking the pulse of the room with each turn. He was not serving, but instead acting as maître d' and host. He disappeared into the kitchen just as there was a tap on a microphone, and Alene Elliott took center stage, Tolliver next to her, deferential as always.

"Good evening, honored guests, family, and loyal patrons of the museum. We are so happy to be able to invite you here tonight to our Concorde Experience. At this time, I would like to introduce Mr. Alex Aldeworth, Museum Director, who will explain tonight's festivities, including the silent auction. Mr. Aldeworth?"

"Thank you, Mrs. Elliott. I am humbled to have the opportunity to host you all here this evening. Humbled and thankful to still be here - to still be here after crashing a vintage Aston Martin Vantage and then not getting sacked."

The audience laughed politely and waited for him to resume.

"Tonight, you all were given name tags with the numbers one and two on them. That number will be the group to which you are assigned for your Concorde tour. I know you'll enjoy this experience. Also, as we always accept generous donations to keep up the marvelous work we do here, we are pleased to have a most impressive silent auction selection available. Please write your name and bid on the sheets for the items that interest you the most. We have quite a collection of articles and experiences to offer this evening. Now, if group number one will please follow me, I will lead you out to your pre-flight briefing and deliver your boarding passes."

Oohs and ahs could be heard rippling through the crowd as they dispersed and headed toward the plane, the auction tables, or the bar. Reggie was scanning the crowd for Audrey and Candace when she spotted Audrey at the end of the auction site, greeting wandering guests.

"Look, Tucker, there's Audrey. Let's go check in."

Tucker followed her silently, and it wasn't till Reggie glanced back that she caught sight of just a sliver of her in the crowd. Lydia Kent-Williams was eyeing Tucker from across the room as she nodded politely to an older gentleman talking animatedly before her. Reggie reached back and grabbed Tucker's hand and pulled him through the crowd.

"Hang on, Reg, I'm coming. Everything alright?"

"Yes. I just thought that maybe you'd be more comfortable..."

"Somewhere else? Somewhere out of Lydia's view?"

"Well, yes. I wasn't aware that you had seen her. Better?" asked Reggie, surprised at his composure.

"I don't think this is the place to panic just because a former employee is present. I will say, though, Reg, I didn't quite recognize her. She's... changed somewhat."

"How so?"

"She used to wear these large spectacles, which I rather got a kick out of. She looked like a sexy librarian about to be bad in the stacks. They are not in evidence this evening, leading me to believe that she is sporting contacts. Also, her hair is lovely. She's done something to it. It used to be somewhat curly and out of control, but it's smooth as a baby's bottom tonight.

"Um, so you didn't see her at the gala at all?"

"Well, there wasn't much time then, was there, what with Weatherford, royalty, and a mass of premium guests in the midst of an angry chef, and then a murder."

"Let's just enjoy this and keep our eyes open, shall we? Audrey seems to have gone now. Oh, there she is with her personal bodyguard, Constable Petry. He is quite handsome, don't you think?"

"I say, she seems to be quite enjoying his company. All well and good if you like that tall, dark, and handsome type," he said, eyeing her sideways. "Everyone seems to be having a splendid time, thank God. There's Candace with people I don't know. Must be Brooklands patrons. There's something different there. Ah, I know. She's left those massive spectacles behind. She looks lovely and certainly in her element."

Reggie followed Tucker's gaze and saw a beautiful young woman rather than the bookish, bespectacled administrator they were used to. Reggie continued scanning the perimeter and the middle of the room. The guests were enjoying themselves with the food, drink, and historical aspects of the museum. Additional docents had been added to answer questions and facilitate donations.

"Say, Reg, why don't we go up to the member area and have a look 'round."

"That's right; you haven't been up there yet. Let's go. We'll skip the elevator and take the stairs. They're right over here."

They passed a few people on their way, and when they reached the end of the corridor, they took a left turn and found themselves in the quaint art deco bar. Small groups of people milled about the private area while several others took in the evening air on the patio overlooking the paddock. They grabbed a glass of champagne and wandered toward the French doors to the patio.

"You mark my words, they'll know who did it soon enough," a woman's voice announced. "I can say who it was this minute, you know. There are people here who should watch their step, you mark my words, I say."

Tucker glanced at Reggie and peered around the door to see Dame Flora Abbington in all her orange glory. She was capturing the attention of a small group of listeners while others wandered through, pretending not to eavesdrop on the conversation. They hovered for a minute and sipped their drinks.

"She best watch *her* step," said Tucker. "We don't know who did it, so how could she?"

"Do you think she knows something we don't?"

"Bless me. How could she?"

"Well, they did say she was the biggest gossip in the county. We'll question her later, but right now, we should go back downstairs. The first group should be finishing, and then we're up."

"Right then. Lead on, Reg."

They retraced their steps back into the bar and started toward the exit. As they slid past a large man with a cane, standing in front of them was Candace.

"Hullo. Fancy meeting you here," said Tucker. "You look smashing this evening. We were just getting to know your quaint member bar here."

"Why, thank you for the generous compliment. And yes, it's lovely, isn't it? Do you need anything? I was just checking on things up here. Everything's humming along beautifully downstairs."

Reggie noted that without Candace's glasses, the beautiful green eyes from their first meeting shone more brightly in the light from the patio. Reggie was thrilled with the turnout and the event, and let Candace know before they hurried downstairs for group two's Concorde adventure. On the way, they ran into the Tiptons, long-time clients and friends, just disembarking.

"How was it?"

"Oh, just marvelous," gushed Lady Tipton. "Such history and romance. Such a shame they no longer fly. What a wonderful way to travel. I know you'll enjoy it," she said, patting Reggie on the arm and flashing a beautifully white smile.

They received their debriefing and boarding passes and joined Dulcy, Laird, and Dahlia at the bottom step. The Elliotts, Porters, and Tolliver were further behind, along with some of the loyal Farthing customers who were staples at their events. Further down the line, Lydia Kent-Williams conversed with a young man whom Tucker did not know.

They found their section and settled in, awaiting the start of the video presentation. They watched the other guests find their seats. Olivia Weatherford was glancing around as though lost, and Tucker waved her over to see if he could help.

"No, no. Just trying to find my seat and wondering where Flora has gotten to. She's on this flight. Doesn't that sound fun? On this flight. As though we're actually taking off."

"Maybe they lost her luggage," quipped Tucker.

"Oh, you silly thing, how amusing. We're right over there if you see her."

She glided to her reserved spot with a wave and accepted another glass of champagne from the "stewardess". She settled comfortably back in the dark blue leather seat and propped her feet on the lower rest with a contented sigh. The lights dimmed, and the movie began with the history of the British Air shutdown of the iconic machines, their disassembly, move, and reassembly at the museum.

"This is the part I'm excited for," said Reggie. "I love take-off. It's such an exhilarating experience."

"Maybe that's why they call it a 'Concorde Experience'."

It was over all too soon, and the passengers deplaned, marveling over the true-to-life simulation of their flight.

The party was in full swing in the club, and guests were bidding rapidly on the auction items. Waiters were still splashing champagne into guests' glasses, which Tucker figured was the reason for the voracious bidding.

"Hello, Mother, how was your flight experience?"

"Oh, it was wonderful. It's just as I remember it."

"You flew on the Concorde, Alene?" asked Reggie.

"Yes, dear, I had a few occasions that actually called for it, so that's what we did. Wonderful way to fly. By the way, have you seen Flora? Olivia was a bit miffed that she had missed her flight, so to speak. She's stalking her like a hound after a fox. I don't honestly know how you can miss her in that dreadful gown, but it was what she wanted, so whatever makes her happy. Please let me know if you see her."

"Mother, last time we saw her, she was on the patio of the member bar. She was... gossiping, you know. I thought she would be right behind us. Let's go back up and take a look."

"I think I'll come with you," said Alene.

Tucker caught Laird's eye as he ushered the women up the stairs. Jennings and Tolliver saw the communication and changed their paths to follow. The bar was in full swing, and the sound level was escalating into the hall. They could hear the different English dialects emerging with each glass of champagne.

"I don't see her in here," said Reggie. "She may still be on the patio."

They weaved through the guests and opened the door to the deck. The night air had gotten cooler, and most of the attendees had retreated inside. Everybody except for one - a woman in a flamboyant orange gown sitting alone at the end of the patio, gazing out over the paddock.

"There you are," said Alene. "Do you know Olivia has been looking everywhere for you, Flora? You should get inside, dear; it's getting nasty cold out here. Flora?"

But Flora didn't hear. Flora was cold, but only because she was dead.

###

They stood frozen in time with Flora frozen in death before them. Jennings appeared out of nowhere with brandy. Tolliver was acting as a buffer between the door and the death scene, directing guests to the far side of the patio so Flora would remain hidden in the shadows.

"Find DCI Campbell," said Laird. "Dulcy went inside to get Constable Petry."

"As he's stationed in the security offices, don't you think he's seen this?" asked Tucker.

"What do you want to bet that this area is also 'out of range' of the cameras?" said Laird.

"Good point. Bollocks. Where's Reggie?"

They scanned the patio and found Alene at a nearby table, sniffing into a handkerchief, Reggie at her side. She was doing her best to console Alene without attracting attention.

"Sad, isn't it? Such a lively old dame," said Tucker. "What do you think happened here, John?"

"She talked too much, and I'm pretty sure she knew nothing. Her claim to being the gossip of the county got her killed. What did you hear her saying earlier?"

"She was telling a group here on the terrace that she knew who the killer was. You and I both know that's not true."

Laird was moving cautiously, taking care not to disturb anything while checking Dame Flora for signs of violence. It was then that he moved her face fully into the light and saw it. A sizable, swollen mark at her left temple, just above her ear. She looked peaceful in the dim light, but nothing was peaceful about the blow to her head. Tucker looked down at the still body and felt for a pulse. Nothing. As he did so, he kicked something sticking out from under the folds of her gown. He gently raised the soft material to reveal a roundish object at her feet. It was a champagne cork.

"That's a funny thing to be here. Well, maybe not awfully funny since that's the main beverage this evening, but why would one be here? Don't they remove the corks inside, then serve?"

"Go into the member area and tell the man in charge of the bar not to throw away any of the champagne bottles, but not to touch them either."

Tucker did as he was told as Reggie watched from Alene's side. Jennings reappeared and gently lifted her from her perch.

"You're wanted downstairs, Mrs. Elliott. Please accompany me to the Barbara Cartland room, ma'am."

Alene let Jennings lead her away like a child while Reggie eyed Tucker from her seat. She watched Tolliver across the way, deflecting guests, and made her way to him.

"You're doing a great job, Tolliver. Here we are again. Poor Flora. Anything I can help with?"

"No, Miss. Luckily, it's colder, and the guests are deciding not to take advantage of the patio now. I assume the proper channels have been notified, and we can expect the DCI shortly."

"Yes, Tolliver. I'm glad you're here. I'm afraid it might be me you'll need to babysit next."

Tolliver steadied her and led her back to the chair she had abandoned. As she was about to sit, she bolted back upright and headed for Flora; Tolliver followed closely.

"What is it, Miss?"

"Look, it's her purse, Tolliver. It's just there by the railing in the corner. You almost don't see it in the dim light. She must have dropped it when..."

She reached out to pick up the contents, but Tolliver stopped her before she could touch anything.

"Here, Miss. Take my handkerchief. You can't disturb anything here. And not to be disrespectful, but with the way things have been going, you'd be picking up pieces of evidence, and DCI Campbell would catch you in the act. We don't want that, now do we?"

"No, we bloody well do not," said a harsh voice behind them.

DCI Campbell was present and accounted for.

31

Chapter 31

Audrey Spitz: What if we're being watched by the killer? What if he was in here? Maybe he stole my Peanut M&Ms.

Nick Spitz: I stole your Peanut M&Ms.
-Murder Mystery, 2019

Guests were gathering and asking questions. Why had everything stopped? Why were the constables here? What had happened? A hush had come over the crowd in the member bar as Constable Petry addressed the group. The patio door swung open, and Olivia Weatherford stood on the threshold, gazing at the group and the orange gown.

"Flora? What's happened? Is she alright? Why is she...

"Olivia, please come with me," said Tucker. "There's been an accident. Please have a seat here."

A hand shot through the two with a snifter of amber liquid glistening in the patio lights.

"Thank you, Jennings. Spot on, as usual. Have you seen Candace and Alex?"

"I believe they have been located and are coming now with Miss Audrey."

"If you would please relax here, Olivia, someone will be with you shortly."

As if on cue, Alex and Candace appeared in the doorway, silhouetted by the back lighting of the bar. Alex turned and shielded Candace from the sight. He led her to the other side of the patio to a seat in the moonlight. Again, a snifter of brandy appeared at the ready.

"What's happened? Not again, Alex, it can't be. Who is it?" she asked, peering over his shoulder at the crumpled figure.

Audrey had been stuck to Constable Petry but made her way to Candace and Alex's table.

"It's so awful. Who would want to hurt that harmless old thing?"

"From what I understand, she wasn't being harmless on the porch earlier," said Alex.

"What do you mean?"

"I mean, she was boasting that she knew who killed Winston Weatherford," said Alex. "She said she knew who did it and certain people should watch their step."

Alex turned to watch the activity at the other end of the patio. DCI Campbell was issuing instructions as Tucker and Laird stood close by, their heads bent toward the conversation. Laird was hurriedly scribbling notes as Campbell dismissed the constables and returned to them and the body.

"So, when was the last time either of you saw the woman alive?" he asked, taking out his own notebook.

Alex's attention swiftly turned to the doorway as Dulcy popped her head out, glancing from side to side. She dashed to their table, avoiding the scene at the other end.

"The guests are in shock, Alex. They're being questioned by the constables and then being shown out. Would you like to say anything or just leave it?"

"I think you should go down, Alex. You should represent Brooklands and assure them that it was just an accident. I don't want them frightened into thinking this has something to do with the museum."

"But it does have to do with the museum. It happened here. Tonight. Again. But you're right - we need to go down and take charge."

"You might want to assure them that the tea launch and gala will go on as planned," suggested Dulcy. "That should reassure them. If Farthing's isn't intimidated, they shouldn't be either."

"Good Gawd, we're not going to say it like that, are we?" he asked.

"No. Just let them know that it was an unfortunate accident and that we are looking forward to the festivities next week for the launch. We'll add something to it."

"Like what?" asked Alex.

"I don't know, but you'll think of something."

"Hope you think of it by the time you get downstairs," thought Dulcy.

She watched them walk away, wondering if the launch would get off the ground or if DCI Campbell would crash their party before it even started.

###

Alene was being questioned in Candace's office while Douglass stood behind her, hands on her shoulders. He wasn't sure if he was steadying her or himself. The constables were efficient and discreet, and he was thankful for that. He wondered how this would impact future events.

"So, you hadn't seen her since you arrived, is that correct, ma'am?"

"Yes. I was making sure everything was running smoothly down here. The main activities were on this level and outside. The member bar was an extra treat for the guests. I hadn't been up there until I followed my son, who was actually looking for poor Flora."

"Yes, then, with whom did she arrive, Mrs. Elliott?"

Alene had to think. She really didn't know in which vehicle Flora had ridden from the Porters.

"I don't really know. Jennings. Jennings would know; he arranged the transportation. He would know in which car she had been placed."

The gentlemen scribbled in their books and checked the facts. Douglass hoped they would be satisfied so they could return upstairs for an update. He wondered how this would impact next week's gala and if it was even worth trying again since it seemed like every time they scheduled their party, it blew up on the launchpad.

"You may go, ma'am, sir. We know where to find you if we have any more questions."

She said her goodbyes to the remaining guests and hoped they had enjoyed the festivities, even with the tragic event. She could see the questioning glances as they headed for the exit, and she vowed to forge ahead with the gala no matter the persistent troubles.

"Oh, Jennings, there you are. Do you remember to which car Flora was assigned for the ride out here?"

"Yes, ma'am, she was in the vehicle with Olivia Weatherford, Miss Audrey, and Constable Petry. I remember because she was flirting with the constable, ma'am. Quite brazen, if not slightly humorous."

"Oh dear, sounds like Flora. Thank you, Jennings. How are things... out there?"

Just as the words left her lips, a gurney burst into the bar, scooting the attendees aside like the Red Sea. Forensics had arrived, along with the coroner. Dame Flora was being prepared for her last ride from Brooklands. Tucker leaned over the railing and noted the coroner's van right outside the door. He wondered if it would be the senior coroner or if the task had gone to one of the other specialist judges. Either way, it looked like it could be a tedious night for someone.

"Whaddya reckon, Laird? Think they'll call this straightforward?"

"More than likely, but I'll get with McCallum shortly and see what he says. It's pretty obvious what happened."

"Maybe to you, mate, but the big question is who? Someone out there is trying desperately to keep something hidden. There's a deeply hidden secret we need to uncover."

"We need to track down that mechanic. Let's take that photo to Campbell and see if he shows up in any of their books. There's a connection to someone or something there."

Most of the guests were dispersing and heading for the exits, while others remained in clumps on the patio, waiting for their dismissal. Constable Petry was chatting with DCI Campbell, and Alene hoped they now had tabs on Flora up until her untimely exit.

"Audrey, dear, what did you discuss on the ride over? I know you were in the car with Flora. Was she... gossiping? What was the conversation?"

"Nothing in particular, ma'am. She was excited to see the tour, as was Mrs. Weatherford. They were talking about the event, and Mrs. Weatherford had shared her experience of being on the Concorde. It was all very chit-chat, nothing out of the ordinary. Is that what got her killed, Mrs. Elliott?" she asked wide-eyed.

"We shall see, shan't we?"

DCI Campbell was talking with the coroner and finishing the details of the removal of the body. Other constables were with forensics, bagging champagne bottles and taping off the bar as they combed the inside and outside areas.

"Don't forget her purse," said Reggie, pointing to an apricot bag with a chain strap hidden in the half-light of the corner.

Campbell sent a man to pick it up. He was carefully lifting the evidence when a small round object rolled away and rested against the base of the railing. The constable lifted it with his tongs and held it out to Campbell.

"Whaddya reckon this is?"

Tucker and Laird examined the piece with curiosity.

"That, my friends, is an earring," said Reggie, poking her head in their midst.

"Stop that gurney," commanded Campbell as the attendants were leaving the scene.

The DCI lifted the sheet and inspected Flora's ear lobes. He gave a grunt, lowered it, and made a quick scrawl in his notebook.

"Well?" asked Laird.

"Two rather large, orange earrings still in place on the woman's lobes. No go."

Reggie elbowed Tucker, who scanned the women still present on the deck. He observed no missing jewelry and nudged Campbell.

"I see no one up here with a missing earring. You'll have to catch the bar patrons before they make their getaway, yes?"

"Telling me how to do my job again, eh, Elliott?" he said, radioing the lower level to hold the downstairs attendees till he arrived.

"We'll be in touch, Elliott, mark my words."

"Oh, I have no doubt, Campbell, no doubt at all."

"Well, dammit," said Reggie.

"I know. That's a bit of a disappointment. Maybe someone down there is missing the thing."

“No, that’s not what I was talking about.”

“What then?”

“Be careful what you wish for.”

“What do you mean? Did you wish for something, love?”

“When your mother showed me the invited guests, it reminded me of a list for a murder mystery game. You know, where people play act, and there’s a body, and they figure out who did it?”

“Yes, Reg. Where does the wish come in?”

“I wished for a Concorde party that did not have a real dead body at the end.”

“Not your fault, love. Wishes don’t kill people.”

“Someone wished her dead, Tucker.”

“And we’ll find out who, Regina. You’ll see,” he said, leading her by the hand to the others.

“Better find out who before next weekend, then.”

All Tucker could do was nod and squeeze her hand.

###

Security allowed them into the Barbara Cartland room, where the supposed innocents were huddling by the warmth of the fireplace. Other than stare at their glasses, they weren’t sure what to do.

"This is ridiculous," said Delia Porter. "We have to do something, Alene. Dahlia, you've been in this situation before. Don't you have any suggestions, darling?"

"Oh, mother, this is so much different than what we were faced with."

"How so?"

"We were being taunted by someone who was playing tricks on us and wreaking havoc at every turn. Reggie was even dosed from having taken my drink. Oh, bugger. It is like this. I didn't even see it. Thank you, Mother."

"You're welcome, darling. Now, let's come up with something useful before someone else dies."

"I think that's a bloody good idea," said a voice from the doorway."

"So, what do we do here, Campbell?" asked Tucker.

"Yes, I'd like to know the same," said Alene, rising to the occasion.

"I'd like to know as well," echoed Alex.

Candace stood by Alex and grasped his hand in agreement.

One by one, they rose and lined up with Delia, pressing DCI Campbell to make a decision.

"You can't do it," he said.

"If you're saying what I think you are," said Alene Elliott, "you will stop me over my dead body."

"That's exactly what I'm afraid of, ma'am."

###

It was a hectic week of planning for the relaunch, or, as it were, preparing for the attack. The group had grown smaller, as necessary, since Tucker, Reggie, and Laird were unsure whom they could trust.

DCI Campbell was outnumbered, outvoted, and outclassed when it came to solving not one but two murders. The postmortem on Dame Abbington was underway even as the drop-down date for the tea gala was approaching.

"I should think this would have been straightforward," complained Tucker. "Why the holdup?"

"They have decided that with respect to everything else that has come to pass, they can't just ignore toxicology on this. Even though it looks obvious, they refuse to take any chances on missing key evidence."

"Well, Laird, don't you have a thing with McCallum? Can't you find out anything?"

"I don't have a thing; I have a relationship."

"That doesn't sound any better, mate. Go poke him so he'll talk."

"Now, who sounds worse?"

"Do your job, Laird."

"I don't have a job here."

"Exactly. So do what you do so well. Extract information, Agent Laird. You're our only hope."

"Contrary to popular belief, I am not Obi-Wan Kenobi. I'm a visiting journeyman who begs on the kindness of other lawmen."

"Then go do it. Reggie is after me to stick her nose in even further. I beg of you. Save me from her."

"Fine. I'll visit McCallum. What are you going to do?"

"I'm going to catch up with Tolliver on those personnel files. It's the only thing out there I can grab onto. Alene has detained Reggie, and God knows when I'll be able to get my hands on her."

"If only we could find out where that mechanic is and who owns that earring. Those seem to be our only two leads."

"Then I've got to go to Brooklands," said Tucker. "I'll take Tolliver. He's the least likely to get into more trouble. Reggie's like a DCI magnet. If I leave her with Alene, she'll stay safe and..."

"Out of your hair?"

"Well, yes. As soon as we're done with the files, we'll run out there and take a look 'round. Tolliver will know what to do. He's an even-keeled chap. He'll know exactly how to proceed."

###

"Actually, sir, I have no idea what to do next. Do you have any ideas, clues, hunches?"

"Damn, Tolliver, I was counting on you to be the smart one. Alright, never mind. What have you found here?"

"I've only just finished with the lab personnel, sir. I shall now be starting with the rest of the staff."

"Do you think that's necessary? Do you suspect someone of something?"

"No, sir, but I just like to be thorough. I've been going through the files in great depth so far. I really don't want to break from that tack, sir."

"If it works for you, Tolliver, you do whatever you need to. I learned in Las Vegas that when you're on a scent, it would be useless to try to stop you. You're a human bloodhound."

"Thank you, sir. I think."

"Now, Tolliver, we need to go out to Brooklands. Before you say no, hear my reasoning."

"I wouldn't dream of doing anything else, sir."

"Right. I'm not sure, but I think I may have just been insulted."

"Not that you know of, sir," said Tolliver with a faint smile.

"You silly old git. C'mon, I'll buy you a beer in the member bar, mate. You are a damn good sport."

"Yes, sir," said Tolliver, picking up his coat and trying to hide the happy grin that touched his soul.

###

Seated comfortably in the conservatory at the Porters, Alene, Dulcy, Reggie, and Dahlia were poring over the guest list while Jennings popped in and out with refreshments and encouragement. They were hoping the lists of the past would provide a clue to the present. Many of the same people from the first launch and the Concorde party would be attending, with a few additions to round out the group. Since Reggie and Dulcy were outsiders, they were trying to spot a trend among people, places, and pasts.

Laird had gone to see McCallum, the FME, who had no new information on anything, much less Flora Abbington's toxicology. It was much too soon to do any more than stick with the straightforward conclusion of a blow to the head. DCI Campbell had taken the picture of the mechanic to run through the computer while forensics labored over the champagne bottles.

Things at Brooklands had returned to a semi-normal state, with Candace attending to daily activities and Alex resuming director duties. The story of the mechanic had rattled him, and he dove back into the security tapes, hoping to find a clue about the man with the short-lived employment. Could he be connected to the mysterious figure seen sneaking into the building the night of the gala?

Audrey was almost one hundred percent and had returned to work, where April and Gillian were fussing over her. And even though Constable Petry had been relieved of his full-time bodyguard duties, it did not deter him from taking Audrey to dinner and double-checking her house upon leaving her each day for the night. Audrey was beginning to think that someone trying to kill her had been the best thing to happen all year.

"So, sir, what's the plan? Go to the garages, study the tapes with Mr. Aldeworth, visit Candace, visit the member bar?"

"Why, Tolliver, I would think you'd know the answer to that," he said, pressing the elevator button. "Second floor, women's apparel, fine jewelry, and member bar."

"Very amusing, sir. Did you get the card from Miss Dahlia?"

"No need, mate. Farthing's Fine Teas is now an official museum member. Actually, it's a family membership, but then again, it is family, isn't it?"

"Yes, sir. Shall we enjoy the patio, or would you rather stay indoors?"

"I've an idea, why don't we start indoors and chat up the servers and then go out to the patio to see things in the light of day?"

"Brilliant, sir. Exactly what I would have suggested."

"Hello, sir, are you a member?"

"Yes, by God, I am," exclaimed Tucker. "See here, my brand new membership card."

"Oh, yes, Mr. Elliott, Mr. Aldeworth let me know you'd be stopping on. So pleased to have you as a member now, sir. May I show you to a table?"

"Of course... Miss Emma," he said, reading her name tag. "And please bring us each a bottle of your Brooklands ale. Cheers, love."

Emma scurried off while Tucker and Tolliver settled into their seats and observed the other patrons. Different discussions were wafting through the bar, but nothing had to do with the events of the Concorde party. Emma returned in no time with the ale and a bright smile.

"Will there be anything else, sir?"

"Well, I was just wondering..."

"Yes, sir?"

"How is everyone doing after the, uh, incident the other night. You know, the Concorde party. I know it must have been an awful shock for you all."

Emma looked over her shoulder and around the bar before lowering her voice to Tucker and Tolliver.

"We're not supposed to discuss it, sir, but since it's you asking, it's been quite a trial here. What with constables running all through the building and the bar and questioning us over and over. I swear we don't know anything helpful."

"See, the one thing you must understand, Miss Emma, is that you may think you don't know anything helpful, but even one small detail could change the course of the whole investigation. Did you know that?"

"Why, no, sir. I couldn't even think. Whatever would we know that the police haven't found out?"

"That's the beauty of it, you see. One never knows what small detail may have been noticed but nothing thought of it. Let's see, for example, that night, Dame Abbington had been out here chatting with other guests when we left her. When we came back from our tour, she was sitting at the end of the patio by herself. As you all mingled amongst the attendees, any one of you could have seen something that didn't quite fit but thought nothing of it. Understand?"

"Oh, yes, sir, but I don't recall anything out of the ordinary. Just guests being guests; ladies chatting with other ladies, men talking motor cars, couples discussing their recent trips."

"What did you notice Dame Flora talking about?"

He could see the wheels turning in the girl's head and hoped for all that work, she might recollect something, no matter how small.

"No, sir. She was just out there on the patio chatting away like a canary."

"What was she chatting about, Emma?"

"Oh, I don't think I'd like to say, Mr. Elliott."

"She was gossiping about the murder, wasn't she?"

"Yes, sir. It was quite... brazen, really."

That was the second time "brazen" had been used to describe Flora and her behavior. Tucker thought it was an interesting observation.

"How, so?"

Again, Emma looked around the bar and her tables before lowering her voice and setting down her tray.

"She said she knew who killed the man. The one who was at your tea gala. Mr. Weatherford. And that they should watch their step."

"Yes, Emma, we overheard that as well. We thought it foolish to spout off that kind of claim. Foolish and dangerous. Obviously, it was for her. Who else did she talk to? Anyone in particular that you may have noticed?"

"Let's see, she was talking with that nice couple, the Tiptons, and Sir Harrington and his wife, Lady Harrington, and I saw her talking with Candace, and then she left to go to the toilet. I heard her say she was woozy from the champagne."

Tucker shifted closer to Emma while Tolliver leaned in to hear more clearly.

"Do you remember when that was, Emma?"

"Oh, yes, sir. The passengers from the first Concorde tour had started to come into the bar, and the others were going downstairs for their turn. We were to be alert because it would get busy again."

"When did she come back to the bar?"

"I don't really know. I was rushing about, and I don't remember seeing her until..." she finished with a visible shudder and shook her head. "It wasn't until Mrs. Elliott and you found her."

"Emma! These are for table eighteen, please," said the girl at the bar.

"Thank you! I have to run, sir. Sorry I couldn't be more helpful."

"Please don't be sorry; you've been a great help, love."

Tucker sipped his beer and digested this latest tidbit. Tolliver did the same, wondering how it all fit together.

"She was woozy and went to the toilet. Then she was dead. What did she do in between the time?"

"I don't know, sir, but we need to look at the security tapes for the bar and patio. Maybe they'll show us to whom she was speaking and for how long."

"Yes, exactly," said Tucker, chewing his nail. "That's where Alex is, isn't it?"

"Yes, sir. He was trying to dig up information on the mechanic chap. Could be difficult since he wasn't here for long. Not even any forms on him, from what the garage chap said."

"Give it a thought, Tolliver. Anyone here you don't recognize? Someone who didn't seem to fit in?"

"I'm not sure I could pinpoint that, sir. Not without the tapes."

"Finish your beer, Tolliver. It's time to visit security."

###

They came down the hall, stopped in front of the old security room, and grinned. They had thought this was the place where the answers were. It had taken them a minute to get used to the fact that this was just a side room—no live scanning screens, just a lovely display of a bygone time and a place to watch videos out of the way of the live security team. They found Alex immersed in tapes, pen and paper next to him, with various notes scrawled across the top.

"Hullo, there," said Tucker, tapping on the door.

"Oh, please, come in. I've been scouring these bloody things with hardly a sign of anything useful. Dashed disappointing. How are you getting on?"

"We were enjoying a bottle of your Goldstar ale. Marvelous stuff. So, nothing helpful here?"

"Not anything new, you know. I went back to look at the person who had sneaked into the outside building during the tea gala, but nothing more conclusive than what we had. He's got to be connected with all this. Couldn't possibly be a coincidence."

"I don't believe in coincidences, Alex, and you shouldn't either. Have you looked at the tapes of the Concorde tour?"

"No, I was just getting to those. Why? Are you onto something?" he asked hopefully.

"Not sure, but it's worth a hard look, right?"

Tucker and Tolliver related their chat with Miss Emma in the bar and the fact that she thought she knew nothing.

"And she said all that and still didn't think it important? We'll have to question every server in the place, you know."

"Yes, yes, we will. And I should think before DCI Campbell has a chance to scare them half to death. May we please see the tapes from the bar area?"

"Yes, they should be right over here. I'll have to look at the camera angles. I'm not sure how many are up there or which ones are on the patio. Just a minute."

They watched eagerly as he flipped switches. Monitors blinked on and off, showing views of the museum from different locations. Finally, he settled on a couple of angles that featured the bar and patio area, where patrons could be seen mingling, walking in and out, and interacting with the servers.

"These are quite useful. You can see exactly which guests are being served by which servers and where they're spending most of their time. Oh, there's Flora over by the doorway where we left her."

"If I may, sir, I see the Tiptons, the Harringtons, as well as Miss Bimmi, Miss Sommers, and there's Miss Candace just inside the bar."

"Yes, that's where we ran into her as we were leaving for the tour. She was checking on things upstairs. Let's see how long she stayed in the bar."

They watched as guests weaved in and around each other, stopping to hug and chat. Flora flitted like a butterfly from one group to the next, pollinating her outrageous story about knowing the killer's identity.

"There's Candace. She's meeting, greeting, smiling, nodding, and now she's talking to Flora. She's listening to her tell her story. Oh my, she looks gobsmacked. Well, I think that's how most everyone reacted to her, quite honestly."

At that point, Candace moved beside Flora and bent to listen to her with her arm around her shoulder. Her back was to the camera, and they lost whatever vantage point they had to see their faces and their conversation.

"There's Emma," said Tucker. "She's stepped in between them now. She's refilling Flora's glass. Whoops, that's quite a bubble explosion. What a horrid waste of champagne."

They watched as Flora was flicking her champagne-covered hand and bobbing for the glass to sip the overflow. Emma handed her a cloth napkin and apologized profusely. Flora waved her off, and Candace maneuvered her to a seat where she could sit and properly dry her hands.

"Now, Candace is giving her a small pat and moving through the crowd again. Well, nothing really telling, is there?"

They noted several other guests watching Flora as she guzzled champagne and patted her face with the napkin. The lights had been dimmed in a party fashion, and it was getting harder to make out faces and names in the low light.

"Wait, sir. She's getting up; she's heading for the bar. There's Emma pointing her in the direction of the toilet; she teeters through the door and off to the ladies' room."

They observed more wandering patrons, cheerful servers, and exclamations of delight over the exhilarating Concorde tour. It had been a boring ten minutes or so until they caught sight of a flamboyant orange gown stepping onto the patio. Dame Abbington was back in all her colorful glory. They could see the outline of someone wrangling her in, taking her hand, and chatting with her as she laughed and waved them away. Guests were starting to move inside as the wind picked up, and the air was chilling down. They watched as the orange Flora blob moved to the railing before her, then off to the side. It was here that the camera angle cut off, and they could no longer see Dame Flora.

"So there's no footage of anything that happened in that area. I don't understand. She was bludgeoned with a bottle for God's sake. Why can't we see it?" fumed Alex.

Just then, a figure came out from the far doors of the patio. It was hidden in shadow and moved quickly to the railing. It was difficult to tell if it was a man or a woman. They then pressed themselves against the rail, out of the camera view.

"Bloody hell! Why can't we see who it is? I shall have them adjust these angles so we have a proper view of the whole area before the gala," said Alex. "You can't tell who or what it is."

"Obviously, they went down to where Flora had taken a seat, and the rest is what we know," said Tolliver. "We just have to watch for this person to go back the way they came and return to the bar."

They watched, and they waited, and they watched some more. But no one returned the way they had come. From the bar or otherwise.

32

Chapter 32

Mark Halliday: Well, you forget detection and concentrate on crime. Crime's the thing. And then you imagine you're going to steal something or murder somebody.

Tony Wendice: Oh, is that how you do it? It's interesting.

Mark Halliday: Yes, I usually put myself in the criminal's shoes and then I keep asking myself, uh, what do I do next?
-Dial M for Murder, 1954

"We are days away from the relaunch, and we have no idea what's happening here," said Alene Elliot.

"Oh, I wouldn't exactly say that, Mother. We have a murder by poison, an attempted murder with the same substance, and a bludgeon death of the county gossip. I think we have some idea as to what's happened."

"Do shut up, Tucker, you're not being the least bit helpful. But thank you for the chilling recap. Now, can we get down to business, please?"

"Of course, Mother, what did you have in mind?"

"We have a gala coming up, I hope. Any news from DCI Campbell?"

"Not so far. I think he has his hands full," said Laird. "I saw McCallum yesterday, but it's too soon to have any information on Flora. They're knee deep in champagne bottles and not even sure what they're looking for."

"And even though Miss Audrey has recovered, we don't know any more than we did before. I should think she's still at risk," said Tolliver. "It's not enough to have the murder weapon. We need to know who used it and why, ma'am."

"What about Weatherford? The same questions apply to him. Even with everything we've tried to do, we're still no further along in finding out what happened there," said Reggie.

"Something has to gel here," said Laird. "We have facts, actions, and theories. Something has to tie it all together to point to someone."

"What if it's not just a someone?" said Dulcy. "What if it's more than one someone? There's got to be a common thread. We just have to find it."

"Well, what have we got?" asked Tucker. "Let's see, Reggie, take a note."

"Really, boss? Got a pen and paper?" she asked, feeling the sleekness of her skin-tight dress.

"I'll do it," said Laird, taking out the ever-present small notepad and pen.

"Let's see; we'll start from the beginning. In order, we have:

- J. Winston Weatherford, murder victim
- botulinum toxin, weapon
- mysterious cup that disappears and reappears, but we know why now

- Water pitcher that turns out to only be a water pitcher
- Cameras that show mostly nothing except for one character sneaking into one of the buildings - man or woman?
- Alex's crash on the track
- Cut brake line
- Alene finds Weatherford's paperwork is hers
- Bella and Roswyn are questioned by Alene with no outcome
- Weatherford funeral, where the vial shows up again
- Audrey is poisoned with the same vial
- Tucker and Reggie go to Audrey's and find the top to the vial
- A sample of a beverage is taken off the nightstand for analysis
- The Concorde Experience and the murder of Flora Abbington
- Fatal blow to the head
- One earring found near the body
- A champagne cork found under her dress
- Awaiting toxicology reports on Flora
- Forensics working with champagne bottles
- Review of security tapes provides little information

"But what ties any of it together?" asked Dahlia.

"That's the big question," said Dulcy. "There's no way to get anywhere without knowing why. If we knew that, then we'd probably know who."

"It seems impossible. Nothing fits together. Maybe we should call DCI Campbell. He must have information we don't. It's just getting him to share it, and that will be difficult," said Reggie.

A slight knock outside the study rattled the group. The door opened, and Myra stuck her head in, bristling slightly as they stared her down.

"Beg pardon, ma'am, but it's the DCI gentleman as wants to see ya. Shall I let him in, then?"

"Oh, of course, Myra. Well, bless me, just who we needed. And you don't hear me say that ever."

The door swung wide, and in strode DCI Campbell, who stopped up short as they continued to stare.

"Blimey, the lot of you all together. Saves me a bit of time, that does."

"What can we do for you, Inspector?" asked Alene.

"We need to have a bit of a chat. We have some new information and now another murder, so things do seem to be going in the wrong direction."

Alene shifted uncomfortably in her chair and shot Tucker a warning glance.

"There goes our launch," thought Tucker.

"Please, Inspector, have a seat. I have a feeling this is going to take some time," said Alene.

"We were just putting all our facts together, Campbell," said Laird. "We're trying to find a common tie that will point to someone and provide us with a motive. So far, nothing."

"I see. Well, we've been having a day with our champagne bottles and have come up with very little as well."

"What did you hope to find, Campbell?" asked Tucker.

"Well, we have nothing forensically as we've yet to find any hair, skin, or blood on any of 'em. Obviously, someone wiped the murder weapon. Even a bottle with smudged fingerprints or traces of evidence would be ideal, but we're not seeing that either. There is one thing we found, and this is a crucial bit of something, let me tell you."

"Go on," urged Reggie.

"We combed the area and managed to find the old Dame's champagne glass. Fingerprints were positive, but so was something else. Her glass turned up with Dilantin in the residue. Not something the average person would be quaffing at a party."

"I've heard of it, but exactly what is it?" asked Dulcy.

"It's a drug for epileptics, an anti-seizure medication, if you like. Causes drowsiness or sleepiness, ya see."

"So if she took it with alcohol, it would accelerate the effects," said Laird. "Explains the video a bit, doesn't it?"

"What video?"

"In the security tapes we viewed, we see server Emma refilling Flora's glass. It fizzes up, and she has to sip it to stop the overflow. She does seem a bit unsteady after that, but we all thought she was indulging too much."

"So that if someone wanted to whack her on the side of the head with a bottle, she'd be too stupefied to realize it," said Tucker.

"That's right. At her age, she just might be dropping off to sleep within fifteen minutes and wouldn't have the wherewithal to fight someone off. It'd be an easy piece of work just to walk up and do the job. In that dark corner, with all the chatter and people moving indoors, no one would see it. She'd likely not scream out. Our murderer just slips away, and Bob's your uncle."

"Oh, poor Flora," said Alene, squeezing Douglass's hand. "She never could keep her mouth shut."

"What about the photo?" asked Laird.

"Yes, anything on the mechanic chap?" added Tucker.

"He was not in the books. No record, or he just hasn't been caught yet. And as far as the earring goes, we didn't find anyone with missing jewelry. We're looking at prints and DNA now."

"That leaves us right where we started, then. Well, except for having another body," said Reggie.

"And Audrey would have made three. Is your man Petry still on her?" asked Tucker.

Reggie smirked, causing him to redden and rephrase his question.

"Is the man still guarding her?"

"He's not exclusively watching her, but I think she's still in danger. We don't know who dosed her. And dose her someone did. The residue you brought us was indeed the botulinum toxin, Miss Reggie."

"So who cleaned the cup?"

"Still out there for us to sort out."

"What about Weatherford?" asked Tucker.

"We know a lot of people were not keen on the man. We need to inspect his business dealings to find out who he may have cheated or offended, which could end up being a rather long list. The gent was just a plain wanker it seems. Even his missus didn't like him."

Alene had listened to all this with as much detachment as possible, but the time had come to jump in with both feet. Her launch was at stake, and they needed a plan.

"So, Inspector, what type of infiltration are you planning for our gala this weekend? We've much the same guest list as the first one, with some minor exceptions due to schedules, but I would think your murderer will be in the midst of things. How shall we flush him out?"

"Or her," said Reggie.

"You're hell bent on proceeding with this, aren't you, Mrs. Elliott? My inclination would be to stop the whole thing, but if we do that, then we may never find the guilty party. So, I'm going to let you have your tea gala, but make no mistake - we will be there in force looking for any wrong move by anybody. I also urge extreme caution with this killer loose. Two deaths and three attempted murders spell desperation in my book. We need to know who's desperate."

They looked at each other, trying to imagine what person out there could be so anxious to keep something hidden.

"I think we need to continue to review personnel files," said Tucker. "Tolliver, I know you're working on that, and hopefully, you'll find a small spec somewhere that'll lead us to someone."

Tolliver had remained silent, considering a new angle. It's probably not the employees they should be worrying about but the former employees. Wouldn't the same go for the Weatherford company? Who held a grudge, besides most people who knew the irritating old man?

"I have a plan, sir. And with your permission, I would like to interview Bella and Roswyn. I believe I have some new questions for them."

"Whatever you need, mate. We're getting down to the wire here. Thank you, DCI Campbell, for working with us on this. Mother, why don't you ask Olivia to tea and see what she might have on present and former employees."

"I'll be going, then," said Campbell. "If anything comes up, you must call me. I'll be reviewing the security tapes. We'll need to reposition some of those cameras so the area has better coverage. Can't have any more of this missing corners malarkey. Ta."

He abruptly exited the study, and with a slam of the front door, he was gone.

###

The rush of activity leading to the launch brought few leads and little new information. They felt as though they would never sort out the facts. Tensions were high, along with the anticipation of the gala, and time was running out for them to solve the puzzles before the six p.m. party.

Tea with Olivia turned into scotch with Olivia and a promise to put her man onto the personnel files, old and new, in hopes of finding some connection. The research documents were still buried in their respective safes, and although it was a breach of confidence and ethics, it paled in comparison with the murderous activities of late. The documents would stay hidden, bound by a tacit agreement between the two women.

Tolliver had met with Bella and Roswyn, but not before combing through their personnel files for background and work history. What little he found could have had either of them guilty of securing botulinum toxin from previous or past work connections or helping someone else to do so. He decided to plod back through the files of those other than the lab assistants and was headed back to the computer when he ran into Audrey at the elevator.

"Hello, Miss. How are you feeling today? Getting back up to par, I hope?"

"Oh, yes, Tolliver, much better today, thank you."

"Do you need any help with launch plans?"

"Oh, I don't think so. I'll be running out to Brooklands shortly to meet with Candace. We're adding some special touches for the guests this time."

"We'll also be needing to adjust the cameras, Miss. We want to make sure there are no dead spots," he said, instantly regretting his word choice.

"Of course. I'm sure Alex will be happy to do whatever we need."

Tolliver returned to his computer, wondering if Audrey had nerves about the poisoner still on the loose. If she did, she wasn't showing them. Tucker and Reggie were relaxing in the conservatory at the Porters' with Dahlia, Dulcy, and Laird. Jennings was gliding in and out with refreshments but also keeping an eye on them. They were out of sorts and stymied. It was a state that Tucker was never very good with. Reggie was preoccupied with Audrey's safety but had no suggestions. Dulcy was working a crossword puzzle while Laird was contemplating the missing earring. All they had were suppositions.

"What's a six-letter word for deadly brew?" asked Dulcy.

"Really, Dulcy? Forest? Trees?" said Reggie. "It's poison. How ironic."

"No, it's got nothing to do with woods but... oh, I see. The answer is poison."

Dulcy scribbled down the word, rested back in her chair, and tossed the puzzle aside. A light mist fell outside, making the room feel dark and damp despite the cozy foliage and full-length windows.

"Alright then, let's change the subject, shall we? What are you lovelies wearing Saturday?"

"Well, I'm wearing my new woolen suit," said Tucker.

Dahlia gave him a glare that would have soured milk as Laird grinned behind his notebook.

"Certainly nothing orange," remarked Dulcy.

"I'm thinking about shopping," said Reggie. "Who wants to go, other than Mr. Woolen Suit here?"

"Oooo, I'd love an outing rather than sitting here in the rainy day gloom. I know just the place. C'mon, ladies. Let's leave these young men to it and have a spree."

"I thought they'd never leave," said Tucker. "Jennings! Two scotches, neat, please."

"Here's to a quiet afternoon," said Laird as they clinked their glasses and reveled in the peace of the conservatory.

###

Forty-five minutes later, the rain had subsided, and the women were window shopping on the High Street. The specialty shops and boutiques were mesmerizing with their trendy fashions and accessories. They were enjoying their leisurely afternoon shopping crawl.

"Hey!" said Reggie. "There's Candace."

"Where?"

"Right over there by that little dress shop. She must be shopping for the party as well."

They watched her at a window display and then move on to the next as if the windows would answer her questions. It wasn't until she came closer and entered the local pharmacy that something about her seemed different.

"That's not Candace," said Dahlia.

"Of course it is. It's the same reddish hair, glasses, and jerky way she moves. That's our Candace," said Reggie.

"That's Lydia Kent-Williams," said Dahlia. "C'mon. If I'm not right, I'll buy you both a round at the pub down the street."

The ladies marched across the road and peered through the pharmacy glass.

"I don't see her," said Dulcy. "She must've gone to the back."

"Let's go," said Dahlia.

"No, she'll think we're stalking her. Plus I don't want to have to get into a conversation," said Reggie. "Did you know Tucker still has her number in his phone?"

"No, I didn't. Hmmm, well then, you go wait in the pub, my dear, and Dulcy and I will track her down."

"Not on your life. I'm going with you," she said, shoving Dahlia toward the door.

As they entered, a tiny bell tinkled, and Reggie wanted to ignore it as the woman behind the counter greeted them.

"Can I help ya there?"

"Uh, no, just picking up a couple of things. Thank you, though."

They were looking at the aisle markers, trying to decide which one when Reggie nudged Dahlia and moved behind her. Dulcy retreated down the first aisle and beckoned Reggie to follow. Dahlia kept an eye on the girl while pretending to examine the available hosiery. She watched as Lydia chose an eye powder and lipstick and went to the check-out. She was oblivious to anyone else. She casually left the shop, turning to the right on the High Street.

"Follow her," said Reggie, pushing Dahlia toward the exit.

"Whatever for? She's just shopping. Get hold of yourself there, love. You're just pissy because she dated your boss, and that was years ago."

"Yes, I'm sure you're right. I see happy hour starting somewhere. Out you go!" she said, thanking the woman at the register.

They walked out into the brisk air,, bracing themselves against the cold. Someplace close would be ideal. It was good that there were public houses on every corner.

"Right up there. That looks like a cozy little pub."

They found a nice corner with an overstuffed couch and a ratty wooden table that looked as though it had been there since the Norman conquest. Dulcy volunteered to go to the bar, and Reggie and Dahlia sank into the cushions and organized their parcels.

"Here we are. Three pints of Taylor's," said Dulcy, placing them on the uneven slats of the table."

"Don't look now, but there she is," said Reggie, nodding her head toward the bartender.

Sitting at the corner of the mahogany bar next to a well-built young man, Lydia Kent-Williams swirled a large glass of red wine and listened intently to her companion. They were in deep conversation, heads bent together, oblivious to their surroundings.

"Wouldn't you like to know what's going on there?" purred Dahlia, leaning over the table.

"Not especially," said Reggie, quaffing her beer and turning her back on the couple."

"You know she'll be at the tea gala. You'll have to meet her sooner or later."

"Let's make it later, shall we?" she said, taking a healthy measure of beer.

They were enjoying their beverages and going over gala details when Lydia and her gentleman friend slid off their stools and headed for the exit. Reggie lowered her gaze and watched out of the corner of her eye as they passed dangerously close to their table. When they had reached the door, the young man shifted to usher Lydia before him. As he turned briefly toward them, Reggie had a flare of recognition. Where had she seen this man before? He looked vaguely familiar. She shook it off and went back to her drink. Maybe it would come to her later.

"Oh, they're gone," noticed Dulcy.

"Yes, they just left a minute ago."

"What's up, Reg? You have an odd look on your face," said Dahlia.

"Maybe it's just gas from the beer," chuckled Dulcy.

"It's nothing. Something struck me, but I can't put my finger on it. Probably just my overactive imagination."

"Oh, something new," laughed Dahlia. "Alright lasses, my turn for the round."

33

Chapter 33

My world was calm, well-ordered, exemplary. Then came this person with chaos in her wake.
-Mary Poppins, 1964

As they walked into the Edwardian Club, it was a deja vu moment. The tea sample table was again off to the left. Guests milled about, and laughter and congratulations filled the room, just as before. Eerily present as ever was the friendship bench out front, which served as the official greeter. Missing from the landscape were J. Winston Weatherford and Dame Flora Abbington. The party was definitely not diminished by this circumstance, and Tucker was pleased that everyone had accepted the hurried invitation.

"May I say that you look even more stunning than usual, Miss Winter?" said Tucker.

"Yes, you may, except that you should say it louder since no one else heard you."

He steered her toward a bar station and ordered scotches neat. He was observing the scene when Dulcy, John, Dahlia, and a handsome newcomer seeped into their midst.

"Hello, all. May I introduce Spencer Evans? He and I met at the Concorde party, and he was lovely enough to escort me this evening. Spencer, may I present Miss Regina Winter and Tucker Elliott?"

"Yes, I'm well aware of Mr. Elliott's accomplishments," said Spencer, shaking Tucker's hand. "Nice to meet you, Miss Regina."

"And what accomplishments might those be, Mr. Evans? The ones in the business sector or the 'other headlines'?"

"Both, actually. I have enjoyed reading about all of your... feats."

"Brilliant. Don't let him near Mother, will you?" whispered Tucker in Reggie's ear.

Reggie was only half-listening as she scanned the crowd for the high-profile guests she knew Tucker would need to greet. She was also looking for not only Candace but also Lydia Kent-Williams. After all, she had a new shade of lipstick to preview this evening, and Reggie wanted to see how it complemented her brilliant red hair. She glanced over the tops of the evening dresses and tuxes and spied a well-turned-out Candace in an attractive off-the-shoulder green gown with generous layers of fabric in soft folds. Her hair seemed lighter, and she wondered how she could have mistaken Lydia for her.

"Look there, Tucker, there's Audrey with her bodyguard, Constable Petry."

"He looks more like a lovesick puppy, if you ask me."

"Don't be mean. I think it's sweet of him to dote on her like that."

"I dote on you that way, love. And I don't look lovesick."

Reggie laughed and pecked Tucker on the cheek.

"I love how you can always make me laugh. Let's just hope he remembers what he's really here for. I take it DCI Campbell is hiding out in the security center?"

Tucker was still working through her laughing at him when the man himself popped into the doorway toward the back of the club.

"Everything alright there, Campbell?" he said, sidling up to the copper.

"Oh, quite. Just getting a bead on the company you're keeping. Anything interesting happening?"

"Lord, I hope not. Let's pray everyone behaves this time 'round and we find out something useful instead of ending up with another body."

DCI Campbell winced and glared ominously at Tucker, who was well aware of it but ignored the insulting stare. He hoped that he had not jinxed his own gala.

"Who's minding the store if you're lounging out here?" Tucker asked.

"My men are everywhere, Elliott. Don't you see?"

Tucker surveyed the room and indeed noticed elegantly dressed men and women filtering through the honored guests. The communication cords spiraling out of their ears were a dead giveaway. As he ticked off the guest list in his head, his attention was captured by a demure beauty speaking with a rather tall gentleman from the bottom stair of the member bar steps. Was that...?

"Campbell, look just there. On the lower stair, speaking with the tallish gent with the glass of champagne. It's Lydia Kent-Williams."

"Yaass, I see," he said, taking out his notebook.

A flip of a few pages revealed a short dossier on the young lady, which included not only her appointment with the Farthing's Fine Tea firm but a notation Tucker must have missed from earlier discussions.

"Does that say Weatherford?"

"Yes, it does. I wanted to talk to you about that. Did you know that she held a post with his company in the research and development area?"

"No, I did not. I thought she went back into a more specialized field, you know, cosmetic chemistry, or some such pastime."

"Not a pastime but a full-blown position with his brands until she apparently was sacked. She seems to have quite a few of those, with Weatherford's being the last in a healthy line of them."

"Don't tell me; she was using company materials for her own pet projects."

"Yes. Apparently when the old man found out, she was out the door like shit through a goose."

"Thank you for the lovely visual, Inspector. Where did she go from there?"

DCI Campbell handed Tucker the notebook while he fished for his pencil in his rumpled tux. Tucker was just happy to see that he actually knew what a tux was.

"I don't see anything here. Where is she working now?"

"She appears to be in between engagements," said Campbell.

"Well, keep an eye on her. I was actually surprised to see that Mother invited her to this bash after what she'd just learned."

"Yeah, right. I believe, according to your mum, that's the reason she's here, so we'll be watching."

DCI Campbell slipped off to the security center while Tucker leaned against the wall, observing the guests. He watched as Olivia Weatherford gave Alene a hug and moved off to her next greeting. Dulcy and Laird were enjoying Chef Dumont's lavish hors d'oeuvres. Dulcy chatted happily while Laird brooded over the roomful of attendees. Tucker shook his head and chuckled at the man's predictability.

"Reggie! Over this way, love. What are you up to, then?"

"I've been playing detective," she said, a mischievous glint in her eyes.

"I thought we agreed you'd behave."

"I am behaving, honestly. Oh, look, Lydia Kent-Williams, Tucker. Why do you still have her number in your phone contacts, by the way?"

"I don't, I mean I did, although it came up the other day, didn't it? I thought I'd deleted that," he finished weakly.

"Did I tell you we saw her on the High Street?" she continued, ignoring his discomfort. "She was shopping and then met a young man for a drink at the Black Horse. She didn't see us, but we saw her. I could swear I knew the man she was with, Tucker, but I just couldn't place him."

"Crikey, Reg, shopping and a drink. Shall I have Campbell slap the cuffs on her this minute?"

"Ass. Don't take me seriously, then. Just you wait; I'll solve this before you do."

She flicked her hand at him and flounced into the crowd as Tucker watched appreciatively. He still had his eye on her when he saw Candace talking with Alex. They looked engrossed in a deep conversation interspersed with wild gestures and wide eyes. He wondered what could be so intense on such a festive occasion. He followed Reggie toward them, then swung away at the last minute.

"What did I just hear?" he thought, glancing back at Candace's streaming hair. His imagination was getting the better of him.

"Tucker! Come over here, please," said Reggie. "You need to settle a bet."

He glanced again at Alex and Candace, who seemed to have calmed down. It was probably just his runaway imagination. A quick round of the venue confirmed that all was well, and the guests were having a wonderful time.

"Must get a hold of myself," he said.

"Regina, love, with what may I assist?" he said, darting another glance at Alex and Candace, who were no longer where he had spotted them.

"Tucker, please correct me. I say Farthing's was established in 1662 when Catherine of Braganza came over from Portugal to marry Charles. She brought tea then, and it became so popular that 'afternoon tea' soon became all the rage. Tucker? Did you hear me?"

"Oh, yes, it was back then. The early Farthing's hopped on the wagon and started working with India to bring it here under our name," he said distractedly, staring across the room.

"Thank you, Tucker. Would you please excuse us?" said Reggie, pulling him by the coat sleeve to a quiet corner.

"What the hell was that, boss? Are you okay?"

"You only use 'boss' when you're trying to reprimand me for something, Reg. Listen, I think..."

A tap on a glass and a high pitch of the microphone stopped him from completing his sentence. When he looked again, Candace was standing with Audrey, smiling and waving as Alene was about to start her welcome speech. Again.

"Oh, no worries, Reg. I think my mind is running away with me. It's just that I thought..."

"Welcome, friends, neighbors, patrons, and family. I'm so glad you could join us tonight for our... tea launch... again," she said, chuckling.

There was a wave of polite laughter as the crowd remembered the eerie events of the previous gala. Alene took heart and continued her speech.

"I'd like to thank Brooklands Museum for their hospitality and their never-ending patience. Please remember to join or renew your membership to help preserve this unique place in time and history. Now, if you'll indulge me, we are proud to present our newest line of teas. You'll find them all presented on the table to your left. Please help yourself to the sample packets and the prepared demi cups that the servers are circulating among you. And don't forget to look for these fine teas coming to a shelf near you. Thank you all for coming, and cheers!"

Tucker heaved a sigh of relief while squeezing Reggie's hand. She pressed back, both of them blotting out the memory of what had happened at the last gala.

"Blimey," said Tucker, exhaling. "Don't think I realized just how stressful that bit was last time. You alright there?"

"Yes, I'm fine, but what were you about to say to me before she spoke? You're not your usual self, Tucker, and I was afraid something had happened again."

"Come over here with me. Where's Dahlia, Dulcy, and Laird?"

"They're right over there talking with Douglass and the Porters. Tucker, what is it?"

"Do you see Candace and Alex?" he said, bobbing his head like a nervous bird.

"They were right there a minute ago, but... they're gone. I'm sure there was something they needed to see to. C'mon, boss, don't run crazy on me now."

Tucker nodded and squeezed Reggie's arm while he scoured the crowd for Lydia Kent-Williams. He was not feeling well in his body or his spirit.

"Oh, sir, there you are," said Jennings. "This way, Mr. Tolliver, he's over here."

Tucker remembered seeing Jennings running interference here and there, but it was the first time he'd seen Tolliver all night. The thought spooked him, and he wondered why he was so late arriving for such a big event.

"Tolliver! Where've you been, mate? I don't recall seeing you at all. What've you been up to?"

"I must speak with you, sir, and you, Miss Reggie, if you have a moment. I think it may be most important, possibly a threat to the event tonight."

"Well, when you put it that way. Where have you been? Let's just step over here."

"I'm glad to know you missed me, sir, but what I have to say may change the course of the evening."

"C'mon, Reg, let's go. Jennings, stay close, please."

Tucker led them to an alcove where they could be seen but not heard. He had a rather sick feeling in his stomach. Unbeknownst to him, Reggie had the same feeling.

"Sir, it's the personnel files. You know, I was digging deeper into them, and I found something unusual."

"Which would be?"

Tucker always wished that those dispensing the bad news would get to the point quickly and efficiently.

"Miss Lydia Kent-Williams, sir. I took the liberty of reading through her file and then casting the net a bit further, if you can forgive the fishing analogy."

"Tolliver!"

"I decided that an extensive background check was in order. It seems that jumping from job to job is not her only outstanding characteristic, in addition to a state hospital stay, sir."

At that point, Reggie began quivering and jabbing at Tucker's coat sleeve.

"Yes, love, I know, he needs to speed it up a bit. Will you please just wait one minute while he gets to the point?"

"Tucker, I know where I saw the man who was with Lydia at the Black Swan. Because there he is, and the last time I saw him was in the mechanic's garage the day I spun out in the Austin Healey."

Jennings was off like a shot, with a serving tray and an attitude, following the man Reggie pointed out. He was casually sauntering through the crowd as if on holiday, and Jennings was now hot on his trail.

"Alright, love, Jennings has that one. Now, Tolliver, go on, please."

"There's a reason you all think there's a connection somewhere," he said, hurrying in a truly un-Tolliver-like fashion. "Sir, Miss Kent-Williams and Candace Corbyn are sisters, in fact, twins."

"Oh, my God," said Reggie. "No wonder we thought we saw Candace yesterday. Oh, my gosh! The green eyes, the glasses..."

"Both of them with contact lenses," added Tucker.

"Her hair was different tonight," said Reggie. "Candace's hair was lighter. It wasn't as brassy red as Lydia's. They have the same movements, the same gestures. How did we not see it before?"

"If I may say, sir, Miss Lydia is dangerous. She's a bit of a chameleon and has quite the history. She was also a Weatherford employee who was dismissed under rather suggestive circumstances."

"Yes, Tolliver, I think we're starting to see the trend. Where's Candace?" he asked.

“I saw her head toward the cafe, sir,” said Tolliver.

“Where’s Alex?” asked Reggie.

“He was with Candace the last time I saw them. It was some minutes ago now.”

“And where is Miss Kent-Williams, sir? There’s something else you should know. She was not only a Weatherford employee, but there were questions of... harassment during her time there. It could be a powerful motive, sir.”

Tucker spotted Laird leaning against an automotive display while Dulcy chattered away to an older couple. One raise of his eyebrows and Laird was across the room before Dulcy could break her conversation.

“What’s happening?”

“Dunno, but stick close. We’re looking for Candace, Lydia, and Alex.”

“I saw Alex and Candace head towards the member bar. Get up those stairs, Elliott,” he said, drawing his gun.

“I just hope we’re in time,” said Tucker as he and Laird shot up the stairs with Reggie bringing up the rear.

###

In the security center, DCI Campbell was watching the events unfold on the video screens. He located his closest constable and made his move.

“Walters, we have a situation. Member bar, now. Collins, you have the center here. Keep a watch on these screens and call for backup. Jennings is out there with his eye on the other chap."

He shot from the room, taking the stairs two at a time. The scene in the bar was like a movie. The audience was frozen in place, watching as Lydia Kent-Williams held Candace and Alex at gunpoint. He nudged his way to Tucker and placed a hand on his shoulder.

"No sudden movements. She's obviously unhinged, and any interference could cause her to use that."

Tucker held onto Reggie while Laird kept his hand on his gun. Constable Walters edged closer to the scene as Tolliver filled in his space.

"Lydia, please," began Candace.

"Shut up, you twit. You couldn't do as you were told, could you? Instead, you left him alive with everything he knows," she said, pointing the gun at Alex.

"I told you I wouldn't tell a soul," said Alex softly.

"And then you tried to blackmail me, the both of you. You think I didn't know what you were doing behind my back?" she shrieked as the two cowered before her.

"Lydia, please see reason. We never blackmailed you. It's all in your mind. You'll never get away with any of it. Everyone knows now," said Alex. "Why don't you just hand me that gun, and we'll get you some help?"

As Alex reached for the weapon, a shot rang through the bar, and Alex crumpled to the floor, Candace flinging herself next to him.

"You there! Stop!" yelled DCI Campbell as the scene turned to chaos.

Laird trained his gun on the woman, but to everyone's surprise, she pressed a button, an entryway opened behind her, and she was gone. Constable Walters had raced to Alex, moving Candace away while Laird kept an eye on her. Sirens could be heard in the distance while Alex writhed in pain on the ground.

"What was that?" said Reggie, watching Walters staunch the flow of blood on Alex's shoulder. "Where'd she go?"

"Jennings!" yelled Campbell into his radio. "Where are you?"

A rasp, then a calm, controlled voice, rang out over the radio.

"DCI Campbell, she's down here. It was a dumbwaiter. She's with Stewart, and they're heading for a motorbike. I've alerted the other constables."

"Who's Stewart?" asked Reggie.

"The mechanic chap," said Campbell. "They're barmy if they think they can run. Let's go, Walters."

Walters joined Campbell as the others rushed to Alex's side, making sure he lay still. Candace was huddled in a heap, crying and shaking.

"It's alright, Candace, they'll catch her. I think Alex will be okay, but he's starting to go into shock. Where are those EMTs?"

In the distance, the sirens were getting closer, breaking the quiet of the country night on their way once again to Brooklands. Tucker leaned over the patio railing as the scene outside took a crazy turn. A wave of rising voices could be heard floating up the stairs from the guests, as they began to question the unfolding events.

"Stay with them," said Tucker to Laird as he grabbed Reggie's hand and flew down the stairs.

Tucker ran past curious onlookers and past the "friendship bench" to join Alene and Douglass, who were watching the events with the Porters. Dahlia and Dulcy were cornered at the entrance, while constables held back the curious onlookers. The roar of a powerful engine engaged, and DCI Campbell directed his men to follow.

"Stop them now!" he yelled as a motorbike swung out of the paddock, heading for Test Hill and the remnants of the racing course.

"They'll never get out that way," said Reggie. "Test Hill is only good to a point, and then it curves back around to here."

They watched anxiously as the two climbed the darkened hill, followed by Campbell's men. A string of cycles scaled the hill, disappearing into the darkness past the tree-lined viewing area.

"Put those blockades in place at the bottom of the hill!" yelled Campbell as the ambulance broke onto the scene.

Party goers flooded the entrance as the constables pushed them back to make room for the EMTs with their gurney. The onlookers held their breath as the sound of raging engines ricocheted off the hillsides of the overgrown track. DCI Campbell stood locked in place behind the barricades as the motorbike engines grew louder in the near distance.

"Hold fast there, men. You AFOs be ready, but don't shoot unless I give the word."

The engines were coming closer. The noise resembled a large hive of bees bouncing off the wooded hill. One lone cycle was speeding ahead of the bevy of bikes gaining ground, their headlamps lighting the Brooklands night sky. The lead motorbike was approaching the barricades, but rather than slowing, it accelerated, preparing to ram the barriers.

"Take care, gents! They're coming through," yelled Campbell.

As the crowd watched, the lead bike slammed through the barricade, throwing steel barriers across the concrete slabs.

"The tire, Hollins, shoot the tire."

Hollins took aim and, with precision timing, squeezed off a shot. The bike skidded onto the other section of the old course, careened off a tree, and, with a last burst of acceleration, splashed into the river. The sounds of bubbles echoed through the night as the stunned crowd jumped into action.

"Stay back," ordered Campbell, while the team of constables raced to the edge of the river with flashlights.

Reggie buried her face in Tucker's shoulder and gave a short gasp as the party goers all began talking at once. Tucker moved to take a step, but Reggie held him fast.

"You're not going over there, Tucker. There's nothing you can do. Come with me, and let's find Laird."

They pushed through the crowd while shouts of rescue and recovery could be heard on the wooded riverbank. The EMTs were rushing to the newest scene, leaving Laird to monitor Alex. Candace was holding onto him while being questioned by one of Campbell's men. The story would come out, but for now, a sedated Candace would remain with Alex.

"That was quite the event," said Laird, with a sour smirk.

Tucker and Reggie leaned over Alex as he lay still on the cart.

"You've got to stay off these things, mate," said Tucker. "Doesn't do to take a gurney ride every other week."

Alex tried to smile, but only winced as he shut his eyes and held onto Candace's hand. Jennings arrived with his rescue brandy and was handing it out to the group.

"Jennings, where are you getting this stuff? I know they don't serve it here," said Tucker.

Jennings smiled and refilled Tucker's glass as he headed for the stairs to secure the Elliotts. The EMTs came back for Alex, bumping him over the uneven ground to the ambulance. Tucker, Reggie, and Laird followed and poked their heads out the front door for an update.

"There you are!" cried Dulcy. "I was so afraid. I didn't know where you were."

"Just tending to business," he said, grasping her hand and holding it tight.

In the glow of the searchlights, they could see a tired-looking DCI Campbell making his way back to the Edwardian Club. He stopped in front of Tucker and Reggie and shook his head slowly. Tucker could feel Reggie shudder while Dulcy sniffled into Laird's chest.

"You've got a lot to answer for," said Campbell to Candace, who Constable Collins was holding.

She slowly shook her head without meeting his eye.

It was going to be a long night.

34

Chapter 34

Murder's never perfect. Always comes apart sooner or later. And when two people are involved, it's usually sooner.
-Double Indemnity, 1944

It had indeed been a long night and a long couple of days for everyone. Piece by piece, the story came out from Candace, Bella, Roswyn, and Alex, with help from Tolliver's background check. It was a story built over a lifetime that had snared them all.

Laird spent some time with FME McCallum, DCI Campbell, and information from the personnel files Tolliver had so painstakingly uncovered. Dahlia and Dulcy went to Brooklands to cook and deliver age-old tea room recipes for Candace and Alex to use for future fundraising events for the museum. Tucker and Reggie crashed in exhaustion before settling down to work on their upcoming shoe launch in the States. Alene Elliott and Olivia Weatherford quietly agreed to keep the research papers locked in their safes, hidden for the foreseeable future. It would be Olivia who suffered most from the trauma of the investigation as many unsavory details came to light regarding not only J. Winston's business dealings but his personal relations as well.

Rather than sit by and idly watch, Rodger and Delia Porter had commandeered the situation and extended a no-regrets invitation for a post-gala gathering in the Porter manor conservatory, Jennings presiding.

The glamorous greenhouse sparkled with tiny white lights softly twinkling around the perimeter, making the plants glow a brighter green than usual against the constant patter of rain against the windows. Upon his arrival, Tucker was stationed in his customary comfy chair, sipping the neat scotch delivered punctually by Jennings. The guests trickled in one by one after depositing soggy rain gear on an oversized coat rack at the entrance.

"DCI Marvin Campbell," announced Jennings as the last of the expected guests arrived.

"Marvin?" said Tucker, chuckling." "You don't strike me as a Marvin."

"That's DCI Marvin to you," said Campbell with a sly grin.

Alene and Tolliver entered, heads bent and conversing in low tones as they joined the grouping by the windows. They stopped when they saw DCI Campbell and Tucker and wondered if their discussion was for Farthing's employees only.

"Welcome, DCI Campbell," she said, taking her seat. "So nice to see you under much better circumstances."

"Well, ma'am, for some," he said cagily.

"Alright, mate, you've been tight-lipped for the last few days sorting through this. Out with it. What's all this been about?"

"What is that simply cracking smell?" said the man, ignoring Tucker.

Jennings was rolling in a massive trolley with no end of marvelous tidbits. He set out plates and tools on the handy sideboard, nodded, and retreated to the door.

"Uh, Jennings, if you don't mind, I'd like you to stay a bit. If that's alright with you, Mrs. Porter."

"Oh, of course. He'd listen from the hallway anyway," she said, winking at the man.

Jennings had the grace to look contrite for two seconds, then positioned himself just outside the circle.

"Uh, Campbell?" coughed Tucker.

"Oh, yes, right. Well, you certainly know how this all ended, but I'm sure, as my Aunt Mary's eyes, you haven't heard how it started. Quite the story, eh Laird?"

"It is a rather distressing tale. I only learned a few additional facts today while in to see McCallum. Miss Lydia Kent-Williams was a paranoid psychotic by all accounts and as devious as they come."

Dulcy grabbed his hand during this and squeezed in support. The usually stolid FBI agent looked a bit frayed at the edges.

"Oooo, this is likely to get quite juicy," said Dahlia, sitting back in her chair and sipping her drink.

They cozied up as the detective inspector hitched up his chair, took a refill from Jennings, and sank back with a sigh. The Elliotts and the Porters were helping themselves to the buffet while Olivia Weatherford gratefully accepted the brandy offered her by Jennings as Campbell continued. She relaxed her usual ramrod posture in anticipation of hearing a sequence of events that would lead to the heart of the matter, most likely with James Winston Weatherford at the center of it. She would not be wrong.

"First, to put your minds at ease, there was an earlier question as to who prepared the tea samples at the first gala," said Campbell. Tolliver slowly nodded, remembering the DCI's loud and clear voice in the Brooklands kitchen accusing Alene of the deed. "Audrey helped the serving staff prepare them, and there was no funny business since it was only the one cup. Speaking of which," he said, glaring at Reggie. "You have been exposed, Miss Winter, seeing as Miss Candace exposed herself during our 'chats'."

"Ahem," coughed Tucker.

"Ah, bloody hell. You know what I mean, Elliott. I've chosen to not - what do you Americans say - sweat the small stuff. I'm willing to let it be."

"Thank you, DCI Campbell," she said, making sure to properly address the man giving her a pass. "I appreciate your graciousness in excusing my behavior in stealing the cup."

Tucker rolled his eyes and shot a short stare at Laird, who returned the sentiment.

"Shall we get the autopsy results out of the way for Flora Abbington, Inspector?" he said.

"Right, yeah. Well, the old bird really should've kept her mouth shut. She sealed her own fate trying to be the mouth of the south of Essex. She knew nothing and paid for it. I'm sorry, Mrs. Elliott, ma'am. Mrs. Weatherford. The autopsy showed that she had indeed been given a great dirty dose of dilantin which would have made a woman of her age quite shagged. It was a quick and evil thing to do, but a swift whack to the temple was all it took.

She died of a blow to the middle meningeal artery, which takes only the slightest of knocks in the correct spot to cause death. If it helps any, she probably didn't feel a thing."

The group bowed their heads in silent prayer for the harmless woman who wanted nothing more than to be relevant in her social circle.

"It probably didn't help that she bellowed about that planted vial all over my husband's wake. She really did need to do better wearing her hearing devices."

"Yaaas, I'm afraid that was quite the misstep. She drew a great deal of attention to herself, and when she spouted off at the gala, that was all she wrote."

"Speaking of the funeral," said Tucker, "what was the reverend trying to say? We thought he was trying to tell us all something, didn't we, Dad?"

"Yes, son, Rodger and I both, and Tolliver. We all thought he was trying to lead us to something but couldn't quite say it. It must've been a sacred trust. You know, the confidentiality of the confessional."

"Ah, and there's where our story begins," said Campbell as Jennings silently appeared by his side, filling his glass. "We may never really know. We believe he was trying to give you a hint. Having known of the indiscretion, the births, the adoptions, it's more than his collar is worth to discuss such a confidential matter, but yes, I think you're right in your assumptions."

Oh, lordy," said Dahlia. "I'm thinking this is where the tough parts come in."

DCI Campbell nodded, giving her a knowing look before he stared into his scotch. He heaved a lengthy sigh before continuing, causing the group to gather even closer as they waited for him to continue.

"Tolliver, you were the one who landed on this, so why don't you start us off?" he said.

Tolliver looked as though he would rather pop into flames than take up the story thread. With a nod from Campbell, he looked around the group and exhaled.

"Alright, if you'll allow me to take a breath, sir, I'll tell you what I know, what I didn't want to know. But in the end, it was what helped to keep all of us out of the nick. Ma'am, Mrs. Weatherford, with all due respect, I've found some things that won't be pleasant to hear."

"I can take it if you can, Alene," said Olivia, gazing at her friend with a prideful look.

"It's time we heard the truth, Olivia," said Alene, grasping her hand tightly in hers.

Tolliver eyed DCI Campbell, who nodded and waved at him to continue. When Tolliver hesitated, the DCI helped him with a jump start.

"So, Tolliver here has done some excellent work in digging up Miss Kent-Williams' roots, so to speak. We had some help from Candace, mind you, but all the same, it's a sordid story starting with an affair between a young Miss and an older gent which produced a set of twins. These children were immediately put up for adoption to avoid any embarrassment to the family."

At this point, Campbell bowed his head to Tolliver and sat back with his scotch. Tolliver set down his glass and cleared his throat as the others looked on in stunned silence.

"Let me first say that I am sorry for the details I am about to reveal because I know they will cause pain. Please don't shoot the messenger."

"I think we have enough bodies at the moment, Tolliver," said Tucker.

Alene shot him a reproachful look and nodded for Tolliver to continue.

"To understand our recent events, we must go back some years—twenty-five, to be exact. A young lady of good family had been seduced by an older man. It's a common story. However, the matter was handled quickly and quietly, and the baby girls were split up and adopted. As I'm sure you have surmised, one child went to the Kent-Williams family and the other to a nice suburban family of good community standing."

Tolliver shifted uncomfortably and eyed the group.

"Lydia Kent-Williams and Candace Corbyn had different upbringings, but both managed to be successful in their own right. Lydia was a bright child as well as an excellent student. She attended secondary with Miss Dahlia, as we know."

"Yes," said Dahlia. "She was a rather homely young thing and had no end of a time being picked on by the other girls. Mean girls, you know? But she was brilliant and excelled at her studies enough to get her through in record time and was shipped off to Oxford after that. I'm sure she was glad to leave there. We weren't sad to see her go either; she could be quite nasty when she wanted to be."

"As I think we had covered before, she took a first at Oxford but not without some controversy as she was accused of plagiarism. It was sorted out, and she eventually received her degrees with firsts in biological chemistry and forensic chemistry. With such a pedigree, it was easy for her to find work in the private sector. She went to Penders, where she made some brilliant discoveries and was highly valued for her work."

Tolliver stopped here and took a sip of his drink while his audience digested the story.

"Until she wasn't," added Tucker. "Let me guess; she was caught pursuing her own projects using company time and resources and was sacked forthwith. Am I correct, Tolliver?"

"Yes, sir. The first of quite a few times this would happen, including her stint at Farthing's and her... liaison with you, sir."

"So, meanwhile, where is Candace?" asked Dulcy.

"Candace had a pleasant childhood; public education, childhood friends, annual holidays to the shore and such. She managed to study art and photography, learn French, and excel in her science and business courses at East Sussex Lewes, much like the sister who would shortly enter into her life. But unlike Lydia, Candace did not have the scholarship intellect and worked at the area shops to supplement her income and pay her tuitions. Lydia was on several scholarships and being from a peerage family, did not worry about money."

"So, how did they come to find each other?" asked Reggie.

"As happens so often with twins, there seems to be a telepathic bond which can drive them to search for what they feel is missing in their lives. And though they may grow up separately, they often share similar qualities and characteristics as if they were raised together. Our Candace and Lydia found each other quite by accident. Where Candace knew early on she was adopted, Lydia's parents decided it wasn't necessary for their daughter to know this detail."

"Rather a large detail, don't you think?" said Tucker.

Campbell shrugged while Tolliver nodded, both acknowledging the dangers in keeping information from someone.

"I've seen it over my years," said Campbell. "Human nature never fails to rear its ugly head in many of the cases I've seen. A human being can be counted on to make detectable mistakes due to it. In fact, where would I be without it? Twins can be alike, twins can be different as the sun and the moon, but at the end of the day, human nature will win out."

"So, Tolliver, what was the fateful moment?" asked Reggie.

"Lydia was always an unsettled thing. No matter how much she achieved or how much attention she garnered, there always seemed to be something missing. Candace worked hard at college and was happy, well-adjusted, and well-liked. As she got older, the question began to haunt her as well. Where was she born? To whom did she belong? She loves her family dearly, but the urge to discover her birth parents became too great, and as many young people do, she started to investigate. It didn't take long, but she found her birth mother and decided to pay her a visit."

"Oooo, Gawd, I bet that was quite a day," said Dahlia. "How did that go?"

"She didn't want to cause distress, so she contacted the woman and set up an appointment, making sure the woman knew she didn't want anything other than to meet her."

"And she didn't know she had a twin, did she? Until then?" said Dulcy.

"Yes. Perceptive thing that she is, she could see there was something the woman wasn't saying. In the end, she told Candace about Lydia."

"Did she tell her Lydia's name?" asked Alene in surprise.

"No, she lied and said she wasn't told what became of the other child. Candace thanked her and went on her way, knowing exactly what she would do."

At this point, Jennings refilled their glasses and waited patiently for Tolliver to continue.

"One thing about Candace is that she may not have had Lydia's innate brilliance, but she is resourceful. At Lewes, there is a legal department. A young man who took a fancy to her received his education there, and she immediately went to see him. He managed to get hold of the records and made a copy for Candace. They were no longer sealed, and she was able to find out quite a lot of information."

"I think this is where it gets sticky," said Tucker to Reggie.

"Indeed, sir," said Tolliver. "They now had the name and the address of the ancestral home. Her gentleman friend used that to track down Miss Lydia. Imagine the surprise when she found she was working in the labs of Farthing's Fine Teas."

Tolliver took a sip of his drink and waited for the revelation to sink in with the rest of them.

"Yes, but how did they meet?" asked Dulcy.

"Elliott? You want to take this one?"

"We had been in discussions with various places where we considered hosting the tea gala. I handed that off to Audrey, and Candace invited her to Brooklands to view the facilities."

"But by this point, we had already secured a venue," added Alene, "but Audrey gave it a nice review and recommended it for future galas. It took some time, but we finally worked it out to be our location this year."

"Meanwhile, Candace was getting to know Audrey, staying in touch and offering her special discounts and free visits to keep her interested."

"All the while keeping Audrey close to gain information on Lydia," stated Alene.

"Exactly, until one day Candace paid a visit to the Farthing's offices, where Audrey was gracious enough to give her a tour and explain what we do there. She expressed her interest in the research and development side, detailing her experience with the state-of-the-art science facilities at Lewe's and her understanding of the processes."

"So, our Audrey was also gracious enough to give Candace a tour of the labs, I'm guessing?" said Tucker.

"Yes, sir. At this point, she was introduced to Bella, Roswyn, and a young lady who looked suspiciously like her."

"That must have been a shock," said Olivia.

"Yes, ma'am. Lydia hadn't a clue, and Candace was able to finally see the sister she never knew. At the time, that was all she was interested in. At some point, the time would come to formally meet her and discuss their... genetic link."

"Speaking of," said Olivia. "Aren't you forgetting a rather important detail, Mr. Tolliver?"

"Yes, ma'am," he said quietly.

"Who's the father?" she blurted out.

The room had fallen to a hush, with the receding raindrops the only sound to be heard.

"The time did come to formally meet when Candace went to sell the idea of Brooklands to the competition to Farthing's Fine Teas."

"The Weatherford Brands," stated Olivia.

"Yes. Candace finally got up the nerve to formerly meet Lydia by using the same ploy she did with Farthing's - visit the firm on the pretense of selling Brooklands as a meeting venue."

"But that wouldn't be something the girl would handle for us," said Olivia. "That would be one of the assistants or even Winston himself."

"Yes, but on the day Candace went to meet them, Lydia was in Winston's office and was now formally introduced to her. Candace told her she, too, had a background in the sciences and would love to chat about their experiences sometime. She handed Lydia her card and left it at that."

"Then they met when?" asked Tucker.

"Lydia was curious. She liked talking about science, especially with someone like-minded. There was also something about Candace that caught her attention even though she couldn't put her finger on it at the time."

"But then something happened, didn't it?" asked Olivia.

"Yes, as in previous jobs, Lydia was misusing resources and was discovered by the lab staff. She was taken before Winston, who immediately discharged her, never knowing the one thing that Candace knew."

"And that was?" asked Tucker.

"That James Winston Weatherford was her biological father," said Tolliver with a sigh.

35

Chapter 35

All's well that ends okay.
-8 Mile, 2002

Jennings nimbly refilled Olivia's glass as the meaning of his words sank in with a thump.

"I knew it. He was a reprobate of the first degree, and I am the fool of a woman who allowed it."

"You're a rather rich fool," said Tucker, rudely.

"Tucker Farthing Elliott! I taught you better than that," snapped Alene.

"Apparently not, Mother."

The room erupted in laughter and released the tension that Jennings could have cut with one of the medieval daggers hanging in the hall.

"So, Tolliver, how did Lydia find this out? Or did she?"

"Well, sir, she happened on Candace's card as she was packing up her things at Weatherford's. Since she was back in the job market, what did she have to lose by calling her? Brooklands hosts a fair amount of companies for events, so it wouldn't hurt to pick her brain a bit."

"There's something else, isn't there Tolliver?" asked Reggie, as Tolliver was not meeting their eyes.

"Yes, Miss. As we've mentioned, Lydia was carrying a secret that was eating at her by the day. She didn't have many friends, and if this Candace proved to be a sympathetic soul, maybe she could confide in her."

"Oh, Gawdy Gawd, here comes the secret," muttered Dahlia.

"They decided to meet. Lydia went to Brooklands to see the famous museum and pick Candace's brain. It was there up in the member dining room that she decided to tell Candace everything."

Tolliver took another sip of his drink and wiped his brow, which was beginning to sweat with the humidity of the conservatory. Or maybe the challenging details of the story.

"It was a rough start since Candace could tell there was something serious on Lydia's mind. Not wanting to pry, she began the conversation by asking Lydia to tell her about herself. This opened floodgates that Candace was not ready for. Before she had a chance even to broach the subject, Lydia launched into her job loss at the hands of a tyrant who mistreated her and took advantage of her."

"In the business sense," clarified Reggie.

When Tolliver stared straight ahead without a word, Alene grasped Olivia's hand while Tucker let out a long low whistle.

"You can't mean..." said Dulcy.

"As we've said, Lydia's mental state was not up to taking on the burden of Weatherford's sexual advances, much less his harassment. It was taking a toll on her, and in the midst of it all, he fired her."

The color was coming back into Olivia Weatherford's face in rushes. What was stark white began to flush red into purple, a color no well-bred English woman would be caught with.

"My dead husband was... having relations with that girl?" she hissed.

"We don't know the extent of it, but it would seem so, ma'am. Candace was shocked and angered by this admission and vowed she would help Lydia. But first, she had to know why Candace would do so. It was at this juncture that Candace produced the paperwork detailing their relationship and that of Weatherford."

"She must have gone right off the rails," said Dahlia. "I can't even imagine."

"Lydia, rather than being upset, was relieved by this information. She knew there was something out there that had eluded her, and here she finally was - sitting in front of her. An ally who could help her get even."

"So, how did we get from here to a murder?" asked Dulcy.

"Lydia bided her time. She had to formulate a plan. Candace was willing to help her, which is all she saw. Candace was willing to help Lydia make contacts, find another job, and then decide how to deal with the harassment issue. She didn't know how damaged Lydia was and never dreamed she was thinking of murder."

"You said she was back in the cosmetics industry, Tucker. So, Candace helped her find another job?" asked Reggie.

"She provided a few introductions but in the end, a company approached Lydia and she was offered an opportunity in a field to which she was quite accustomed."

"A field that would make botulinum toxin easy to get," said Laird.

"Exactly. Lydia began seeing more of Candace and more of Brooklands. She was introduced to Alex and got to know her way around the Edwardian Club," said Tolliver.

"Enough to know there was a dumbwaiter in the bar. The Stewart chap? He was a puppet to her. He did anything he was told," added Campbell.

"He was the man in the security tapes!" exclaimed Reggie.

"Yes. She would need help with the body, and it had to be someone more substantial than Candace. All Candace thought she was doing was confronting Weatherford, accusing him of his actions, and letting him know that he would pay for them."

"Legally," said Laird.

"I don't understand how we never saw it before," said Reggie. "When you place them side by side, they're hard to tell apart. How did we miss that?"

"It was a subtle thing," said Campbell. "Anytime she was around Candace, she wore her contact lenses and dyed her hair a few shades darker to hide the resemblance. She was quite astute, that one."

"Too bad she didn't use her powers for good instead of evil," said Dahlia. "So, what actually happened that night?"

"May I get anyone anything?" asked Jennings before Tolliver took up his tale again.

Glasses raised around the circle, and after Jennings had topped off everyone, it was time to hear the rest of the story.

"As we know, Weatherford had raised a few hackles with some of the attendees at the gala."

"Don't forget the chef," said Dahlia.

"Of course. We can't leave Chef Dumont out of the list of the offended," said Alene. "Good thing I carry cash."

Tolliver began recreating the events of the evening, including Weatherford offending royalty and rock stars alike.

"What helped break the whole thing was when Audrey recalled seeing him come back into the club, pouring something into a cup, and wandering off toward the back of the building."

"Yes," said Reggie. "We thought he had gone to the Sunbeam Cafe."

"Where he had actually gone was to keep his meeting with Candace, who had slipped him a threatening note. She would meet him upstairs, where she would accuse him of his transgressions and tell him that he would pay."

"But it wasn't Candace, was it?" said Tucker.

"No, it was not. It was Lydia, hair smooth, colored yet again, and large spectacles looking exactly like Candace. Stewart was the one we had seen in the tapes entering the building. He had been at the party earlier, keeping an eye on things until he was needed. Under all the heavy wrapping was a tuxedo."

"So, when we saw him on the tape, he was getting ready to help Lydia," said Reggie.

"Yes, Candace and Audrey were waiting for Alene to start her presentation and had no clue Lydia had gone to dispatch Weatherford."

"But he was sent out of the building. Wouldn't she lose her chance to confront him?" asked Reggie.

"Yes, but Lydia was still inside, and she figured he'd just be waiting out on the bench, and as soon as things got underway, she'd go out and confront him there."

The thought of the bench flitted through their minds, and they winced from the memory.

"He reread the note, went back into the gathering and up to the member bar. 'Candace' was waiting for him with a lethal glass of champagne while Stewart was hiding in the shadows."

"But the cup!" said Reggie. "The toxin was in the cup under the bench. And he had a tea packet in his hand."

"Yes, she put the toxin in the glass of champagne and also in the cup. She also put the packet in his hand as a message that it was one of you, the competition, who had killed him."

"Ugh! Horrible woman," spat Alene.

"This 'Candace' accused him of sexual misconduct but said she wouldn't tell if he paid her off, something he readily agreed to do. To seal the deal, they toasted to it. As he realized something was wrong, Lydia took off her glasses and told him who she really was and watched as he writhed in pain and died on the spot."

"Oh, lord, but how do you know all this, Tolliver?" asked Tucker.

"When they found Weatherford on the bench, Candace panicked. She confronted Lydia, who proudly described the scene down to the last detail. She threatened Candace if she told a soul, telling her the same could happen to her. When Alex saw a figure entering the building on the tapes, Candace knew who it was and was afraid we'd figure it out. She tried to downplay the tapes with Alex, fearing he would be in danger from Lydia."

"Too late," said Tucker.

"Candace was afraid and confided in Alex, begging him not to go any further with the security cameras. He thought they should go to the police, but before they could do that, the brake line was cut."

"So what about the body?" said Dulcy.

"Lydia had learned about the dumbwaiter one day while up in the bar with Candace. What a perfect way to get him out to the bench with Stewart's help. Being out of the range of the cameras, it was perfect."

"Which is how Lydia whacked Flora on the head and then disappeared from the scene," said Reggie.

"Yes, I'm afraid so. Lydia had dropped the Dilantin in her drink, which made her so tired she sat for a rest. Then she came back - the figure on the tapes in the dark - hit Flora while she was out cold, wiped the bottle, and escaped down the dumbwaiter."

"Losing her earring in the process," added Laird, who up to this point had been silently taking it all in. "The other one was found in her apartment."

"What about the cork under her seat?" asked Reggie.

"Nothing special about it," said Campbell. "Just a cork rolling around on the deck after going missing from a newly opened bottle."

"So, I take it Stewart was responsible for the oil slick on the track with the Austin Healey," said Reggie. "Why didn't the cameras pick that up?"

"We may never know, but it's a good bet he's our man there," said Campbell. "We believe that 'Jeffrey' managed to disable the one camera which would have shown him spraying the oil on the course. The security people are being questioned further on that. It would have been easy for him to strip off the garage uniform to one like the other security blokes wear and offer to give the guard a toilet break."

"What I don't understand is why they tried to kill Audrey," said Reggie. "What did she have to do with any of this?"

"Audrey is a smart lass," said Campbell. "She was beginning to ask questions because she saw Weatherford re-enter the building, and then he was dead. At the funeral, she was there with 'Candace'," he said with a twinkle in his eye.

"Oh, no, not Candace," said Reggie. "Lydia. Lydia who planted the vial in Mrs. Weatherford's pocket where she knew it would be found. Dame Flora helped her out there, didn't she? But where was the real Candace? She wasn't at the funeral."

"No, she unwittingly used their twin likeness to beg off of the funeral, nearly getting Audrey killed in the process. Lydia was more than happy to accommodate Candace as it paved the way for her to take out Audrey. Simple task to squirrel away a minute amount of the toxin to use when she got her chance. Which she did."

"And you hauled me off to the High Street like a common criminal, Detective Inspector, accusing me of God knows what," Olivia said.

"I wasn't accusing you of anything," smiled DCI Campbell. "I was just trying to keep you safe."

Olivia's mouth opened and shut and opened again, but she decided better of it. She leaned back and swallowed a considerable measure of brandy.

"So, it was Lydia who went out to eat with Candace, took her back to her house, fixed her the 'warm milk' and left her to die," said Reggie.

"Yes. Audrey has finally begun to remember a few things," said Campbell. "Lydia left but kept the milk on the nightstand, thinking Audrey would just drink it. When Audrey woke the next morning, it was still there. She took a small sip, but it tasted so bad she took it to the kitchen and dumped it, rinsing it out with water and bleach. Then, she began to feel ill. If you all hadn't come along, I'm not sure she would have made it. She's only started remembering what happened. She was bloody well mad at Candace; I can tell you that much. We disabused her of that notion quickly."

"Where is Audrey?" asked Dahlia. "I thought she might be here this evening."

"She's on a date," smiled Campbell. "With Constable Petry."

They laughed and relaxed while Jennings wheeled in a dessert trolley loaded with scrumptious treats.

"My goodness. That's enough to make you gain weight by just looking at them," said Dulcy. "Give me one of those, please."

"So, what about the research?" said Douglass. "What's to become of the... papers?"

"What papers?" said Alene and Olivia, with a quick glance between the two of them.

"Alright, then. So, what's to become of Bella and Roswyn? Safe with their jobs for now?" asked Tucker.

"Oh, hell no," stated Alene, causing Delia to choke on her eclair. "They have been summarily dismissed. I will not have deception in my company."

"But you never proved they did anything," said Tucker.

"It's a matter of principle, son."

"So, uh, Mummy," began Tucker.

"Oh, here we go. Whatever it is, Tucker, the answer is no. Emphatically."

"May I please keep my lab room jib door?"

"Again, hell no. And take out the one in your office. How do you come to think I'm that stupid?"

Tucker lowered his eyes into his scotch and clamped his mouth shut.

"So what shall we do about our personnel, ma'am?" asked Tolliver.

"Personnel, Sydney?"

“Replacements for Miss Bella and Miss Roswyn.”

“Oh, that. Steal them from the competition!” she said, giving Olivia a sidelong look.

“Oh, no you don’t, old woman. Over my dead body,” she said, rising to her feet.

“No, no, no! That’s how all this started,” said Tucker, separating the two women.

“Oh, Tolliver,” cooed Reggie. “How about another scotch, and you can tell me all about Las Vegas...”

The End

Turn the page for a sneak peek at the newest Tucker and Reggie Mystery Series, Strangled in the Vines.

36

Strangled in the Vines

"A good friend just told me that the key to a successful marriage was to argue naked." -LeAnnLeAnn Rimes

"You told me he'd leave me alone."

"And he will, Lauren. I promise."

"You better make sure; there's been a lot of planning and preparation for this wedding. I'm going to hold you to your promise. I don't want any issues."

"Don't worry; I'll make it so he never bothers you again."

Bill sat on his tractor and glanced at the vines shining in the evening light. They were beautiful at this hour as the sun set over the lake and left a warm glow over the property. He wished he hadn't heard the conversation. It didn't do to know too much about your guests, especially those paying a premium for a fairy-tale wedding in a vineyard.

"I'm going back to my room now. Take care of it, Peter. I don't want to have to have this talk again."

It was all he heard, but it was enough. He threw his leg over the tractor, slid the key into his pocket, and left the equipment to be garaged later. He slipped around the side of the building and stared into the waning light at the herb garden. They were gone, and their troublesome conversation with them. He brushed his hand through his hair and headed toward the pavilion. It would be a beautiful rehearsal dinner. For most of the guests, anyway.

* * *

Caterers were refilling the buffet, wine flowed throughout the event space, and guests were telling stories of how they met the bride and groom. It was a beautiful scene, and Bill was observing from a back patio as guests wandered through to the sitting area, remarking on their favorite pieces of art hanging on every wall. A young man saw the piano and began a rousing melody, filling the winery's space. Bill stood off to the side, wondering which of the guests was the cause of the harsh exchange earlier.

"What are you up to, boss?"

"I'm being attentive."

"You're being nosy," said Daisy. "I know that look. What's up?"

"I'm being a good owner and making sure everyone is happy and taken care of."

"That's my job as manager."

"Well, then, go manage," he said with a huge grin.

"You're sure you're okay?"

"Yes, I'm going to make one more round on the tanks and then settle in. You all have this."

"Oh, by the way," she said, wheeling around on him, " I have good news and bad news. Which do you want first?"

Bill gave her his "go-ahead if you must gaze."

"The people in number three and four have decided they want to be with the rest of the guests at the other hotel, so they have canceled their rooms."

"Okay, that isn't optimum, so what's the good news?"

"Two couples heard about us in town and wanted to book in. Since those suites are now empty, I told them they could take the rooms. They paid in advance for a few days. Does that work for you?"

"Yes, but do they know they'll be in the midst of a wedding?"

"Yes. They thought that was 'charming' and are looking forward to it."

Bill smiled, shrugged, and headed toward the path to the fermentation tanks.

"Thank you, Daisy," he said, continuing on his way, darting a glance at the festivities in the pavilion.

"Who has the wedding jitters? Them or me?" he muttered.

Why couldn't he seem to ignore that niggling feeling in the pit of his stomach?

* * *

"So, Reg, brilliant shoe expo. People were flipping for flops everywhere. Well done. Mum will be pleased to see her pet project off life support and gaining strength every day. Now, I have a surprise for you," he said with that familiar glint in his eye.

"Oooo, where are we going?"

"Why do you think we're going somewhere?"

"You have that maestro look about you, which means you've been orchestrating something somewhere. So, where are we going? England, west coast, back to Useppa?"

"Conneaut, Ohio."

"Huh? Where is that?"

"About an hour east of Cleveland. Pretty country, so I'm told. It's up by that big lake up there."

"You mean Lake Erie, you silly Brit?" said Reggie.

"Yes, love. That's the one, so pack up, and we'll grab Dulcy and Laird and take a lovely drive."

"Where are we going again?" asked Dulcy as they climbed onto the freeway and rolled east.

"It's a B&B."

"Oh, I see, since I know nothing about those," she said. "So glad we're taking a break from me managing Dahlia's B&B to go to a different B&B. Good idea."

"Lot of sarcasm today, I see. It's also a winery."

"It's a boutique family winery in a picturesque country setting. They have fine wines, tasty bites, a laid-back tasting room, live music, casually elegant lodging, and special events."

"Wow, sounds great. How do you know all this?"

"I'm reading the brochure," said Reggie. "Oh, look! All the rooms come with hot tub spas. Now, that sounds amazing after standing in flip flops for eight hours a day for three days. Maybe we should have our next corporate meeting there."

"Well, there is an event this weekend," said Tucker quietly.

"Oh, dear. Why do I detect a kink in the works?"

"It's a wedding, Reg. We're the only guests not involved."

"A wedding!" said Dulcy gleefully. "How fun. Won't that be fun, John?"

John Laird leaned back against the seat, a grim straight line where his mouth would typically be. He was staring at the back of Tucker's head with the look he reserved for intimidating criminals during an FBI investigation. Tucker sneaked a peek in the rear-view mirror and smirked. It humored him to see the commanding FBI agent squirm occasionally.

"Alright, my navigator, how are we doing?"

"Turn left onto this road coming up, and then it'll be on your left."

The elegant sign by the road ushered them into a quaint setting with a car park filled with trucks of caterers, bakers, florists, and other sundry wedding personnel. A gentleman watched as they scouted for a space and wandered casually over to them.

"Good afternoon. You must be the Elliott party. Welcome to the Buccia Winery. We have quite a group this weekend, so if you'll follow me, I'll put you right over here. Come in when you're ready, and we'll get you a glass of wine."

He strolled back to the entrance and supervised as deliveries were being dispatched to various areas of the property.

"What beautiful weather," said Reggie, glancing around the car park to the vineyard.

She wandered to the building's edge and stared past the sun streaming through the glistening vines. Rounded green grapes were dangling from every cluster, and she wondered what variety each one represented.

"C'mon, love, time for wine. We'll get the bags later."

"Hello, folks," said Daisy. "You must be the Elliott's. Bill said to give you a glass of welcome wine, and then you can check in or wander the property if you like. We have a wedding here this evening, so a lot is happening in the pavilion and arbor area. Now, what do you all normally drink?"

Once the wine choices had been sorted, they stepped through the art gallery and out to the grounds. A group of musicians was setting up on the dais, and streams of bows and roses cascaded off the pergola by the first row of vines. The accompanying wine barrels were also decorated with greenery and glasses, looking like pages from a magazine. At center stage was the arbor, waiting patiently for the guests of honor to exchange their vows.

"Oh, look, they're having their pictures," said Dulcy. "This really would be an idyllic setting for a wedding, wouldn't it? Don't they look wonderful?"

The bridal party had been stationed near the middle front row of vines while a man with cameras dangling from all sides gave directions and tipped heads at attractive angles. The bride and groom made a stunning couple, she with her long auburn hair and pale blue eyes and he with his blond curly hair and magnetic grin. At center stage, they towered over the smiling faces surrounding them—all but one, so it seemed.

"Hmmm," muttered Reggie.

Tucker leaned in, but she said nothing else, and he decided it was in their best interests not to encourage her. She had seen something, but what, he couldn't say. Nor did he want to know.

"Huh," said Dulcy.

Tucker glanced at Laird, who coughed and stepped away from the Kodak moment. He dutifully followed and stood behind the women while they eagerly watched the proceedings.

"They've seen something," said Laird.

"Yes. I suggest..."

"Running?"

"More wine," said Tucker, grinning.

Dulcy and Reggie never noticed them slinking away to the inside counter as they leaned shoulder to shoulder, observing.

"Hmmm," repeated Reggie.

"Hmmm," echoed Dulcy.

"What did you see?"

"I don't know, Reggie, it's just that..."

"Where did those two go?" asked Reggie.

What Dulcy had seen would be lost as Tucker and Laird emerged from the wine room with new glasses and a large bottle indeed.

About the Author

Jacqueline Farthing Galvin is a versatile author who is also known by her pen names Jacquie Galvin and Mama Galvin. She is the President and CEO of Live Life's Rich Moments. Jacqueline has been on a literary journey for over 30 years and has self-published over 100 works across various genres.

Her works include captivating short stories, heart-racing mystery thrillers, informative feature articles, and descriptive travel narratives.

Jacqueline's literary journey started at a unique intersection, where she skillfully balanced her passion for writing with running a freight business and excelling as a medical representative.

One of her most recent literary gems, the award-winning ***Grace for Grant: A Journey with an Old Soul***, masterfully navigates the deeply moving odyssey of her family, marked by the loss of her 19-year-old son, Grant.

You can connect with me on:

- https://www.jacquelinefarthinggalvin.com
- https://x.com/jgalvin9111?s=21&t=5zNRjrFniociQg3h66OR-A
- https://www.facebook.com/farthinggalvin
- https://www.instagram.com/jacquiegalvin

Subscribe to my newsletter:

✉ https://jacquelinefarthinggalvin.com/bookclub

Also by Jacqueline Farthing Galvin

A Tease of Murder

Murder for Afternoon Tea: Episode I - The Last Cup of Tea

Murder for Afternoon Tea: Episode II - Welcome to my Underground Lair

Murder for Afternoon Tea: Episode III - Finally

Death in Paradise: Secrets of the Croquet Club

The Brooklands Motor Course Murders

Strangled in the Vines

Tucker, Reggie, Dulcy, and Laird head to a quiet, cozy vineyard in Ohio, only to find themselves in the midst of not only a posh wedding but vintage trouble. When the groom is found no longer aging like a fine wine on his wedding night, it's sour grapes all around as the list of suspects grows faster than the winery's upcoming harvest.

Reggie and Dulcy are fermenting their own trouble by meddling in police matters. After Reggie discloses what she heard through the grapevine, more possible suspects bloom like the spring vines. Much to the dismay of Tucker and Laird, Dulcy and Reggie dig deeper into a barrel of suspects. At the same time, Detective Kerrigan would like nothing more than for the disruptive duo to put a cork in their investigating.

When another body is found strangled in the vines, the four work to discover the guilty party before another victim is stomped out. It's a narrow miss for Dulcy and Reggie as they close in on a killer who's trying to keep his secret bottled up. Will they expose the murderer in time, or will it be a harvest of their own deaths? Find out in the latest Tucker and Reggie Mystery Series!